"Time travel, ancient legends, and seductive romance are seamlessly interwoven into one captivating package."

  –*Publishers Weekly* on Midnight's Master

"Dark, sexy, magical. When I want to indulge in a sizzling fantasy adventure, I read Donna Grant."

  –Allison Brennan, *New York Times* bestseller

5 Stars! Top Pick! "An absolute must read! From beginning to end, it's an incredible ride."

  –*Night Owl Reviews*

"It's good vs. evil Druid in the next installment of Grant's Dark Warrior series. The stakes get higher as discerning one's true loyalties become harder. Grant's compelling characters and continued presence of previous protagonists are key reasons why these books are so gripping. Another exciting and thrilling chapter!"

  –*RT Book Reviews* on Midnight's Lover

"Donna Grant has given the paranormal genre a burst of fresh air..."

  –*San Francisco Book Review*

Smoldering Hunger

Smoke and Fire

Dragon Fever (novella)

Firestorm

Blaze

Dragon Burn (novella)

Constantine: A History (short story)

Heat

Torched

Dragon Night (novella)

Dragonfire

Dragon Claimed (novella)

Ignite

DARK WARRIORS

Midnight's Master

Midnight's Lover

Midnight's Seduction

Midnight's Warrior

Midnight's Kiss

Midnight's Captive

Midnight's Temptation

Midnight's Promise

Midnight's Surrender (novella)

Dark Warrior Box Set

CHIASSON SERIES

Wild Fever

Wild Dream

Wild Need

Wild Flame

Wild Rapture

LARUE SERIES

Moon Kissed

Moon Thrall

Moon Struck

Moon Bound

Historical Paranormal

THE KINDRED

Everkin

Eversong

Everwylde

Everbound

DARK SWORD

Dangerous Highlander

Forbidden Highlander

Wicked Highlander

Untamed Highlander

Shadow Highlander

Darkest Highlander

Dark Sword Box Set

ROGUES OF SCOTLAND

The Craving

The Hunger

The Tempted

The Seduced

Rogues of Scotland Box Set

THE SHIELDS

A Dark Guardian

A Kind of Magic

A Dark Seduction

A Forbidden Temptation

A Warrior's Heart

DRUIDS GLEN

Highland Mist
Highland Nights
Highland Dawn
Highland Fires
Highland Magic
Dragonfyre (connected)

SISTERS OF MAGIC

Shadow Magic
Echoes of Magic
Dangerous Magic
Sisters of Magic Boxed Set

THE ROYAL CHRONICLES NOVELLA SERIES

Prince of Desire
Prince of Seduction
Prince of Love
Prince of Passion
Royal Chronicles Box Set

MILITARY ROMANCE / ROMANTIC SUSPENSE

SONS OF TEXAS

The Hero

The Protector

The Legend

THE DEFENDER

SONS OF TEXAS, BOOK 4

DONNA GRANT

This is a work of fiction. All of the characters, organizations, and
events portrayed in this novel are either products of the author's
imagination or are used fictitiously.

THE DEFENDER
© 2019 by DL Grant, LLC
Cover Design © 2018 by Charity Hendry

ISBN 10: 1942017499
ISBN 13: 9781942017493
Available in ebook and print editions

www.DonnaGrant.com
www.MotherofDragonsBooks.com

Kiev, Ukraine

The click of the hammer on the pistol behind him was piercing in the silence of the corridor. And it stopped Lev in his tracks.

He glanced at the hallway three steps ahead on the right, and the door eight steps to his left. Either one could get him to the next level of the theatre, but not without taking at least one bullet in the process.

"Don't be a hero."

The very feminine, very American accent brought him up short. Before he could respond, the woman repeated her statement in perfect Ukrainian, and then again in Russian.

It was lucky for Lev that he spoke all three, though his Ukrainian was rusty.

"Turn around," she demanded.

Lev waited until she said it in Russian before he slowly turned toward her. The moment his gaze landed on her, he knew this was no ordinary woman. This was someone who had seen war up-close and personal.

It was there in her deep brown eyes, in the set of her jaw, and the way she held the gun as if it were an extension of her hand.

He noted her thick, wavy, caramel-colored locks with the top pulled back away from her face to fall with the rest of her hair down the middle of her back. Her heart-shaped face was classically appealing, the kind of beauty that made men do anything just to be with her.

She was of average height, but there was nothing average about her. Lev would've believed she was just another patron at the ballet with her form-fitting black gown, the pearls dangling from her ears, and black stilettos.

Except for the gun pointed at his head.

Their gazes locked, clashed.

If he were going to get out of this and complete his mission, he would have to think fast.

The COM in his ear crackled before Callie said his name from the underground base in Texas where the rest of the Whitehorse team was located. When he didn't answer, she called for him again. But this time, she was cut off mid-sentence.

Which meant his link to the outside world had been disabled.

———

6 Hours Earlier...

Lev adjusted the bowtie at his throat while trying not to tug at it as he glared with distaste at his reflection in the mirror. He wouldn't mind wearing the tux if he didn't have to have something around his throat. It reminded him too much of being choked.

He stopped his thoughts before they could travel down that bumpy—and disturbing—road. It was no use griping about wearing the tuxedo. There was no way around it. He turned to where his cell phone sat on the table near him and checked it.

Another day without hearing from Sergei. It pained Lev more then he liked to admit that he hadn't heard from the old man. Though that *old man* wasn't just anyone. Sergei Chzov ran the Russian mob at the docks in Dover, Maryland.

And Lev was his *Brigadier*. His captain.

Which made it doubly hard not to be by Sergei's side. Lev had watched over Sergei for more than twelve years. Sergei was, in fact, the only family Lev had.

And Sergei wasn't even blood.

Lev set the phone down and walked to the open bottle of vodka. He poured some into the glass and downed it in one swallow. The alcohol slid from his throat into his belly with a warm rush.

His eyes closed as he set the glass down and thought about the events that had led him and Sergei from Dover to Texas. It wasn't that Lev didn't want to join forces with the Loughmans. It was simply that his first duty was to Sergei.

Except they'd discovered the Saints. The worldwide organization that had manipulated their way into every government in the world to secretly become the biggest power player of all. And they were out to control the population by using a bioweapon that would sterilize women.

Luckily, all four Loughmans—Orrin, the father,

and the brothers Wyatt, Owen, and Cullen—had taken the bioweapon, Ragnarok, and killed the scientist who could recreate it.

The Loughmans had been joined by four feisty women, and it just happened to be Mia who got Lev and Sergei into this mess. But only because Mia reminded Sergei of the daughter he'd lost.

It went against everything in Lev to help Mia and Cullen Loughman—and eventually the entire Loughman bunch—but he had never gone against Sergei's orders. And he wasn't about to start now.

Lev blew out a breath and opened his eyes. He had much to make up for. While he couldn't bring Sergei's daughter back from the dead, he could—and would—protect Sergei until his dying breath.

First, Lev had to finish his mission in Kiev. Then, he could return to Sergei's side.

The moment his phone vibrated, Lev spun around and grabbed for it. "Hello?"

"You sound irritated."

At the wispy voice thick with a Russian accent despite years in America, Lev relaxed for the first time since leaving Maryland. "Sergei."

"Cullen and Mia have kept me up-to-date. It seems you're to attend the ballet this evening."

There was no humor in Sergei's voice. He knew just how much Lev hated having anything near his neck. "That's right."

"Are you all right?"

Is that why Sergei called? Was the old man worried about Lev? There was a hint of a smile on Lev's face as he walked to the window and peeked through the curtains to the city. "I'm fine."

"You know what *fine* means, right?"

This time, Lev chuckled because the conversation harkened back to the very first one between the two of them. "Freaked out, insecure," he began.

Then Sergei joined him and finished with, "Neurotic and emotional."

They both fell silent. Lev's thoughts went to the night Sergei had found him, and the fact that he was still alive because of the Russian.

"I should not have made you go," Sergei said.

Lev let the curtain drop closed. "I could've refused."

"We both know you would not have done that."

No, he wouldn't have. Sergei was his *Pakhan*. His boss.

Sergei sighed heavily. "If I was younger, I would be there with you. Hell, I would have gone in your place."

"I know."

"This is a fight everyone must join, no matter how much we wish we did not have to."

Lev turned his head toward the mirror and met his own gaze. "I know."

"You are not your father, Lev. You are not in Russia. No one knows where you are. Remember that. All of it," Sergei said, his voice deepening with emotion.

"I don't make the same mistakes twice. You don't need to worry about me."

Sergei made a sound at the back of his throat. "Of course, I worry. You are the son I never had."

Lev clenched his teeth as emotion swelled within him. Neither of them had ever spoken this way, and he wasn't prepared for it now.

Before he could form a reply, Sergei cleared his

throat and said in no uncertain terms, "I expect you back home. Get your mission completed and return to your post."

"Yes, sir," Lev replied.

The line went dead. Lev slowly lowered the phone to the table and tugged on the bowtie and the collar of his shirt. He then went to his bag and opened it, pulling out a Sig Sauer 226, a Colt M45A1 close-quarters pistol, as well as two knives.

He strapped the Sig in his shoulder holster and the Colt to his ankle holster on his left foot. He slid one knife into a sheath on his right calf, slipped the other into a scabbard on his left forearm. Then he put the COM in his ear.

"Check," he said.

Instantly, Callie responded. "I hear you loud and clear, Lev. Good luck."

He took another shot of vodka, looked at himself in the mirror one last time, and then made his way out of the hotel room.

Lev didn't doubt for one moment that the intel Callie discovered was sound. It was Orrin Loughman who had trained and recruited her for his company, Whitehorse. She was damn good at her job. Lev could work his way around the internet, but there were places Callie could get to that he didn't even know existed.

The summer air smelled sweet and fresh as he got into the cab that would take him to the theatre. Lev was used to moving in the company of questionable people. But the Saints were an entirely different matter altogether.

Anyone could be a part of the Saints. The organization might have begun with the leaders of the world, but they had methodically and meticulously made their way down the ranks to everyday, normal people.

But few knew the real drive behind the Saints. Right now, none of that mattered. Because tonight, Lev had to stop the assassination of one of Ukraine's new political figures.

It seemed that Denys Stasiuk had unknowingly stumbled upon the Saints. Without even knowing it, Stasiuk began to call out those who supported anyone involved. The politician's stand against such a clandestine powerhouse had made international headlines. More and more of the country's other politicians were standing with Denys.

It caused a fervor that the Saints couldn't ignore. Because if one stood against them, then others might, as well. After all the work the Saints had done to take control, they weren't going to let go easily.

Frankly, Lev would rather be searching for the book that contained the names of all the top brass of the Saints. He wanted that volume so he and the others could go after the organization.

But he feared that it might take more than that to bring the Saints down once and for all. Since his group was no closer to locating the secret book, they had decided to thwart the Saints' attempt at taking Stasiuk's life.

It had been a long while since Lev was in such a situation, but he was ready for it. Perhaps it would remove some of the regret he lived with.

The cab pulled up to the theatre. Lev paid the driver and got out of the car. He adjusted the sleeves of his shirt while letting his gaze move around the area.

Men decked out in tuxes, along with women in dazzling dresses and jewels, made their way up the stairs on the outside of the building to the entrance. Long banners declaring the ballet hung from the roof and billowed in the slight breeze.

For just a heartbeat, Lev was taken back to his childhood as his mother dragged him to the ballet. He missed those times with her. If only he'd known then what he knew now, he wouldn't have put up such a fuss. He would have drunk in every second with her before she was ripped from his young life.

Lev drew in a deep breath and released it.

Callie's voice sounded in his ear. "Everything looks good so far. I still wish Maks or someone else was there backing you up."

"Don't need it," Lev muttered.

"Maybe not, but I'd feel better if you hadn't gone alone."

Lev didn't remind her that their team consisted of just eleven people, not counting Sergei. They were already stretched too thinly.

"I have the schematics pulled up," Callie continued. "Owen and Wyatt have already picked out the places they expect the attack to originate from."

Lev slowly walked up the long flight of steps. "You sure it's a terrorist group?"

"That's what I saw in the chat room on the dark web. But it's the Saints masquerading as terrorists."

"Then they'll be a part of the audience, and possibly part of the ballet troupe."

Callie made an inaudible sound. "Wyatt said the same thing. That's why I got you tickets in a box. It'll give you the advantage of looking around the theatre.

It should also give you time to make your escape and get to Denys Stasiuk since he's in the box directly above you."

"If I was going after him, I'd use a sniper," Lev said.

"There's too much chatter for just a hit. No, they'll want to make an example out of him."

Lev pulled his ticket from his pocket to hand to the attendant. With a nod of his head, he entered the theatre. "Here we go," he whispered.

2

There was no turning back. Though Reyna had known that the moment she joined the Saints five years earlier. The pearl dangling from her earlobe brushed against her neck as she made her way up to the balcony seats.

At one time, she would've been ecstatic to attend the ballet. She'd always loved to watch dancers. While she'd been in a few classes when she was a child, it had soon become apparent that she didn't have the skill for it. Yet she remained because her love for it was so strong.

Perhaps if she'd known her skills lay elsewhere at such a young age, she would've left dance.

Her gaze was trained on the stage and the closed burgundy velvet curtains, but her mind was going through her plan. There was no fear or excitement within her like there used to be before such a mission. Her first twenty or so assignments, she'd vomited before each one. Once she'd settled into her role, the fear and anxiety turned to anticipation and exhilaration.

She was dead inside now. Had been for some time.

The lights flickered twice to alert everyone that the show was about to begin. Reyna drew in a deep breath as the lights lowered and the first strings of music from the orchestra filled the air.

For the next forty-five minutes, she let herself pretend that she was a normal person taking in a ballet like everyone else. The music, the performers, the dancing was all magical. She wanted nothing more than to watch the rest of the show.

But her internal clock reminded her that her desires didn't matter. Reyna got to her feet and made her way past other patrons to the aisle. She then walked out of the doors and turned right.

After a quick glance around to make sure that no one was watching, she entered through a door marked STAFF ONLY. Holding her long skirt up, she quickly navigated the stairs in her stilettos.

When Reyna reached the bottom, four armed figures in solid black garb waited for her. One handed her a pistol. She took a moment to look at each of the men before giving a nod that set the night into motion.

One of the men spoke into a transceiver, letting the other groups know that the operation was a go. Reyna released the magazine of the gun and saw that it was still fully loaded with jacketed hollow point rounds.

She slid the magazine into the weapon and pulled back the slide. At that moment, her men were barring doors to make sure no one could get in or out of the theatre.

"Ma'am."

That was her signal that it was time for the next step. Reyna didn't want to interrupt the ballet. It reminded her of the world she'd been in before, the life she'd had. The dancers and the crowd watching were oblivious to the chaos that was about to descend.

She lifted her skirts again and continued down the remaining stairs that brought her backstage. The dancers making their way to the stage shrieked when they saw her and the black-clad men—and the weapons.

Reyna ignored them, knowing that the soldiers behind her would gather the stragglers. She kept walking, past the stage manager with her headset. She flashed a confused look when she saw Reyna.

Reyna met her gaze and lifted her finger to her lips as she strode past. The woman's mouth fell open as her hands dropped to her sides, and the clipboard clattered loudly to the floor.

Reyna's men rushed past her and onto the stage as Reyna stood in the wings, her gaze locked on that of Denys Stasiuk. He wasn't her target. She was there to ensure that no one else tried to do anything heroic to save the day.

The disconnected sound of the orchestra as they quickly stopped playing was only overshadowed by the screams of the audience members. The dancers were too shocked to do more than try to leave the stage. But they were soon met with more men and guns.

Reyna waited as Emil walked out onto the stage, looking as if he owned the place. And for the next few minutes, he did. She didn't listen as he began telling the crowd that he and his soldiers weren't there to kill everyone. That they were after one man: Stasiuk.

Every eye in the theatre turned to the box where the politician sat.

All eyes, except for one person's. Reyna zeroed in on the man casually sitting in the box directly below Stasiuk's. He sat too calmly. He wasn't bothered by the screams, the men, or the guns. Obviously, he was someone well acquainted with violence. More telling was the way his gaze moved over each soldier as if memorizing their faces.

Reyna didn't know if he worked for Stasiuk or if he just happened to be at the ballet, but men like him were exactly the reason she was there. She needed to get rid of him before he compromised the mission and unraveled everything she had worked for. Not once did she think he was a Saint, because she was in charge of the mission and knew every individual from the society there.

She smiled when the man moved quickly and silently out of his seat and then disappeared from the box. Reyna took another moment to look at those in the theatre. She glanced at her counterpart on the other side of the stage and got a shake of the head to confirm that nothing was amiss.

Reyna whirled around and made her way back to the stairs. No doubt her target would try to come at them from the top. There were men up there, waiting for just such an attack, so she wasn't worried.

Until she reached the top and found herself staring at two dead soldiers. Less than twenty feet away were another two, also deceased.

"Who are you?" she murmured about the unknown man.

She'd been right that he had gone up, but who did he work for? Few in the world actually knew who the

Saints were or those who were part of the organization. Anyone who spoke out against them either intentionally or not was eliminated, swiftly and most times, violently.

Which is precisely what was happening to Stasiuk.

Except no one would know that the Saints were actually behind this takeover. Only Stasiuk and those who worked with him would know the truth. The rest of the world would believe they were some terrorist group who would be taken out the very night they showed up.

The quiet of the hallway didn't bother her. She knew her target was near. Reyna glanced down at the two dead men at her feet before she walked to the second set. All four had been killed without a gun.

That didn't mean the unknown man wasn't armed. It only meant that he hadn't wanted to bring attention to himself and give away his location. Reyna was shocked to feel a little flurry of interest in her stomach. She hadn't had such a match in...a very long time.

She silently made her way to the next doorway and squatted down before slowly peering around the corner. There was no sign of the man. She waited a few more seconds, but still, nothing.

Reyna straightened and cautiously walked to the next door. She tested the doorknob, only to find it locked. Methodically, she checked each of the doors down the hallway. With every one she found locked, she knew she was closing in on him.

Except when she came to the last hallway and looked around the corner. There was no one. She narrowed her gaze. He was here. She knew it. And she *would* find him.

She turned her head to look back the way she'd come. Then she tried to imagine what she might do if she were in his shoes. Her lips turned up in a smile because she would hide until the coast was clear, and she could make her way down.

Reyna stepped through the doorway and flattened herself against the wall. It wouldn't be sight that alerted her to his presence. It would be her hearing.

She closed her eyes and strained to hear every detail. She picked up Emil talking below, though she couldn't hear his exact words. Minutes ticked by slowly, but still, she didn't move. Then, the softest of clicks had her eyes flying open.

If she hadn't been listening for it, she never would have heard it. She peered around the corner and saw a figure walk out of a room. His back was to her. Just as she was about to step around the corner, she saw him start to turn her way. Reyna ducked back out of sight before he could see her.

Reyna waited and then spun around the corner, lifting her gun. The man had his back to her once more. She spotted one of the Saints' transceivers in his hand, so he knew where they were.

She lengthened her strides and stopped about ten feet from him. Then she pulled the hammer back on the gun. The click was shockingly loud in the space, but it had the effect she'd been going for.

"Don't be a hero."

She inwardly winced at her use of English. Reyna knew better than to make such a move. She repeated the statement in both Ukrainian and Russian as she stared at his thick, midnight hair and incredibly wide shoulders.

Then he turned to face her. She had seen his face from a distance, but it didn't prepare her for an up-close viewing. He was sinfully attractive. From his piercing blue eyes to the hard-as-granite jawline to his lips.

For a heartbeat, she forgot where she was and what she was supposed to be doing as she became lost in his eyes. The sound of a gunshot below brought her back to the present.

"Who are you?" she asked in Russian since that seemed to be the dialect he responded to.

He twisted his lips and shrugged one shoulder.

She took a step closer and put her bag down, keeping the pistol aimed at his head. Then, she lowered it between his legs. "Don't make me ask again."

If it were possible, his eyes went even icier. Then, in a deep, rich voice he said in Russian, "My name does not matter."

"Then tell me who sent you."

His hands might be raised because she had a gun pointed at him, but he looked bored. "No one."

As if she expected him to answer any differently. And even though she knew the next answer as well, she still asked, "Are you alone?"

"*Da.*"

Whether it was a lie or not, she couldn't chance the mission going south. "It just isn't your lucky day."

She didn't want to kill him, but she didn't have another choice. Too much hinged on this night. Just as she was about to pull the trigger, the man shifted, coming right at her.

Before Reyna knew it, she was on the ground with the man on top of her. He knocked the gun from her hand and reached into his jacket, but she batted his arm away and got to the weapon first.

She slammed the butt of the pistol against his jaw, which only angered him and caused a muttering of cuss words to fall from his lips. Despite his size and bulk, she still managed to get on top once more. But she didn't keep the advantage for more than a second before she was on the floor again.

Using all the hand-to-hand combat skills she'd acquired over her years of training, the two of them battled. He was good. Very good. Perhaps the best she'd ever encountered—and that said a lot.

But she had to win. She had to succeed. There was no other option.

It was that desperation that had gotten her this far. And it was what eventually showed her the opening to elbow him in the side of the head. The blow caused his body to slam against the wall, dazing him.

That was all she needed to get to her feet and have the gun pointed at him once more. She was breathing heavily as she found her footing and realized that she'd lost a shoe in the fight. But she was more worried about where her gun was than her heel.

A strand of hair fell into her face. She tasted blood in her mouth. The man had gotten off several good hits. She would be sore tomorrow.

"Hands up," she told him.

He blinked several times. No doubt trying to stop the room from spinning. It gave her the opportunity she needed to find her gun. Now, with two weapons pointed at him, she met his gaze.

There was no anger at being defeated, no resignation at the thought of losing his life. Only an emptiness she knew all too well.

She slid her finger to the trigger, and yet she couldn't seem to pull it. Never in her life had she hesitated. Why was she now? What was it about the man that brought back feelings she hadn't felt in years?

"Slowly remove the rest of your weapons," she ordered.

He blinked and gingerly pulled out another pistol and two knives that he then put on the floor and slid over to her.

After she'd picked up the gun and the blades and put them in her bag, she shifted to the side to get her shoe. That's when she saw the COM in his ear. The best solution would be for her to kill and forget him. But it might be wiser to figure out who he was working for and how many others were there.

That kind of knowledge would get her right where she needed to be with the Saints.

"It seems luck is on your side, after all," she told him.

3

S he had shocked him.
　　And that wasn't something that happened easily. Or often.

Lev saw her move her finger away from the trigger on the gun, but she didn't lower either of them. She might have given him a reprieve, but she wouldn't hesitate to shoot him if he gave her a reason.

"Move," she ordered.

Her Russian was impeccable, without even the slightest accent. That was a skill of someone who had spent considerable time in Russia—and had an excellent tutor. If Lev had to guess, he suspected the woman worked for some American intelligence agency. Most likely the CIA.

He climbed to his feet, only to be forced to put his hand on the wall since he was still slightly dizzy. No one had ever rung his bell quite like the American. He wanted to hate her for it, but he found himself impressed with her.

He'd gotten the upper hand several times in their fight, but she was resilient—and determined. She gave no quarter. He hadn't pulled any punches either. The fact that she'd been able to take the hits he'd dealt her and still keep coming at him said something about her training.

Her elbow to his temple wouldn't have knocked him on his ass. Neither would slamming his head into the wall. But both? Yeah, they'd done the job adequately. It meant that she was used to employing anything and everything around her to her advantage.

While he utilized his mind and brute strength.

She'd won this round. The next was still up for grabs. And Lev intended to come out on top of that one.

He grudgingly walked to the stairwell he'd climbed earlier. Most likely, she would take him to the others. Fat lot of good he would be to Stasiuk now that he too was caught. It seemed that the politician wouldn't be the only one dying this night. Looked like Lev would be another body for the Saints to drive home their point.

And Lev couldn't even tell Callie or anyone back in Texas what was going on or warn them. Then again, they'd realize that something was wrong when he didn't answer through the COMs, and then when they saw his and Stasiuk's bodies on the news.

Just before Lev was about to go down the stairs, the muzzle of the gun pressed into the middle of his back. "Stop," the woman stated.

He turned his head to the side to try and get a glimpse of her. "Where do you want me to go?"

She didn't answer immediately. From what little Lev could see of her face, it appeared as if she were attempting to decide what to do with him. That could mean that she intended to try and get information out of him. She would soon learn that it didn't matter what kind of torture they put him through, he would tell them nothing.

Lev heard her mumble a curse word. He bit back a grin. "Problems?"

"Down one flight of stairs," she barked.

He made his way down and glanced at her as he turned on the switchback. She didn't seem fazed at maneuvering in heels and a long dress. In fact, she acted as if she dressed like this for every mission. She certainly fit the part well.

Once they reached the next level, she moved in front to face him. Then she positioned one of the pistols right at his groin. She raised a brow, silently telling him that she wouldn't hesitate to shoot off his balls if he dared to make a move.

Since Lev was partial to his man parts, he kept silent as she opened the door just wide enough to look through. She told someone in Ukrainian that they were needed below.

As soon as the sound of boots faded, she pushed the door open wider with her shoulder and motioned at Lev with the gun to follow.

He had the opportunity to escape. He'd had it while she spoke with the soldier despite the gun pointed at his cock. But he hadn't taken it. Mostly because, while she thought she could get intel from him, he knew he could get information from her.

When he was through the door, she moved behind him again. He started walking, their pace quick. It was obvious that she intended to get him out without anyone seeing them together. It was ballsy.

And he reluctantly admitted to himself that he respected her for it.

With remarkable ease, he watched as she

navigated them around soldiers without anyone seeing either of them. In no time, they reached the door to exit the theatre. Except it was chained.

She didn't even pause. Lev frowned as she nudged him to walk to the left. Soon, he was descending into the lower section of the theatre below the stage. He had to bend over in some places just to move, but she effortlessly made her way through the maze of props and beams.

Not long after, Lev figured out where they were thanks to Callie getting the schematics of the theatre. There was a door toward the back that was no longer used. That's exactly where the woman was taking them.

When they reached it, he stopped, thinking that she had the key to unlock it. Instead, she pulled a pin from her hair and handed it to him.

He held it and gaped at her. "You want me to do it?"

"I'm not exactly going to put my back to you, am I?" she replied.

Lev blew out a breath and dropped to one knee to pick the lock. It took him longer than usual, but he got it done. He heard the click and stood to open the door. She smiled then and motioned with the gun for him to proceed.

"What? No 'well done?'" he mocked.

She came up behind him and said, "Well done."

While it had been said sarcastically, the husky sound of her voice and the fact that her body had been nearly pressed against him shocked Lev so much that he didn't move for a second.

"Come," she ordered.

She walked him to an older-model black

Mercedes and pointed at the driver's side. Once he was in the seat, she climbed into the passenger side and handed him the keys.

"Any destination in particular?" he said snippily.

Her dark eyes cut to him. "Don't like being the driver?"

There was a ghost of a smile on her lips. Lev hated that she found humor in his irritation. Though he had to admit, he wondered what her mouth would look like in a true smile.

He started the engine and put the car in drive. She still had one of the guns pointed at him, but her eyes were on the road. He drove them through the city, Lev turning where she told him until the buildings began to fade into the background.

Neither spoke as they continued down the road that took them farther and farther from the city. Another thirty minutes passed before she told him to take the next right.

Lev nearly missed the road. There were no signs, and frankly, it wasn't much of a road. He drove slowly down the lane as it curved one way and then the other, with dense trees on either side, until he saw the cabin. He pulled in front of it and put the car in park.

The woman reached over and turned off the ignition to take the keys. "Out."

The only person he'd ever been able to take orders from was Sergei. Having to take them from the American was like rubbing salt in a wound. He ground his teeth together and climbed from the car.

She was quick to follow him out, standing just far enough away to keep him from reaching for her gun. The woman motioned with the pistol to get him moving. As he walked to the cabin, he let his gaze wander. There wasn't much he could see in the darkness, but the trees would provide him cover when he escaped.

She raised a brow when he hesitated at the door. He glared at the gun still pointed at him and entered the structure. Lev stood in darkness as she closed the door behind her after entering. There was the sound of something striking something else, then a hiss as light flared to his left. He looked over to see her moving a match to a hurricane lamp. One by one, she lit three others and two candles.

Oddly, they shed quite a bit of light to show the cozy cabin. There were only the necessities, and it looked as if no one had been there for a few months. Which meant this must be a safe house for her.

"Your name," she demanded.

He leaned back against the door and crossed his arms over his chest. "Yours first."

She kicked off her shoes and put her bag and the other gun on the table. "Reyna."

"Lev," he responded.

"Well, Lev, let me show you to your quarters."

He stared down the barrel of the gun she still had pointed at him and dropped his arms to his sides as he pushed away from the door. Lev walked toward her before she motioned to the door on the right. He passed a bathroom and moved into a tiny room with a cot and shackles attached to chains hanging from the wall.

"Fasten them," she demanded.

Lev shrugged out of his jacket and folded it neatly to lay at the foot of the bed. Then he untied his bowtie and tossed it aside. Only then did he turn to face her.

"Confining me is not the way to go."

"Oh?" she asked sarcastically. "I beg to differ. I actually want to sleep tonight. I'm not going to do that unless you're locked up."

"You could ask me to stay."

She let out a bark of laughter. "I might try that next time." Then she held out her palm.

He frowned at the outstretched hand. "What?"

"The COM in your ear, please."

Damn. He'd thought he might get lucky and have her forget about it, though he wasn't sure what good it was since he hadn't heard from Callie since the theatre. Lev reached up and removed the COM to place in Reyna's hand.

She flashed a quick grin of appreciation and motioned to the chains with the gun. He couldn't wait to take the weapon from her. Maybe he'd even tie her up.

The image that flashed in his mind had nothing to do with torture. It was so surprising that he jerked in shock, but he quickly covered it by locking one shackle and then the other around his wrists. He was able to move slightly from the bed to the window, but little else.

The moment the chains were on, she lowered the gun. Her shoulders dropped slightly, and for the first time, he saw her exhaustion. When she walked to check the window, he noticed that she limped.

Had that happened when they fought? Most likely. He hadn't even known he'd hurt her. And, dammit, he didn't want to feel bad about any injuries that he'd given her. He was her prisoner, after all.

Willing prisoner, he had to remind himself.

She didn't say another word as she walked out.

Reyna didn't even close the door behind her. Lev listened as she moved around the bedroom across the narrow hall. It wasn't long before she was in the kitchen making noise.

To his surprise, she returned a short time later with a sandwich on a plate as well as a Styrofoam cup filled with beer. She set it on the table next to him and backed away.

"It isn't much, but I thought you might be hungry."

He was a little peckish now that he had food in front of him. "Why did you bring me here?"

She shrugged. "It wasn't exactly a smart move."

"You want something from me."

Reyna lifted the COM. "Who sent you?"

Lev ignored her and reached for the food. He took a bite, surprised at how good it tasted. He chewed and swallowed before he drank down half of the beer before bringing the sandwich to his mouth once more.

She finally sighed and walked out. This time, she closed the door behind her. He stared at the entrance even as he heard the sound of a chair scraping on the floor. Was she eating her own sandwich? It was too bad they weren't eating together.

He winced. Those thoughts really needed to stop. He had a mission, and it didn't involve an American posing as a Ukrainian.

Lev wiped his mouth after he'd finished his meal. Then he lay back on the bed and crossed his ankles, turning his head to the light under his door as he wondered what Reyna was doing.

4

The meditation wasn't working this morning. Reyna opened her eyes and blew out an exhausted breath while looking at the dense forest before her. All she'd wanted was sleep after she and Lev had gotten to the cabin, but the hours had crawled by with agonizing slowness as she lay in bed.

She couldn't even blame it on her prisoner since he hadn't made a sound at all. Reyna had finally given up and rose, thinking that some meditation and a workout might be just what she needed to focus her mind once more.

The workout had gone great. And even though she was a little sore from her skirmish with Lev, it didn't stop her from her normal routine.

She rose from the deck and slowly moved her gaze from one side of the woods to the other. The cabin was far enough back from the road that someone couldn't just happen upon it. And if anyone did venture down the lane, she had alarms at various places along the drive that would alert her when someone got close.

But if the Saints—or anyone—decided to come

after her, they wouldn't drive up to the cabin. They'd come through the forest. Her years at the CIA had given her a lot of training for just such scenarios, and thankfully, she had made some good friends along the way. Acquaintances that didn't care who she worked for. They only wanted her money.

It was just such a friend that had made the sensors along the drive as well as certain places in the woods. She also had ammunition and guns, but it wouldn't be enough.

She yanked the elastic free from her hair to let the ponytail down. She then shook out her locks and walked back into the cabin. Dawn had just broken. No doubt Lev was awake, which meant she needed to see to him.

Reyna put the kettle on to heat. Then she opened Lev's door slowly and peeked inside to find him standing at the window looking out. The chains clanked together as he drew in a deep breath, his shoulders rising as he did.

She watched him for a few seconds as she recalled how he'd yanked off the bowtie as if the thought of it around his throat had been too much. Even standing in what remained of his eveningwear, he cut a handsome figure.

Quite frankly, she was glad that his eyes weren't on her. He had a way of looking at her that made her antsy, as if he were peeling back her many layers of armor to see into her soul. Lev wouldn't find anything there. She'd lost her soul when she joined the CIA.

Her heart...well, she'd lost that long ago, as well.

"You did not sleep."

His words surprised her. She'd thought he'd been

resting. "I won't fall asleep today if you think that's how you'll get free."

The chains clinked again as he looked at her over his shoulder. Lev said nothing, just stared at her with his frosty blue gaze.

She left the door ajar and returned to the kitchen. She didn't usually eat breakfast, but she found she was starving this morning. She made bacon and eggs, filling two plates. Then she poured two cups of tea. With a mug and plate in hand, she returned to Lev's room.

This time, he faced her when she walked in. She met his gaze and held out her hands for him to take the food. In the blink of an eye, she saw him size her up and determine if there was a way for him to get free.

"The key to the chains is hidden, so I wouldn't suggest killing me. Otherwise, you'll starve," she told him.

Lev shrugged and said, "I've been in worse situations and have gotten free."

After he'd taken the food and turned to sit on the bed, he set the cup of tea down and began eating without looking at her again. Reyna, however, was ready for information. Unfortunately, her stomach rumbled, reminding her that she needed to fill it.

She pivoted and made her way to the kitchen table where she sat. While she ate, she checked the video feed of the cameras throughout the forest from her phone. There hadn't been an alert, but it was a habit for her to look anyway.

Reyna downed the food and found that it improved her mood some. She fixed another mug of tea and drank it as she thought about the day. No doubt her handler from the Saints, Lorraine, would contact her any minute. Reyna had followed protocol for last night, though she had left a little earlier than she was supposed to—with a prisoner in tow.

As if her thoughts had conjured the Saints, her phone buzzed. Thanks to some work from a hacker friend, the Saints—and anyone else looking for her—would believe she was in Kiev. But she knew such technology could only help her for so long.

She answered the phone, gripping it tightly. Reyna had pushed the boundaries very little while in the Saints. This was the first time she had dared to test just how far she could go.

"I thought you'd sound more pleased," said the American woman's voice on the other end. "Everything went according to plan just as you said it would."

Reyna sat forward at the sound of Lorraine's voice, leaning her elbow on the table. "I am pleased."

"The repercussions of Stasiuk's meddling is spreading far and wide. Everyone will think twice about going against us."

"Except they don't know it was us," Reyna said.

Loraine laughed. "Those who needed reminding know it's us. That's what matters."

"That's good to hear."

"You make me look good, Reyna. I knew you were wasted in the CIA. You're much better off with us. Keep up the good work."

Reyna squeezed her eyes closed. "Thank you."

"How do you feel about returning home?"

Reyna sat up straighter, unease rippling through her. "You want me back in America?"

"We're having a little issue that needs to be

addressed. One of our other operatives let us down and was killed. I told them you'd get the job done because you always succeed in whatever I send you to do."

Reyna pulled out her tablet and searched American news outlets for any information. "That's my job. What do you need me to do?"

"You'll get details soon. I worked in a couple of days off for you. Enjoy them while you can."

The line went dead. Reyna shut off the phone and set it aside. She hadn't been back to the US in five years. Not since...

She wasn't sure she wanted to return. In fact, she'd assumed that they would keep her where she was since she had been completing the jobs. Reyna didn't want to think of the people who had died so she could topple the Saints, but it was better than billions dying.

The sound of Lev's chains pulled her out of her thoughts. Shit. He would have heard her conversation. Even if he didn't understand English, he would've known she spoke it. Did it matter, though?

She needed information from him. And after? Well, she wasn't sure what she would do with him then. The best course of action would be to kill him, but she hadn't actually pulled the trigger to end someone's life in nearly two years.

While she didn't hesitate to defend herself, the shots she took only wounded her enemies. It just happened that other Saints fired the killing shots.

That didn't exempt her from the deaths. The fact that she was there, fighting alongside the Saints—no matter *why*—made her accountable.

What it meant for her aloof prisoner, she wasn't sure.

Reyna pushed aside the tablet after not finding anything and rose from her chair. She had two days with Lev. It wasn't a lot, but it would have to do. When she reached the door, she leaned her shoulder against it to find him reclining on the bed, his hands laced behind his head, his ankles crossed, and his eyes closed.

"I need intelligence," she told him in Russian. "I'm prepared to take whatever steps I have to in order to get it."

His head turned toward her as he opened his eyes. Then he said in perfect English without even a hint of a Russian accent, "Then you better get to it."

Damn. She'd really held out hope that he was Russian. Not that she particularly wanted to mess with anyone from that country, but it would be better than someone from the US. Since the Saints infiltrated not only the governments but also the intelligence agencies of both Russia and America, Reyna couldn't trust anyone. For all she knew, Lev had been sent to kill her.

"Did they send you for me?" she demanded.

He sat up, swinging his legs over the side of the bed. "Would you believe anything I told you?"

No. And that was the rub.

"I'm here for the Saints," Lev stated.

Reyna wasn't sure how to take his confession. He could be someone standing against the organization. It was insane and foolish, but a few dared—though they never lived long enough to do any damage.

Then again, he could be a Saint testing her allegiance.

Lev never broke eye contact. "You don't believe me."

"I'm waiting for you to continue."

His head tilted slightly. "Why didn't you kill me at the theatre?"

"Because I want intel."

"On?"

"Whoever sent you."

He blew out a breath. "Free me, and I'll tell you anything you want to know."

"Right," she said with a laugh.

"No one sent me. I came on my own."

Reyna retrieved the COM from the kitchen counter and returned to the doorway. "This says otherwise."

"I didn't say I wasn't working with others. I simply said no one sent me."

"So, who are you working with?"

"Does it matter?" he asked.

She raised her brows and nodded. "It does."

"Again, would you believe me?"

"Give me a reason to," she stated.

One side of his lips lifted in a smile. "What were you? CIA? Secret Service? I recognize the training."

"You say that as if you were trained, as well."

He shook his head slowly. "Why would you get mixed up with the Saints?"

"Why are you here?"

"Do you know what they are? What they're planning?"

She pushed away from the doorway. "Who are you working with?"

He flashed her a quick grin. "You're going to have to do better than that to get anything from me."

"I could probably cut off every one of your fingers, and you still wouldn't tell me anything," she guessed.

His smile was slow as it filled his face. "That's right. Keep asking your questions. I've got some of my own."

"If you won't tell me anything, then there's no point in keeping you around."

"Then shoot me," he said as his smile vanished and he held out his arms. "Or free me. But do something."

She frowned. "Do you think I won't put a bullet in your skull?"

"You had the chance and didn't do it. That means you want something bad enough to bring me out here, chain me up, and keep me prisoner in the hopes you might get it. It reeks of desperation."

"Maybe in your eyes," she retorted. "In mine, I know what will happen *when* I get what I want from you and take it to my superiors."

He lifted one shoulder in a shrug. "I might tell you something, but how do you know it's not a lie? Your plan to gain some advantage with your superiors will be for naught if what I give you is false information."

Damn him for being right. Her ex-partner, Arthur, had said that she didn't have the stomach for torture. He was right, but she didn't have a choice now. Too much rested on her shoulders.

"It's a chance I'll have to take."

Lev tsked. "You're going to have to trust someone, Reyna."

"And you want me to trust you?" She laughed and shook her head. "That's not going to happen."

5

S omeone would have to be the first to bend. It wasn't something Lev did. Ever. But after hearing Reyna on the phone, he had a suspicion that there was a lot about the female she kept hidden.

Much as he did.

Her dark eyes held his as if daring him to be the first to crack. He'd been through so many levels of Hell, that it would take much more than her to break him. And while his instinct was to refuse to budge, he recalled fighting alongside the Loughmans, their women, Yuri, and Maks Petrov against the Saints.

It had felt good to take such a stand, even if it killed him not to be by Sergei's side to protect him. The sooner Lev finished with this, the sooner he could get back to Maryland and Sergei.

Where he belonged.

Because as much as the Loughmans might try and make him feel as if he were part of their group, Lev knew better. He was a loner. Destiny had chosen that road for him. Sergei had given him a home and a place to hone his skills. Lev owed Sergei *everything*.

"You want information?" Lev lifted his arms. "Take these off."

Reyna shook her head of caramel locks. "I quite like walking around without having my gun pointed at you every second."

"I won't attack you or leave."

She barked in laughter. "As if I'll take your word."

Lev glanced down at the floor. He'd planned to wait to show her that he'd picked the locks during the night with the pin that she'd given him to unlock the door at the theatre, but it seemed that now was his opportunity.

He tugged gently, and the shackles fell to the floor. Reyna's eyes widened as her lips parted in shock. Then her gaze jerked to his face.

"You forgot to take this back," Lev said as he held up the pin. "I unlocked them within an hour of being here last night. I didn't harm you or leave when I had the chance. That should prove my word is good."

She closed her lips and swallowed. Anger tightened her features, but he suspected that she was furious with herself more than him. "Who are you?" she demanded. "I've done this job a long time. I don't make mistakes."

"You did last night," he pointed out.

"If I made those kinds of mistakes often, I wouldn't be alive."

She spoke the truth there. Had it been anyone but him, she would be dead. But he didn't point that out. There was no need. She knew.

Lev got to his feet. As he did, he saw the way she took a defensive step back, readying to go for a gun she most likely had stashed nearby.

He ignored her and picked up his empty plate

and mug before he walked past her to the kitchen. Lev set the dishes by the sink and rolled up his sleeves. He had his back to her, but he was aware of her position.

As soon as he had walked into the kitchen, Reyna moved to the fireplace and reached into the bucket of wood for a pistol. Lev didn't say anything to her. If it made her feel safer to have a weapon pointed at him, then he'd let her. For now.

After he'd finished the dishes, he dried his hands and turned to face her, leaning back against the counter. He spread the damp towel out to dry and folded his arms across his chest. The only good thing was that she didn't have the gun pointed at him.

"I don't work for the Saints," he told her. "I came here to stop Stasiuk's assassination."

"You didn't succeed."

He drew in a breath. "I know."

"Even if you had saved him, the Saints would've gone after him again. And again. Until they ended him."

Lev wondered if she realized that she didn't include herself with the Saints. That slip-up might have been done on purpose, but his instincts said otherwise. His gut told him that Reyna wasn't with the Saints, even if she was working for them.

Which meant that she might be undercover. It made sense. Especially given she was so adamant about wanting information to take to her superiors.

"You're probably right," he conceded. "But I would've liked to shove another loss in the Saints' faces."

Her gaze intensified. "Another?"

Lev hid his smile. He'd known that would get her attention. "You heard right."

"Tell me more."

He had leverage to get information out of her, but he decided to hold off for now. It was a calculated risk, one that he hoped would pay big dividends. "We killed the scientist who developed Ragnarok."

Confusion marred her face as she shook her head. "What's that?"

"You must not be very high up in the organization if you don't know about the bioweapon they had developed to sterilize women."

Her nostrils flared as shock reverberated from her in waves. "Was the bioweapon actually developed?"

"Yes. And before you ask, the Saints will never get their hands on it."

"You mean you have it?"

Lev decided to lie. "It was destroyed."

Reyna nodded, her gaze on the floor.

He remembered when he first heard about the bioweapon. He'd been so astounded that he hadn't wanted to believe the news. He'd chosen to ignore things, but it was Sergei who made them enter the fight, first by helping Mia and Cullen, and then by joining the entire Loughman family.

Reyna walked to the table and set the gun down before she opened a cabinet and pulled out a bottle of vodka and two shot glasses. Her hands shook slightly as she poured the alcohol into each glass. Without looking at him, she downed her shot and placed the back of her hand against her lips, her eyes closed.

Lev dropped his arms and made his way to the table. When he finished off his shot, her eyes were locked on him. She once more had her emotions under control. It was the mark of a professional. The more he watched her, the more he suspected that she was CIA. He'd had enough run-ins with them on the docks in Dover to know their look.

"Why did you leave the CIA?" he asked.

She poured another round before she met his gaze. "Sometimes, we have no choice but to walk the path before us."

He knew the feeling well. He'd done it himself. "You've been on this path for some time."

"I'll remain on it until I'm finished."

"Doing what?"

Instead of answering, she drank the shot of vodka. "Who are you working with?"

"I'm not giving up names. We've gotten the notice of the Saints, though. Between the bioweapon, the scientist, and thwarting an attack on us, we've delivered three big defeats. And I'm guessing by your phone call earlier that we're the reason they're sending you back to the States."

"I didn't get any info. I was only told there was a problem that needed to be dealt with in America."

Lev grinned and downed his shot. "That would be us."

"You shouldn't be happy about it. They'll be relentless in their pursuit to bring you down."

He raised a brow. "They?"

Reyna closed her eyes in frustration as she compressed her lips. When she lifted her lids, there was resolve there. Lev waited for her to make up some excuse as to why she said *they* instead of *we*, but to his surprise, she didn't.

She pulled out the chair and sank into it with a sigh. Then she poured another drink and tossed it back. She swallowed, squeezing her eyes closed briefly before she slammed the glass down on the table.

"For five years, I've been careful about everything I've done and said," she told him. "Maybe this is a sign I should get out of the game."

"Maybe you knew on some level that you could trust me? Or you wanted to." He sat opposite her and reached for the bottle. He poured vodka into both glasses and set the bottle between them.

Reyna shrugged. "There are spies within the Saints. I've been one before. They send us to others they're unsure about, those within the organization who have caused someone to look unfavorably on them."

"You think I'm one of those spies?"

"It wouldn't surprise me. How else would you have known about the assassination last night?"

He leaned back in his chair and scratched his jaw. "One of my colleagues found something in a chat room."

Her brows snapped together. "No. No, no, no. That's not good."

"What?" Lev asked, confused. "Terrorists do that kind of idiocy all the time."

She scraped back her chair as she jumped to her feet. "How did you get to Ukraine?"

"I flew," he said flatly. "By plane. Under a fake passport and name."

Her gaze moved to the floor. "They tracked you. That's the only explanation."

"Hold up," he said as he got to his feet. "What are you talking about?"

Brown eyes met his. "The Saints never broadcast their intentions. *Never*. You were set up."

"Shit," he mumbled.

"And by not killing you, they must know I'm helping you."

Lev looked out one of the windows. "My COM. Did you shut off communications?"

She shook her head. "And we don't wear any."

He recalled the radio he'd taken from the soldier. He and Reyna were in the middle of nowhere. The only way out was in the car he'd driven down the drive that was most likely being watched.

"We need to go. Now."

She nodded in agreement. Both sprang into action. Lev went for his jacket, hating that he was in evening shoes and not something better to make a run for it through the forest.

Reyna tossed him a backpack and pointed at the cupboard. He opened the doors and found non-perishable food and bottled water that he hastily threw into the bag. When he turned around, there were four rifles, ten handguns, three knives, and ammunition for each. She was filling another pack with the bullets and nodded at him to do the same.

As he did, he tossed some of the food into her pack. Then they each grabbed two rifles and split the handguns, with Lev making sure he took his knives.

"This way," Reyna said then grabbed her tablet and walked to the back of the cabin.

He watched as she checked the cameras through the tablet. There wasn't any sign of anyone. Yet. But both of them knew the Saints were coming.

"The call this morning was to get your location," he said.

Reyna shook her head. "I have it so that my location shows in Kiev."

"Are you sure no one followed us last night?"

"No, I'm not sure of anything anymore. We should wait until dark."

He raised a brow. "I wouldn't suggest that."

"We'd have the cover of darkness."

"And they'd have night vision."

She smiled and pulled something out of her pack.

He grinned when he saw the night vision goggles. "I still think we should go now. Get out before they even get close. You must have set up a plan if you ever needed to leave quickly."

"We need to get to the Baltic Sea."

Lev calculated the distance in his head. "That's nearly seven hundred miles."

"Passing into Poland."

"And once we're at the Baltic?"

Reyna adjusted her backpack as she put it on. "We travel by boat."

Lev clenched his fist at the thought of getting on a ship. No matter how many times he'd tried, he got violently seasick. Just what he needed.

6

Loughman Ranch
Texas

"There's something wrong," Callie said to the group before her as they stood in the underground bunker beneath the barn on the Loughman property.

Her gaze went to the eldest Loughman brother, Wyatt, who she'd fallen in love with. He stood silently, but she knew from experience that while he might look as if he weren't interested, his mind was working a million miles a minute.

"Should we call Sergei?" Mia asked.

Callie looked into Mia's black eyes and shrugged. "I would."

Cullen, the youngest of the Loughman brothers, shook his head of dark brown hair. "I disagree. Sergei and Lev have a special bond. If Sergei thinks Lev is in trouble, he'll go find him."

Dr. Kate Donnelly's gray eyes widened in surprise before she frowned. "As we should all want to go find Lev. He's one of us."

"Of course, he is," Orrin Loughman said to soothe her, taking her hand in his and giving her a smile. "And we do."

It warmed Callie's heart to see Orrin so happy. He'd taken on the role of father-figure when she realized that her family lacked anything remotely good in them. It was Orrin who had recruited her for the private contract business, Whitehorse. Though none of them could have possibly imagined that it would progress to hunting down a clandestine global organization out to determine who got to have children and who didn't.

Each of them knew this was just the first step in the Saints' plans. It was anyone's guess what they would do next if they succeeded.

Callie's gaze shifted to Owen and his wife Natalie, who had yet to say anything. As the middle brother, Owen usually kept the peace between everyone. Although, thanks to the Saints forcing the family back together, the past had been forgiven, truths had been discovered, and healing had begun.

"I've seen Lev in action," Owen said to the group, his dark brown eyes sweeping over each of them. "He's not easily killed."

Yuri Markovic, a Russian major general who'd left his country to fight against the Saints, snorted from his chair. His gaze was on the mug of steaming coffee in his hands.

"Yuri?" Orrin urged.

The Russian lifted his blue eyes after pouring a healthy dose of vodka into his coffee. "I told you all from the beginning not to send anyone to Ukraine. I said it then, and I still hold to the fact it was a setup."

Callie tried not to be offended, or feel like this

was somehow her fault, but she couldn't seem to shake it. "I triple-checked everything. The chatroom and thread were legitimate."

"None of that matters," Natalie said. Her green eyes looked first at Owen and then at the rest of them. "If it was a setup, the Saints played us good. If it wasn't, then we need to know what went wrong. And, bottom line, we have to discover if Lev is alive."

Owen smiled as he kissed his wife's temple. "You're exactly right, sweetheart."

"If this was a trap by the Saints, then they would've made sure we knew Lev was dead," Wyatt stated.

Cullen frowned. "You're assuming they know who all is helping. And that they would've figured it out despite Lev traveling under a false name."

"They know," Orrin said, his voice soft but carrying through the bunker.

Yuri nodded solemnly. "*Da.*"

"Even Maks?" Kate asked.

All eyes turned to Callie. She threw up her hands in frustration and from a growing concern in the pit of her stomach. "I tried to keep track of Maks, but he ditched the tracker I planted on him."

"As well as the one I stuck in his pack," Wyatt added.

Callie blew out a breath. "I've never seen someone become a ghost like Maks."

"Where was he going again?" Natalie asked.

Once more, they looked at Callie. She hated not having answers. "All he said was that he was headed to do a little investigating on his own and that he'd be in touch."

"That was two weeks ago," Owen said.

Wyatt moved to stand beside Callie. He linked his fingers with hers, giving her the support she needed. "Maks can take care of himself. Trust me on that. Our focus needs to be on Lev."

Mia's lips twisted. "We just said that the Saints probably know each of us. That means they'll know Lev's connection to Sergei, regardless of what name Lev flew under."

Cullen, Owen, and Wyatt all exchanged a look. It was Cullen who pulled out his phone. "I'll call Sergei."

There were tense seconds until Cullen gave a nod as Sergei answered. It was a quick conversation where Cullen warned the old Russian to be vigilant. Then Sergei asked about Lev.

"We lost contact with him during the mission," Cullen told the mob boss.

Callie turned to her computer and sat down. She had been monitoring news outlets in Ukraine, looking for any sign that the assassination attempt on Denys Stasiuk had either failed or succeeded. Oddly, there had been nothing since she'd lost contact with Lev.

But all that changed with a click of a button. She stared in shock at the picture of the theatre bathed in red and blue lights as the authorities sent in tactical units.

"Uh, guys," she said. In seconds, everyone surrounded her.

Kate asked, "What are they saying?"

"It's Ukrainian," Yuri said. "They're talking about a terrorist group who stopped the ballet to make a speech."

It was exactly as Callie had read would happen in

the chat room on the dark web. Was Yuri right? Had this been a setup? Had they sent Lev to his death?

Callie didn't need Yuri to tell her what the reporter was conveying now. It was obvious by the spray of bullets that the authorities were fighting the Saints.

The gunfire was over quickly. Almost too quickly.

"Most of the Saints must have already left the theatre," Orrin said.

Mia shook her head sadly. "The authorities never stood a chance. They walked into a trap."

"I still don't understand how this helps the Saints," Kate said. "They went into a theatre and killed someone. They didn't say they were the Saints, so what do they gain by this?"

It was Wyatt who said, "Power."

"He's right," Callie said. "Stasiuk had made quite a bit of traction within his political party against the Saints. The fact that he ignored numerous threats on his life, as well as his family's, made others realize they should, as well. Stasiuk and those who stood with him believed that they had won against the Saints."

Yuri made a sound in the back of his throat. "And Stasiuk discovered tonight what it's like to walk into a den of vipers."

It was easy for them to feel as if they had made headway against the Saints since they'd won a couple of skirmishes, but the simple fact was that the Saints were a *global* organization.

They had infiltrated not just governments around the world, but also intelligence organizations and police and military forces. Callie feared that the Saints had been building their infrastructure for decades. How were they, just a dozen people, supposed to stand against that?

And win?

As if reading her thoughts, Wyatt put his hand on her shoulder and squeezed. They'd just begun their life together. She wanted a future with Wyatt. To grow old together, take trips, get married, possibly have kids. They might not get any of that.

But if they didn't stand against the Saints, then who would?

"Now we know why we lost contact with Lev," Owen said into the silence.

Callie sat up straighter when the news camera zoomed in on some paramedics wheeling someone out on a gurney, but the sheet covering the face was all the answer she needed.

The room went deathly quiet when they heard the reporter say Stasiuk's name. Each of them knew in that instant that Lev hadn't been able to stop the assassination. But they had yet to determine what had happened to *him*.

"He'd claw his way up from Hell to get back to Sergei," Cullen said.

Callie turned her chair to face them. "Sergei will see this."

"If he hears from Lev, he'll let us know," Orrin stated.

Mia raised a brow, her lips flattening. "I'm not so sure."

"Then we need to remind him we're working as a team," Wyatt declared and looked at Cullen.

Orrin's youngest rolled his eyes. "Fine. I'll call him back."

"No," Mia said as she took Cullen's phone. "I'll do it."

Callie returned her attention to the computer. "Have they said anything about other bodies?"

"Yes," Yuri replied.

Owen asked, "Names?"

Yuri shook his head.

Callie popped her knuckles and rotated her shoulders. "They'll be identifying them soon. That means I get to hack in and find out before the rest of the world."

"Good luck, baby," Wyatt whispered before he gave her a quick kiss.

7

43 Miles from the Polish border

Reyna couldn't remember a longer day. Or one where she was so tense. To her surprise, somewhere between rushing from her cabin into the forest, walking ten miles before hitching a ride in the back of a truck full of manure, and then walking twelve more miles, she had stopped questioning Lev.

She wouldn't say that she completely trusted him, but it was close enough. He'd had plenty of chances to kill her, and he hadn't. That said something—in her mind at least.

"There," he said when they reached the edge of the line of trees.

Across the road was a rundown building that served as a bar in the remote location. Reyna spotted the transport truck. It was covered, which would give them both time to get a little sleep. There was only one problem.

"We don't know which way he's going or when he's leaving," she said.

Lev lifted one shoulder. "Does it matter when he's leaving?"

"Yeah," she said and shot him a flat look. "I'd like to get on the water quickly."

Lev's icy blue gaze slid to her. "Why?"

"You can't be that dense."

"The Saints know by now that we're gone. They'll be looking everywhere for us, especially at the border crossings. Between tonight and tomorrow, they'll double their lookouts."

Reyna blew out a breath. "It's actually worse than that. There are places people used to be able to cross without going through checkpoints, but both the Ukrainian and Polish governments have installed cameras to catch anyone in the act."

"I suspected as much. There is always a way. We just have to find it."

"We're losing light."

Lev nodded as he stared at the truck. "I have an idea."

He darted across the road, and she quickly followed into more forest. Lev lowered his pack to the ground. Before she had time to ask what he was doing, he stealthily walked to the vehicles and proceeded to look inside each one. It wasn't long before he opened a door and pulled out a pair of boots. After comparing the size to the bottom of his foot, he closed the door and moved to the next car.

Reyna knew that his feet must be killing him in the dress shoes, but he hadn't said one word about it. She was exhausted, and she had on hiking boots.

When Lev returned, he had a change of clothes in hand. He shot her a knowing grin and dropped the bundle to the ground to pull out his shirt from the waist of his pants.

She didn't want to seem as if she were ogling him —though he certainly wasn't shy about showing off his body—so she removed her pack and dug into it for a protein bar. Out of the corner of her eye, she saw his bare chest, and the scar that ran down his left side near his heart.

But it was the only glimpse she got before he tugged on the ragged, stolen shirt that was a muted blue from so many washings. Reyna sat and finished off the bar before stuffing the wrapper into the outer pocket of her pack. When she looked up, it was to see Lev bent over, removing his tuxedo pants.

She couldn't remember ever seeing an ass quite so fine before. Reyna hastily looked away and tried to pretend that she wasn't insanely curious about his body. She'd felt enough of it when they clashed at the theatre, but seeing it now in a more favorable light was vastly different.

Lev put on the pilfered pants and boots then looked at her. "Rest here. I'll be back."

"Rest?" she said, offended. "I'm perfectly capable of continuing on."

He stared at her for a heartbeat before saying, "No one is questioning your ability. I plan on going into the bar, getting a drink, and seeing who is driving the transport truck to learn which way they're headed. Since it would be better if I went in alone, I thought you could take the opportunity to rest. Especially since I'll be doing the same inside."

"You could've just said that to begin with," Reyna retorted.

"I'll remember that for next time."

Then he was gone.

Reyna settled back against the tree so she had a good vantage point to see the road as well as the forest they'd recently traveled through. There was a chance that someone could come up behind her, so she made sure to hide herself and their packs well.

As the minutes ticked by and the sky darkened, her eyes grew heavy. She let them close, but she didn't fall asleep. It was enough to rest her body and eyes for what little time they had. No doubt they'd be hoofing it through the night to stay ahead of the Saints.

She wouldn't be there now if she'd killed Lev at the theatre. Even knowing that, she still didn't regret her decision. When she looked down the barrel at him, she'd known in that instant that she couldn't pull the trigger. She didn't know how or why, only that she couldn't.

The only thing that irked her was not completing her mission. And it wasn't as if she had anything to go back to when she reached the US. The Saints were everywhere. They'd find her eventually.

But she'd known that when she joined them. It was the chance she'd taken to get close to them and learn their secrets in order to bring them down.

Unfortunately, she hadn't comprehended just how massive the organization was. She had known it was big, but she hadn't realized just how large. One person could only do so much against a group with their fingers so deep in everything.

Yet she had found out quite a bit in her five years with them. If she could find the right people to trust, her knowledge could do some damage to the Saints.

Especially after someone within the Saints had

secretly directed her down a certain path that had given her more than she could have hoped for.

She heard something and opened her eyes to see Lev walking into the trees. A look at the sky told her he'd been in there for over an hour. She hadn't realized that she'd been resting her eyes for that long.

"Come on," Lev said as he gathered his pack. "We've got a ride."

She smiled. "He's headed in our direction?"

"Yep. He'll be another hour or two, which will give us time to rest. We'll have to jump because he's headed to a border crossing."

Still, that was over forty miles they wouldn't have to cover on foot. And the idea of getting some sleep sounded too good. Reyna got to her feet and lifted her pack. She and Lev quietly hurried to the truck and slipped beneath the heavy tarp that enclosed the back.

"You sleep first," he said. "I couldn't rest now if I tried after having those shots of vodka."

Reyna chuckled and lowered herself to the bed of the truck. She used her pack as a pillow and laid down. Within seconds, she was asleep.

Lev stretched out his legs before him and leaned back against the hard seat. He shifted until he got comfortable and then folded his arms over his chest and crossed his ankles. His gaze kept going to Reyna.

He wanted to know her story. What had brought her to work undercover against the Saints? Or who?

They had traveled a considerable distance that day, but they still had the entire country of Poland to cross. It wasn't going to be an easy passage, and he'd be surprised if they actually made it without being caught by the Saints.

He wondered if everyone in Texas thought he was dead. He would in their place. Had they told Sergei? That thought soured Lev's stomach. He needed to find a way to contact Callie and the others.

Two hours later, Reyna woke and motioned for him to sleep. He didn't balk. His mind was full of all the different scenarios for how the Saints could capture them. He needed to clear his head, and the best way to do that was sleep.

He laid down and, right before his eyes closed, he looked at Reyna. She smiled and took the seat he'd occupied.

It was during Reyna's second rotation of sleep that the engine roared to life. Her eyes snapped open. Lev was sitting beside her, his pistol drawn just in case. But nothing happened. The truck rolled out of the area and onto the road.

She exchanged a look with Lev. "That was easy."

"We should be okay for the next thirty-five miles or so."

"Can you count miles?" she asked, joking.

He lifted his wrist to show what looked like a watch. "It'll keep track of it. I'll need to buy a burner phone to get in contact with the rest of my companions to let them know I'm alive."

"We can do that in Poland."

They bounced along in the back of the truck, each lost in thought. Reyna had set up this escape path within months of being assigned to Ukraine. Her specialty in the CIA had been languages. She picked them up easily. First, it was Spanish and Russian, and then Ukrainian and Belarusian came next. In all, she spoke eight languages.

When she had made the route for her escape, she'd thought she would be doing it alone. Not once had she considered that there would be someone with her. But if she were honest with herself, she'd never expected to have to use the plan.

The Saints trusted very few. It didn't matter how high up in the organization a person was, the Saints constantly listened in on conversations, followed people, and had spies trying to turn them away from the Saints.

"Why did you join them?"

Reyna jerked at Lev's question that pulled her out of her thoughts. She met his bright blue gaze and pulled out a small photo from her pack. The edges were worn and curled from being handled and shoved into her pockets.

She glanced at the picture. It no longer pained her to see Arthur's face smiling back at her, but the memories of their time together, the bond that had developed and turned to love, would always remain.

Reyna handed the photo to Lev. "That was my partner, Arthur. We were often sent into situations where we posed as a couple. During an op, Arthur stumbled upon information about the Saints. He told me, and we did some investigating. Before we got to share the intel with our superiors, the Saints sent someone after him. He was gunned down on the way to get us breakfast."

Lev stared for a long time at the picture before he looked back at Reyna. "You loved him."

"Yes."

"So, you went after the Saints for revenge." He handed the photo back to her.

She ran her finger over the picture before tucking it back into her pack. "It was mostly for Arthur, yes. Yet, during the few days we dug into the group, we found so much more. Then, when the CIA brought me home after Arthur was killed, their questions made me wary."

"Because they were Saints."

Reyna nodded slowly. "I took some leave, and during that time, I quietly dug into the Saints more. After I returned to work, I made sure to find those who I believed were part of the Saints organization and said all the right things. In less than six weeks, I received an anonymous package on my doorstep. It was tickets to Kiev with a note that simply said, '*join us.*'"

"And none of those at the CIA knew what you and Arthur found out about the Saints?"

"They asked me a dozen times in a dozen different ways, but I said that Arthur had been very secretive of late and refused to share anything with me. I hated lying."

"But if you wanted revenge, you had no choice," Lev said.

She raised her chin. "Just because I'm leaving doesn't mean I've given up on getting my retribution."

Lev's stare intensified. "Good."

"Ready?" Lev asked as he and Reyna perched on the back of the truck, ready to jump.

She shot him a look and nodded. "Ready."

They tossed out their packs since it would be easier to jump without them.

"Now," he said.

They both leapt, landing hard and rolling to absorb the impact as the truck drove away. Each quickly got to his or her feet and retrieved their packs before hurrying off the road.

After ducking behind a tree, Lev looked around for any movement. He knew the Saints were out there, waiting. No doubt the bastards would let him and Reyna believe that they were about to get away before they swooped in and killed them.

Lev had known for a while that he'd die violently, but he would do it fighting for Sergei, not out in the wilderness battling a group that never should have been able to gain such power to begin with.

"Clear," Reyna said after looking to her side of the forest.

He adjusted his pack on his shoulder. "Same."

Reyna pulled a map from her pack. It had been folded and refolded so many times that the edges were worn. She then cracked a glow stick to shed some light in the darkness. Lev saw the red marks added to the map along the border of Poland and Ukraine, which must be the checkpoints.

"We're here," Reyna said and pointed at the map.

It put them farthest away from the busiest border crossing, but closer to one of the smaller ones. "If I were the Saints, I'd have very few of my people at the crossings. Instead, I'd station them between the checkpoints to hide."

"I would, as well," Reyna agreed.

"Which means, in order for us to get across, we need to find those waiting." He didn't say *to kill them*, because it was understood.

Contrary to what many in Sergei's employ thought, Lev didn't enjoy taking anyone's life. Each death was a mark against his soul, but he willingly bore the weight because of Sergei.

"The mountains will help us," Reyna said as she tapped the paper, indicating the location.

Lev studied the map before he nodded. "I agree. There is a forest, as well."

"True, but it won't be much use. Both governments took down trees and anything someone could use as cover about twenty feet on either side of the border."

That would leave them exposed when they crossed. Prime opportunity for a sniper to take them out as soon as they showed themselves. But what choice did they have? They had to get to Poland. Everything hinged on them locating the Saints first.

Reyna looked at Lev. "There's no other way."

"We'll get through."

"Your confidence reminds me of Arthur's," she said as she folded the map and returned it to her pack.

Lev raised a brow at her. "Is that a compliment?"

"Definitely. Arthur never saw anything he couldn't do. Except end the Saints."

"He isn't to blame for that. Neither of you understood how far-reaching they were."

She twisted her lips. "I'm not sure if that would have stopped Arthur, to be honest. He hated injustice of any kind. It's why he got into the CIA. He loved the idea of protecting his country. Arthur was very much a patriot. He never shied away from doing whatever it took to keep America safe, and our people free."

"He sounds like a good man. I'm sorry you lost him."

Reyna shrugged nonchalantly as she zipped up her pack. "It's part of the job, right? We knew what we were getting into."

"Perhaps, but I doubt you expected to fall in love."

Reyna stilled and slowly lifted her eyes to his. "No, I never expected that."

Lev had never been in love before. He thought he might have come close once, but that had been a long time ago. Besides, a *Brigadier* really couldn't allow themselves to have that kind of connection with anyone. It gave his enemies something to use against him.

He was good at his position because the only one he cared about was Sergei. And it would stay that way.

Reyna gave him a nod when she was ready to set

out. They began walking, keeping to the trees to stay out of sight. He was glad he'd found some boots. They not only helped him with traction as they began the ascent up the mountain, but they also supported his feet.

"How did you come to be here?" Reyna asked after nearly twenty minutes of silence.

Lev wanted to refuse to answer as he usually did, but something stopped him. He wasn't sure if it was because of the time he'd spent with her, or if it was because he felt as if she deserved to know something after what she'd shared with him.

"I'm not a spy by trade," he said.

She moved ahead of him on the narrow path and glanced at him over her shoulder. "You do pretty damn well. What do you do?"

"I work for a Russian mob boss."

Reyna halted and looked at him. "In the US?"

"That's right."

"That's why your Russian was so good."

Lev shrugged one shoulder. "My father was Russian. I learned the language early."

"You have no American accent, and when you speak English, you have no Russian accent."

"A product of learning both languages at the same time."

She gave a short whistle. "Impressive. And I thought I had a knack for languages. You understood my Ukrainian, didn't you?"

"For the most part. I've not spoken it in ages. How many languages do you know?"

"Eight."

"That's remarkable." And damn if he wasn't impressed.

Reyna flashed him a quick smile and started walking again. "Everyone has a skill. That's mine."

"Obviously, you had other strengths. Otherwise, the CIA wouldn't have made you an operative."

"I suppose. What are your skills?"

"Killing."

She didn't so much as glance his way when he stated the fact. Somehow, that made him feel a little better. It didn't absolve him of his many sins, though. Not that he expected such a thing. He, more than anyone, knew what awaited him when death came for him.

"What do you do for your boss?" Reyna asked.

"I'm a *Brigadier*."

"My time in Kiev gave me an up-close and personal look at the mafia. Do you do the same functions in the US as the *Brigadiers* do there? Here, they're in charge of a small group of men and give jobs out to the *Boyeviks*, the warriors."

The path widened so that Lev could come even with her. He was surprised when Reyna slowed to let him catch up.

"Actually, things are a bit different for me," he explained. "My *Pakhan,* the boss, came over from Russia. He wasn't part of any mafia while he lived there, but his uncle was. He learned a lot, and when he came to America, he took what he knew and used it to create his own mafia."

Reyna looked at him as if she were seeing him for the first time. "You care a great deal for your *Pakhan.*"

"He's more of a father than my own ever was."

"That's nice that you have that relationship."

Lev wasn't sure why he'd shared that with her.

He'd never told anyone else before. "I may be the *Brigadier*, but I also carry the job of the *Two Spies*."

Reyna's eyes widened before she looked forward once more. "Support *and* security for your *Pakhan*. That must keep you busy. Why doesn't your boss fill one of the other roles?"

"Because I get the jobs done properly."

"I see," she murmured.

Lev caught her quick glance in his direction. He wished he knew what she was thinking.

Reyna asked, "Did your *Pakhan* send you here?"

"He wanted in the fight against the Saints, yes."

"And you didn't?"

He shrugged. "It's not that I didn't want to fight them. My job is to protect Sergei and everything he's created. I can't do that from here."

"You're worried about him."

It wasn't a question, so he didn't treat it as such. "I know fighting the Saints is important, but my first duty is to Sergei."

"I think I'd like to meet him."

"He'd like you."

Her head snapped to him as her lips turned up in a smile. "You think so?"

"He's always had a thing for strong, intelligent women."

Reyna's smile grew, making her eyes twinkle in the moonlight that fell through the trees. "I think that was a compliment."

"It was."

The smile was still in place when she looked ahead. "How did you come to work for him?"

That was a story Lev had never shared before. No one had dared ever ask. That was his own doing. He made sure no one wanted to know because he didn't want to talk about it.

"Forget I asked," Reyna said when he didn't reply.

He shook his head. "It's just that I've not spoken about it in years."

"It's fine. You don't need to tell me."

"When my father arrived from Russia, he went to work for Sergei. He lived hard and drank harder. He expected a lot from me, and no matter how well I did, it was never enough. The simple truth was that he went to the US for a better life, but he hated it. He hated everything about America. It didn't matter that my mother loved him more than life itself. It didn't matter that Sergei took him in and gave him a job."

Reyna licked her lips. "And your mother?"

"The gentlest woman I've ever known. One time, when my father was drunk—though not too drunk— he told me that's what drew him to my mother. He loved her. In his own way. He just couldn't find happiness where he was."

"Even with your mother's love?"

"Apparently, love doesn't fix all things," Lev replied.

Reyna tucked her hair behind her ears. "Was it the connection of your father that brought you to Sergei?"

Her question brought memories of that time straight to the forefront of Lev's mind. "I knew Sergei, of course. He was always nice to me back then, but no, I was going for my medical degree."

"To be a doctor?" she asked, her brows shooting up on her forehead.

"I was drawn to it. It was the one thing my father

approved of. I was in my second year when he died of liver failure. He'd always said it would be the alcohol that took him. I was finishing up my final year, getting ready to do my residency when I got word that my mother had been attacked on her way home. Witnesses told authorities that it was a group of men. They beat her so badly that she never regained consciousness."

Reyna stopped to face him. "I'm so sorry."

He looked off into the distant darkness as he halted next to her. "The police took too long to bring the group to justice. When they finally did haul one man in, he confessed to doing all of it. And when I heard his connections to a rival mafia, I knew it was in retaliation for something my father had done. If only they'd come after me. Not my mother."

Lev snorted and slid his gaze to Reyna. "I went to the *Pakhan* of that mafia and demanded the men who had attacked my mother. I wanted my revenge."

"Did you get it?"

"It turned out that my mother's death was just a ploy to get to me. *I* was their target. More than six of them came at me. I deflected as many hits as I could, but suddenly there was a rope around my neck."

Reyna's gaze darted to his neck exposed by his shirt.

There were no scars there, at least not externally. "That's when Sergei and his men stormed in. He not only gave me my life, but allowed me to take revenge on the men who murdered my mother. I followed Sergei back to his home and never looked back."

9

Learning Lev's history helped Reyna understand him better. His roots in the Russian mafia explained a lot. She detected the similarities, as well as the differences, between him and those in Russia.

Reyna waited for him to start walking. His retelling of how he'd nearly died was too smooth. No doubt there was much more to the story. She knew how long it took someone to die by strangulation. How long had Lev had the rope tightened around his neck before Sergei got there? She had a suspicion that it was a long time.

To know that Lev had walked away from a career as a doctor to serve Sergei told her so very much about him. He hadn't said that Sergei forced him to serve, which meant that Lev had decided to do it on his own.

"Do you regret being a spy?" Lev suddenly asked.

She thought about it for a moment before she said, "No. I regret some of my decisions and not always listening to my gut. This job isn't for everyone."

"But it suits you?"

She looked over to find him staring at her. "The CIA recruited me right out of college. I honestly thought I'd be behind a desk translating languages, and I started out doing just that. But they needed someone on a quick mission during my eighth month. My first mission was sitting at a bar in a hotel in Moscow, pretending to be a prostitute while spying on a known KGB spy."

"And you were hooked after that?"

Reyna chuckled softly. "Actually, I was terrified. There were plenty of others who spoke Russian, but apparently, I fit the bill more as a prostitute. Not sure what that says about me."

"That you're beautiful."

His words surprised her so much that she nearly tripped over a root. "Thank you. But I was happy to go back to my desk. A couple of months later, they requested that I join another mission. About once a month, I was being pulled to go on one op or another, and the next thing I knew, I was no longer going back to my desk."

"Is that when you got teamed up with Arthur?"

She glanced up at the moon to see it was just a thin slice in the sky. "I was on my own for nearly three years before Arthur."

"You liked it?"

"Every day was different. There was never a boring day."

Lev pulled a bottle of water out of his bag and drank deeply. "I can see how that would appeal to some people."

"I missed my desk sometimes," she confessed. "I missed being able to talk about work. My family knew I worked for the CIA, but I could never tell them anything. I missed many holidays with my family. I barely made it to my mother's funeral."

"Do you still work for the CIA?"

She shook her head. "When I used the plane ticket the Saints left me, my status within the CIA was removed."

"So, you weren't fired?"

"No."

"Hmm," Lev said. "I wonder if that means you could return there."

She snorted loudly. "Why would I want to, knowing the Saints have a connection there?"

"The Saints are everywhere."

"Exactly. Have you even thought about what you'll do when we reach the States?"

Lev gave her a quick glance. "I'm going to Sergei, and no doubt we'll meet up with my companions to continue the fight."

How could she have forgotten about that? Just because she was on her own didn't mean that everyone was.

"You could join me," he offered.

Reyna was about to tell him that she didn't need his pity when she realized that she did need it if she wanted any chance of survival so she could keep going after the Saints. "I think I will. If your companions are still alive."

Lev merely laughed. "You don't know my friends."

"Who are they?"

"The Loughmans."

That drew her up short. "The Loughmans? As in Orrin Loughman?"

Lev stopped a few paces away and turned to look at her, his brows drawn together. "You know him?"

"I know his name. I saw it in a document that I found recently. I thought he was dead."

"It was close, but he's alive. It's because he fought back against the Saints when they sent his team to Russian to collect the bioweapon."

She grunted. "Ragnarok, right?"

"Yes. He went missing along with the weapon, so the Saints called his three sons back home—after murdering their aunt and uncle as a reason for them to unite."

"Are his sons anything like him? Because from what I read in Orrin's file, he's a badass."

Lev gave her a flat look. "I'll deny it if you ever tell them, but they're even better than he is."

"That's who you've paired up with?" she asked, suddenly feeling as if she might actually succeed in her mission.

"There are eleven of us total. It's not like we have an army."

She smiled and inhaled deeply. "It's just about that. And right now, I'll take anything I can get."

They continued on in silence until they reached the top of the mountain. There they paused, and each drank some water. Lev removed his pack and pulled the knife from the sheath at his wrist.

"Going hunting?" she asked.

He nodded. "Stay here."

"As if. I can hunt myself."

It was hard to make out every detail of his face in the dark, but she didn't miss the frustration. It had been a long time since anyone had acted as if she needed to be taken care of. She wasn't offended by it, though.

In fact, it was sort of sweet. Not that Reyna was looking at Lev with any kind of warm and fuzzies. Her mind was focused entirely on getting to her boat and then making it back to the States.

But she could appreciate a gorgeous face and a fine body. And Lev certainly had both.

"I have no doubt you can take care of anyone, but I was thinking of him," Lev said and pointed behind her.

Reyna's head swiveled to find what he was pointing at. She saw the flare of a cigarette in the darkness, the reddish-orange light highlighting the man's bearded face.

She felt something nudge her. When she looked, Lev was holding out his other knife. The blade was slightly smaller than the one he'd chosen, but no less dangerous.

"The border is just over the rise," she told him.

He held her gaze. "We go together. I'll meet you back here."

She nodded and silently lowered her backpack beside his as he slipped away. With her eyes scanning every shadow, she began quietly making her way toward the man. He was focused on his cigarette and nothing else.

That didn't mean he was alone, however. There was a good possibility that someone else was near. Reyna's eyes had adjusted to the darkness, but she could only see so far in the night.

Reyna reached the man, coming up behind him as he finished his smoke. He pushed away from the tree and snuffed the cigarette out on the bark before tossing away the butt. She didn't give him a chance to turn around.

She reached up and around his neck, slicing his throat with one cut. He was a good foot taller than she was, and while she would've preferred to let him fall, she couldn't afford to. She sagged under his weight as she lowered him to the ground.

The moment she stood, she stepped left and felt something brush against her face right before she heard the thud of something slamming into the tree. Reyna glanced over at the blade sticking out of the bark.

Her head snapped back to follow where it had come from to find a giant of a man coming for her. His face was mottled with rage, his meaty hands fisted.

Reyna yanked the knife from the tree and threw it at him. She'd never been very good with knives, so it was no surprise that it missed him by a foot. Then he was before her.

She ducked his hand and slashed his thigh with the blade Lev had given her, but it didn't seem to faze the giant. Another hand came at her. She dodged that one as well, but the third caught her on the side of the head, dazing her.

The next thing she knew, she was being held up against the tree by her throat, her feet dangling inches from the ground. She still had a hold of the knife and used it on the man's arms, but once more, he didn't react.

It was easy to panic in such situations, but Reyna didn't. She sank her weapon into the man's chest above his heart and kicked his nuts. Suddenly, his hand on her throat loosened, and he fell to one knee.

She landed on the ground and pushed his hand away so she could take a deep breath. As she did, she spotted Lev's longer blade sticking out from the giant's back.

Then Lev came walking out of the shadows like some kind of savior. She'd told him not to be a hero, but it seemed he couldn't help himself.

"Come on," he said as he retrieved their weapons and they ran to their packs.

She slung hers onto her back. "Thank you."

"You would've done the same for me."

They said no more about it as they raced from the safety of the forest into the open area and crossed into Poland. They didn't slow for another five hundred yards.

Reyna was breathing heavily when she looked back over her shoulder. "They'll know this is where we crossed when they discover the bodies."

"That's why we need to keep out of sight of anyone so they don't know which direction we take."

"This way," she told him as they set off again.

10

L orraine stared down at the dead body as the mountain swarmed with Saints poring over the scene. She was in a foul mood. Not only had Reyna somehow managed to escape, but she also continued to elude them.

And to make matters worse, Lorraine actually had to don boots. Not her designer stiletto boots, but *hiking* boots. And she was in jeans—a piece of clothing she usually avoided at all costs. But when the director ordered you to a scene, there wasn't time to do more than grab necessities and hop on a chopper.

She grasped the strand of pearls at her neck and ran her fingers back and forth over the beads as her gaze lifted toward the Polish border. Reyna was out there.

Along with Lev Ivanski.

The fact that both had gotten away was a black mark against Lorraine. And she simply couldn't allow that to happen.

"Well, well, well. What do we have here?"

She stiffened at the sound of Anatoli Kozel's deep voice, heavily accented. She'd thought—and hoped—

that she wouldn't run into him again. But working for the same organization and having the same rank meant that was impossible. Still, she'd managed to avoid him for years. What the hell was he doing here now?

Lorraine turned to face the Ukrainian. It wasn't fair that he didn't seem to age. He still sported the same full head of blond hair, the same broad shoulders and trim build. The same gorgeous face. There were a few more laugh lines around his eyes, but he didn't look anywhere close to his forty-six years.

While she had a costly regimen of facial creams and serums that she used religiously every night to keep her face from showing any signs of aging.

Anatoli's blue eyes crinkled at the corners. "Surely, it isn't so bad to see me. After all, there was a time when you wanted me around."

No matter how many years passed, he wouldn't let the fact that they had once been lovers go. The one thing she would never share with him or anyone else was that he was the love of her life. But she'd chosen her career.

And she hadn't regretted it.

"And I was the one who left," she reminded him. "You always forget that part."

The teasing left his eyes, and they turned as cold as the frigid winter. "Trust me, Lori. I've never forgotten how you snuck out of our bed in the middle of the night. All you ever cared about was climbing the ranks."

It rankled that he used the pet name he'd given her. "You did, too."

His nostrils flared. "But I would never have chosen them over you."

"That's the difference between us."

"That's not the only one," he said, jerking his chin to the bodies. "Look at what you've done to get your position. I went about it another way. Yet we're still equal. I wouldn't have underestimated Reyna Harris."

The dig was one Lorraine felt keenly. "You wanted her on your team, but I was the one who ended up getting her."

"You've also lost her. Along with the American," Anatoli stated.

"I'll find them."

He knelt beside the body that separated them. "Reyna is very good at her job. Even better than you were." Anatoli glanced up at Lorraine. "I tried to warn you about Ivanski."

"Oh, please," she said with a roll of her eyes. "You think because you were notified about Lev leaving the States first that you have some kind of dibs on him?"

"It simply means that I know more about him than you do. You kept your focus on Reyna, but I was doing my homework on those who've helped the Loughmans recently."

Lorraine wished she could say that Anatoli was bad at his job, but it would be a lie. He was damn good. It came easily to him. Much easier than it did to her. If she had allowed her heart to rule, he would have climbed the ranks within the organization while she was left behind. And she couldn't have that.

"I looked into them, as well," she replied. "I know about Lev."

Anatoli straightened and shook his head as he

met her gaze. "If that were the case, you never would have allowed him to reach the theatre."

She crossed her arms over her chest. "Are you telling me that you knew Reyna and Lev were going to team up?"

"What I'm saying is that allowing him in the theatre was your first mistake."

"I had a plan."

"How is that working out for you now?"

She lifted her chin and stared at him defiantly. "You doubt my ability?"

"I think you've let your confidence outweigh your judgment. The Lori I used to know never would have let her quarry get away. She certainly wouldn't be standing here now looking at dead men."

Anatoli walked away, but his words rattled around in Lorraine's mind. The fact was, everything had gone badly from the moment Lev had arrived in Ukraine. If she had ordered Lev to be taken out before the theatre, then she wouldn't have scanned the CCTV footage when his body hadn't been recovered, and she wouldn't have seen Lev and Reyna drive away together.

At first, Lorraine had believed that Reyna was taking Lev into custody, but when she never called, Lorraine had known her prized agent had another agenda.

She'd decided to go to Reyna's apartment in Kiev after pinging her phone. When Reyna didn't answer the door, Lorraine had one of her men open it. There wasn't a trace of Reyna.

That's when Lorraine decided to dig into Reyna's life as a Saint. Everything had seemed on the up and up—almost too much. Lorraine went through tapes, recordings, and everything she had on Reyna.

Reyna hadn't taken a single misstep. Or so Lorraine had thought until she was flipping through some pages and happened to catch sight of documentation showing Reyna visiting the Saints' headquarters in Kiev.

No one but the upper tiers of the organization knew that the building was nothing more than a front for the Saints to use to conduct their business. For all intents and purposes, it was one of three home bases.

Lorraine pulled up the tapes of that day and found where Reyna had entered the building. Lorraine might have been able to dismiss Reyna's visit if she hadn't gone to the archives. Though Lorraine couldn't see what Reyna did there since the recordings had been tampered with.

With that information, Lorraine was able to look at Reyna differently. And there were some suspicious things. It took some time and six different hackers, but she was finally able to locate Reyna when the woman called her. As soon as it was confirmed that Reyna was thirty minutes outside of Kiev, Lorraine knew that her operative was no longer viable and needed to be neutralized.

She couldn't even blame it on Lev. Reyna's actions before he'd left the States proved that.

Lorraine let out a breath as she dropped her arms to her sides. She made her way to the clearing but stopped short of continuing into the Polish forest.

If Reyna were a double agent, someone would have figured that out by now. No one who dared try to infiltrate the Saints by such an action lasted more than a few months. Reyna had been with them for over five years.

But if she wasn't a double agent, what was she? Because she no longer seemed to be with the Saints.

"You're thinking about Reyna," Anatoli said as he walked up beside her. "What happened to her? She was favored to rise within our ranks."

Lorraine shook her head and looked at him. "I don't know. She was vetted, right?"

"By the elders." His brows snapped together in a frown. "Why? What are you thinking?"

Lorraine knew she'd probably regret this, but she needed to bounce ideas off someone. She didn't trust anyone working for her enough, so that left her ex-lover and enemy. Anatoli might use it against her—she would in his shoes. But he'd never been wired that way.

Then again, time changed everyone.

But what choice did she have?

She made a quick decision and said, "When Lev wasn't killed in the assassination at the theatre, I checked nearby CCTV and saw Reyna driving off with him."

"Maybe she realized who he was."

"I have no doubt, but she didn't bring him to me."

Anatoli shrugged, his lips twisting. "Perhaps she wanted to bring him in herself to get the credit."

"I thought that as well, but when I pinged her phone that showed her location in Kiev, imagine my surprise when she wasn't there."

His brows shot up at the news. "That does make things look bad."

"There's more. I began looking into Reyna and happened to discover that she went to headquarters."

Worry filled his blue eyes. "And you didn't send her there?"

Lorraine shook her head.

"Who did she see?" Anatoli asked.

"No one. She went to the archives. I think she's a double agent."

He stared at her for a long minute before he sighed. "I know you're careful when you investigate someone, and I wouldn't hesitate to believe you. However, her going to headquarters without orders from you is telling."

Lorraine faced him, anger and a little bit of worry filling her. "How so?"

"What if she's working for one of the elders? What if she's one of the spies they've sent out to make sure we're doing our jobs?"

Lorraine rolled her eyes, but even as she did, trepidation filled her. "That's insane. We send those spies out with new recruits."

"Why wouldn't they do the same with us?"

"Because we're dedicated."

He quirked a blond brow. "Were you dedicated to the CIA before you joined the Saints?"

Damn him for reminding her of that. He was right. People could be talked into changing sides, bribed, or sometimes even forced. It happened all the time.

"If you didn't tell her about headquarters, then who did?" Anatoli asked.

Lorraine didn't have an answer for that.

Anatoli swung his gaze to the forest on the Polish side. "If she knew the building, then that means she has connections to the elders. They could be sending her on this mission with Lev. It's perfect, actually.

Gain his trust, infiltrate the Loughmans, and then take them out. But,"—he hesitated and slid his gaze back to her—"you could be stepping into a mine field if you keep hunting her."

"If she is working with one of the elders, they would've alerted me by now."

"Are you sure?" he asked.

Lorraine narrowed her eyes on him. "Are you saying someone is trying to set me up?"

"I'm saying you should be careful."

Someone called Anatoli's name. Normally, she would have followed him since this was her scene, but she remained. Her mind had yet to sort through the jumble of Anatoli's theories.

What bothered her the most was that he might be right. In fact, there was a very good chance that he was. Before she continued after Reyna and Lev and possibly signed her own death warrant, she needed to see if she could find out more.

No one spoke to the elders, which would be the easiest thing to do. They contacted you. Lorraine wasn't about to sit around and wait to see if the decision she made was the right one or not.

She spun around and raised her hand to signal for her people to gather up the dead and move out. She needed to remove the hated jeans and hiking boots and get back into her regular clothes so she could think properly when she sat at her computer.

11

They avoided cities, which made their trek even longer. Just a few hours in, Lev saw a village when they crested a hill.

"We're ahead of them," Reyna said.

Lev wanted to agree with her, but the Saints had proven resourceful. "We can't take the chance."

"We're going to need food soon."

"And a cell phone."

She leaned against a tree and finished off another bottle of water. "I know I said we should take the long way around before getting to my boat, but I've been thinking that might not be the right way to go. I think we should head straight for the sea."

"It doesn't matter what we do. We need to expect the Saints to be wherever we are." He set down his pack and grabbed a bag of nuts and a bottle of water.

They'd been walking for hours. He wanted to cover as much ground as they could during the day and find someplace to bunk down for the night. They were running out of forest to hide in. If they were going to make it to the coast, they would need to find another way to do it. Continuing on foot could prove disastrous.

"I know," Reyna said suddenly.

Lev looked at her to find her staring. "You know what?"

"That we can't continue as we are. It's nothing but plains for miles and miles. We're going to have to steal a car."

"How far are we from Warsaw?"

Her eyes widened. "You want to go there?"

"It's better to get lost in a city of hundreds of thousands than a village with just a few hundred."

"We take the chance of being seen wherever we go. But to answer your question, we're about a hundred kilometers from the city."

He inwardly winced. It was much farther than he'd hoped. "We won't be able to wait to get there. We need to get a car now."

"Not in that village," she said.

"Agreed. Let's see what we find next."

She put her backpack on and shifted northwest from their present westerly course. "This way."

They used every bit of cover they had, staying clear of roads but walking near them. Anytime they heard a vehicle coming, they ducked down. Despite alternating from a walk to a jog and back again, the sun was sinking faster than they were eating up miles.

It was dusk when they reached a town. It was large enough that they could get lost in the people, but it wasn't as if they could go in carrying their packs.

"We should split up," Reyna said. "We'll cover more ground that way."

He gave a nod. "I'll get the car and meet you back

here."

"I'll get us some food and a cell phone," she replied with a smile.

They hid their bags in some shrubbery and walked into town. With a glance at each other, they went their separate ways. Lev was surprised that she trusted him enough to get the car. He wasn't sure he would if he were in her shoes. Then again, she was capable of taking care of herself.

After all, she knew the location of her boat. If Lev wanted to return home, he needed her. He grinned. It wasn't that she trusted him, he realized. They needed each other. It was as simple as that.

It took Lev less than thirty minutes to find what he was looking for. He spotted the older-model silver Skoda and made his way toward it. When he tried the door, he was shocked to find it unlocked.

Lev got in and quickly hotwired it. As soon as the engine started, he put it in drive and started back toward his meeting place with Reyna. Once there, he put their packs in the back seat and waited for her to return.

As the minutes ticked by, he grew anxious. He kept looking in the rearview and side mirrors as well as through the front windshield, hoping to see her. It started raining, which made things even more difficult.

Another thirty minutes went by before he caught sight of her in the rearview mirror. He started the engine right before she reached the car and slid into the passenger seat.

"Here," she said and handed him a mobile. "Though I suggest you make the call now and then toss the phone away since I stole it from someone."

He laughed and dialed the secure line to the Whitehorse base. There was an answer on the second ring, but it wasn't Callie's voice. Instead, it was a deep, Texas accent belonging to the eldest Loughman brother.

"Wyatt, it's me," Lev said.

"Lev?" The surprise in the Texan's voice was clear. "I told them you weren't dead."

"Not for the Saints lack of trying. I'm attempting to get home."

"So, they know you're there?"

Lev glanced at Reyna. "Without a doubt."

"Where are you?"

"Right now, Poland. But we're trying to make it to the sea to come home that way."

There was a pause before Wyatt said, "*We?*"

Lev lowered the phone and asked her, "What's your surname?"

"Harris," Reyna replied.

Lev lifted the phone back up. "Reyna Harris. She's an ex-CIA agent who was working with the Saints to get information to bring them down."

"Are you sure you can trust her?"

"She had the opportunity to kill me and didn't." Lev didn't look over at Reyna, but he felt her eyes on him.

He wasn't upset by Wyatt's question. He would've asked the same. Actually, he would've asked a lot more.

"Hang on," Wyatt said. There was a soft click. A moment later, Wyatt said, "I have you on speaker now. Cullen and my father are here."

Cullen said, "Glad to hear from you, Lev. What's going on?"

THE DEFENDER | 85

"A lot. Too much, actually. The short of it is that the Saints are after me, and they've figured out that Reyna has been working against them. They're not far behind us, and we don't have a lot of time to tell you every detail."

"Understood," Orrin said. "Stay safe and check in whenever you can. And let us know if we can help in any way."

Reyna nudged Lev. "Tell them the Saints are coming for them."

Damn, he couldn't believe he'd nearly forgotten that. "By the way, the Saints are sending people after you. Or that's what they led Reyna to believe anyway."

"We're ready for them," Wyatt declared.

"I may be keeping the majority of their attention focused on me right now." Lev knew that would benefit the Loughmans.

Cullen made a sound at the back of his throat. "If that's true, you won't get far from...where are you?"

"Poland," he supplied.

"How far are you from the coast?" Orrin asked.

Lev licked his lips. "Not nearly close enough."

"One more thing," Lev said before anyone could disconnect from the line. "Can one of you call Sergei?"

Wyatt said, "Consider it done."

Lev ended the call before he took out the SIM card on the phone and snapped it in half. Then he threw the cell phone out the window and drove away.

It was then that he smelled the food. He looked over at Reyna, sitting in the last rays of daylight, to see her staring at her lap. "What is that?" he asked.

She smiled at him and held up a sandwich filled

with sausage. His stomach rumbled at the thought of hot food. Reyna handed him half, which he bit into immediately. He'd never felt bread so soft, cheese so melted, or tasted sausage so good before.

Neither said a word as they devoured their food. Lev kept the car pointed north and ate up the miles as darkness settled over the land once more.

"I could eat two of those," Reyna said after she'd wiped her mouth.

He nodded and swallowed his last bite. "Me, too."

She laughed, then leaned over with her napkin and dabbed at the corner of his lips. "You had some sauce."

"Thank you," he said, shooting her a grin. "How did you get the food?"

"I had some money."

"That was fortunate."

She laughed and placed her elbow on the door and her hand against her head. "I'm usually never that lucky."

"Seems like you're always lucky. You weren't killed with your partner, you were able to join the Saints and not be detected as a spy, and you got out of the cabin before they arrived."

"Only because of you." She nodded and met his gaze. "The others I can't refute, but the last I can and will."

"You would've realized it."

She shook her head. "Before it was too late? I'm not so sure." Then she changed the subject. "Your friends are leery of me. I don't blame them."

"They want details, none of which I can supply right now."

She turned her head to look out the passenger

window. "I used to think this job was fun and full of adventure when I was with Arthur. It's turned me into someone who doesn't trust anyone and who sees danger at every turn."

"You see danger because you know firsthand that it's there. Whether it's the Saints or whoever you were trying to bring down working with the CIA, bad people are bad. It doesn't matter their skin color, religion, or where they live."

She dropped her arm and turned her head to him. "But I fully realize now what I didn't when I joined the Saints."

"And what's that?" he asked, glancing at her.

"That I'll never be free of them. I know how determined they are. I know the capabilities and the resources they have on hand. We're just two people. It's like an ant thinking it can withstand a boot."

Lev shrugged one shoulder. "Ants are strong. Together with other ants, they can build bridges. I don't mind being an ant."

"You're missing the point."

He heard her frustrated sigh as she dropped her head back against the seat. "I know exactly what you're saying. If you want to give up, then you might as well get out right here."

"Why would I do that?" Her head swung to him.

"So the Saints can find you. If you want to win, to survive and bring down this organization, then you can't give up. Ever."

She drew in a long breath and then slowly released it. "You're right. I was feeling sorry for myself when I was looking for a phone to steal. I thought that I'd be out of the CIA and living somewhere with a husband and a dog by now."

"No kids?"

A small smile tugged at her lips. "Possibly. I'd want at least five years with my husband to do all the things together as a couple before we even considered children."

"You did say a dog. Lots of people consider them children."

"Hmm," she replied. "Good point. A cat then."

He smiled at the teasing he heard in her voice. "And where would this place be that you lived?"

"Somewhere pretty. I don't care if it's in a city or somewhere quiet in the country. If I had someone I loved, anywhere could be home."

"All I've ever known is city life. The closest I came to the country was when I was with the Loughmans in Texas on their ranch."

She sat up quickly. "Do they have horses? I love horses."

"They have several." He smiled and imagined how she'd react when she saw them.

Suddenly, she reached over and put her hand on his arm. "Thank you."

"For what?" he asked with a frown.

"For pulling me out of my self-pity and making me smile again. I can't imagine being on this journey with anyone else."

Lev gave her a nod and focused back on the road. He cleared his throat. "You should sleep while you can."

She gave his arm a squeeze before her hand slipped away.

And damned if he didn't find that he missed her touch.

12

The slowing of the car before it turned pulled Reyna from sleep. Then she heard the repeated squeak. She couldn't believe that she'd actually slept, but oddly enough, she had. She yawned as she straightened and shifted toward the door.

Her eyes opened to see the rain falling at a steady rate against the windshield, the sky dark. The rapid beat of the windshield wipers let her zero in on the squeak. She yawned again, this time arching her back before leaning her head from side to side to stretch her neck.

Reyna glanced over at Lev's profile. It felt nice to be fed, rested, and relatively safe. She hadn't let her guard down like this since before Arthur was killed.

"How long was I out?" she asked.

Lev glanced her way. "About five hours."

"You shouldn't have let me sleep that long," she admonished.

He shrugged and continued driving. "Why not? I was fine, and you needed the rest."

"And you don't?"

"I didn't say that. I figured one of us should be alert. It's me this time. Next time, it might be you."

She stared out the window, watching the rain fall in the glow of the headlights. "When did it start raining?"

"About two hours ago. At least there are very few people on the road."

"Why don't you let me drive?"

He shook his head. "I'm okay. Thirsty, though. Can you grab a water?"

She twisted in her seat and reached into the back seat and his pack for a bottle. Reyna unscrewed the cap before she handed it to him.

"Thanks," he mumbled before drinking deeply.

She saw a sign for a village five kilometers out. Reyna turned in her seat, but this time, she dug into her pack for the small flashlight she had, and the map.

Leaning over to look at the dash, she saw that they needed to get gas soon. "We're only about an hour and a half from the marina in Gdynia."

"I'm going to have to stop for petrol soon," he said. "We won't make it that far."

"We can refuel in the next town."

They didn't speak again until they reached the small city. Lev pulled into the first petrol station he found. Reyna jumped out and found a restroom while he pumped gas. When she finished, she took over the gas while he emptied his bladder and paid the store clerk.

Reyna smiled when she saw that Lev carried a bag of food and two cups of coffee when he returned. She reached for one of the warm cups and sighed. "You read my mind."

He chuckled and handed her the bag. "Help yourself."

She was so busy digging through the goodies that she didn't realize he'd once more gotten behind the wheel until the engine started.

Reyna got in and shot him a flat look. "Let me drive."

"We don't have that much farther, and I know nothing about boats. I'd rather you rest until we reach the marina. I'll sleep then."

It sounded like a good compromise, so she feasted on the delicious coffee, even if it didn't have sugar in it, and munched on some cookies as he pulled back onto the road.

"How big is Gdynia?"

She swallowed her cookie and said, "It's about two hundred and fifty thousand people. The port is good-sized, as is the marina. I chose it because there are so many boats there. It's easy for someone to lose a vessel that way."

"We just have to hope the Saints don't realize you bought a boat."

She chuckled and offered him a cookie. He took two. "It's not under my name. I paid cash for it and registered it under an alias. They'd have a difficult time finding that."

"Paying with cash was smart. The owner could recognize you, however."

Reyna shook her head. "Not going to happen. I used a wig, appeared twenty pounds heavier, and about ten years older."

Lev's gaze met hers. "This just might work then."

"Don't get too excited," she warned. "They'll

probably have guessed we'd head to the sea. They'll have people at every port. Some obvious, some not."

"We've gotten this far. We'll make it," Lev asserted.

She really hoped Lev was right. Reyna wrapped both hands around her coffee cup, letting the warmth settle into her palms. The dampness of the Slavic countries invaded everything. She missed the heat of Florida at times.

"What are you thinking about?" Lev asked, intruding on her thoughts.

"Home."

"Where is that?"

"Florida," she said, hearing the wistfulness in her voice. "I've been here so long, I think I forgot what it's like to feel that kind of heat on me. Even before Ukraine, I was either at Langley or stationed near Russia. You'd think I'd be used to the cold by now."

There was a beat of silence. "I don't think we ever get used to things we don't like."

"There are things about my job I like."

He quirked a brow at her.

Reyna rolled her eyes and sighed loudly. "Fine. There is nothing I like anymore. Honestly, I've been thinking about home more and more often of late. I kept putting it off until I succeeded here, but I think I've always known that I wouldn't meet my goal."

"I think you've done a fantastic job, especially knowing you were on your own. You held it together mentally and emotionally. Few people could've done that. Hell. I don't even think I could have."

His praise made warmth spread through her. "Thanks, but from what I've seen, you could've done it. I'm surprised you aren't in the CIA or some other government agency. If they knew of you, they'd certainly try to recruit you."

"I didn't say I hadn't been recruited."

Her mouth fell open. "You turned them down?"

"I owe everything to Sergei. And I am happy with him. Why would I want to leave that?"

"For an adventure."

He chuckled, the sound making her grin. "I get all the adventures I could want with Sergei."

"And when he passes? Will you take over?"

The smile dropped from his face. "I never wanted the strain of running such things. There are those who will fight to take Sergei's place, but I won't be one of them."

"I'm pretty sure no one would fight you if you stepped in. You think Sergei will name you to take his place?"

"He knows I don't want it."

"What if he wants you to have it?" Reyna couldn't believe that she was pushing someone to take over a mafia operation, but it was because she knew Lev. He'd be fair.

Or as fair as a mafia boss could be.

Lev's shoulders lifted as he took in a deep breath. "All of Sergei's family is gone. I'm as much a son to him as he is a father to me."

"Then it should go to you."

"I'm better suited for other things."

She shifted to lean her back half on the door and half on the seat. "Being the muscle, you mean? You're forgetting your intelligence. It takes both physical and mental strength for Sergei to do what he's done. Seems like he's been preparing you for a while now."

Lev's head snapped in her direction. His brow

furrowed, and confusion was clear in his eyes before he returned his attention back to the road. "He asked me long ago if I would take over one day. I said no. He never brought it up again."

"Things change. Our world has changed. I would rather you take Sergei's place instead of a Saint."

His hands tightened on the steering wheel so that his knuckles went white. "The Saints will never get close enough to Sergei to do any harm."

Reyna didn't bother to point out that Lev wasn't with Sergei now. Lev was aware of that. There wasn't any need to remind him. She wondered how long the Saints would search for them before they went after Lev's family and friends—including Sergei.

Lev's thoughts must have gone down the same track because his foot pressed the accelerator and their speed climbed. She didn't admonish him. She would be doing the same thing in his place.

"Do you have family?" he asked suddenly.

She looked down at the cup in her hands. "Both my parents are dead. I have an older sister I've not spoken with in seventeen years. I don't even know where she lives."

"So, the Saints won't go after her?"

"I distanced myself from everyone when I joined the CIA. When I became an operative, the only people I interacted with were in the agency, but I was never close to anyone except Arthur. I did the same when I joined the Saints. I made sure there was no one anyone could use against me." She swallowed and lifted her gaze to him. She wondered if Lev had a woman waiting for him back in Maryland. "What about you? Anyone other than Sergei?"

He gave a single shake of his head. "I didn't

cultivate friendships with the men under me. I wanted their respect, not their camaraderie. As for anything romantic...the women I dated didn't last long. They couldn't handle coming in second to Sergei."

The knowledge that he didn't have anyone made her heart leap. Reyna turned her head away while she tried to digest that bit of information. No one had even come close to making her take a second look at them after Arthur.

Until Lev.

Was it his smooth voice? His penetrating eyes? His calm, steady nature that held a violent streak at bay that excited her?

"What about you?" he asked, glancing her way. "You have anyone here? It has been five years."

She smiled sadly. "My anger and hatred drove me at first. I mistrusted everyone, and the deeper I got into the Saints, the more I retreated into myself. They liked that. They wanted operatives to perform a function, and believed that there should be absolutely no attachments."

"That made things easier for you."

"It was a lonely life. I don't think I was fully aware of that until this moment," she confessed, shocked by her admission. "Even when I was around a roomful of others, I was still alone. I didn't write down my thoughts or tell them to anyone."

Lev covered her hand with his. "That kind of solitude can drive a person crazy."

"There were times it felt like I was going mad." She fiddled with the lid of the coffee cup with her free hand. "But then I'd remember why I set aside my life. Yes, I wanted revenge for Arthur's murder, but it became more than that. When I realized how deep the Saints had infected the governments, I realized I couldn't waver from my mission."

He squeezed her hand. "No matter how good you are—and you are very good—even you can't do something like this alone. You need people who have your back. People you can trust."

She looked at his profile, glad that he had to focus on the road instead of looking at her. Because if he turned those bright blue eyes on her, she might tell him that *he* was the one she trusted.

It was a peculiar feeling to realize she trusted, especially when she believed she would never again feel that kind of connection to anyone. Fear, relief, anxiety, and excitement all churned within her.

Her eyes lowered to Lev's hand on hers. She turned her hand around so their palms faced each other. Without hesitation, he twined his fingers with hers.

13

He desired her.

Lev didn't want to feel anything toward Reyna Harris, and yet, he couldn't seem to help himself. First, there had been respect, and somewhere along the way, he'd discovered that he actually liked being around her.

She had a strength of will and character he rarely found in others. She was tenacious as well as rational, a combination that had kept her alive. But she was perceptive, shrewd, and bright.

Not to mention, she was stunningly beautiful.

It was a combination that few men could withstand. And he was one of them.

Lev had liked that she slept. Not because he wanted her refreshed, but because she trusted him enough to fall so fully into slumber that she didn't even know when he pulled over to refuel the first time, an hour after they'd stolen the car.

She would never tell him she trusted him, but it was in her actions. And actions, as he well knew, spoke louder and clearer than any words.

They traveled in silence, their hands linked

together as if it were the most normal thing in the world to do. The more Lev learned about Reyna, the more he was attracted to her. He was just a man, after all.

A man with needs.

When they were forty minutes outside of Gdynia, he asked her, "Tell me about the marina. How many entrances, the layout, and where your boat is."

He listened as she told him every detail he would need. They spoke about where to leave the car, how to approach the boat, and what to do if any Saints were waiting for them.

"We'll be timing our departure to sea at dawn," Reyna said.

"Along with so many others. That could be in our favor."

She blew out a breath. "Or it could work against us."

"What route did you intend to take once you got out to sea?" he asked.

"There's only one route. We have to sail through Kattegat. It's a strait that forms part of a connection between the Baltic and North seas. It's a hundred and thirty-seven miles long."

Lev shook his head as he pressed his lips together in frustration. "There will be Saints waiting for us there."

"I know. It was a chance I took, but I assumed I'd get away before they knew I was missing. And I didn't expect to have someone with me."

"If we go that route, we're as sure as caught."

She shrugged. "It's not like we can go anywhere else."

"Really?" he asked as he looked her way.

Her brows snapped together. "What are you thinking?"

"They'll assume we'll want to get out to sea. The odds are that they'll post dozens of Saints at the strait to find us."

"True," she said with a nod. "It's what I would do since I'd assume—rightly so—that there is no other way."

Lev grinned. "We do have another escape. The Baltic Sea reaches several countries."

"While that's true, we'd still need to cross them, if you're referring to Sweden and Norway. Going any other direction takes us right back toward the Saints. Which only a crazy person would do."

His smile widened.

Her eyes followed suit. "You can't be serious. What are we going to do? Wander from town to town until someone notices us?"

"Nope. We need to find another cell phone."

"For?" she prodded.

"Mia is the best pilot I know. She might have lost her plane, but Sergei can find her another."

"Mia?"

Was it Lev's imagination, or was there a hint of censure in Reyna's voice? "Mia is with Cullen Loughman, the middle brother. Sergei has a soft spot for her since she reminds him of his dead daughter."

"Then it's time we hide this vehicle, find you a phone, and make our way to the marina."

"Agreed."

"The perfect place to hide the car is at one of the warehouses at the port, but it's a forty-minute walk to the marina from there. That's a long time to be out in the open where anyone can spot us."

Lev couldn't disagree with her. "We can't chance leaving the vehicle at the marina. No doubt it's been reported missing by now, or it will be soon. I'd rather not take a chance of bringing it straight to the docks."

"There is a section between the marina and port that might work. We'd still be walking a bit."

"I say we split up."

She wrinkled her nose, showing her distaste for the idea. "I'm not sure that's a good idea."

"It may be the only one. I'll drop you close to the marina. It's still dark, so you should be able to make your way to the boat. The Saints are looking for a couple, not just one person. Do you have a cap?"

"I have a beanie."

"Hide your hair beneath it."

She put her now-cold coffee in the cupholder. "Okay. And what will you be doing?"

"I'm going to drive east to ditch the car. I'll also get a cell phone. And you'll pick me up."

Reyna sat there for a second before she tilted her head toward her shoulder briefly. "It sounds like a good plan. But there's just one tiny problem."

"How are you going to know where I'm at?"

"Precisely."

Lev followed the signs to the Gdynia marina. "Follow the coastline. You'll find me. I won't go farther than ten miles before I hide the car."

"It's risky."

"It's riskier not to do this. If we take the boat out to the North Sea, we're all but handing ourselves over to the Saints. If you want to do that, then I say we just pull over right now and wait for them to find us."

She sighed loudly and gave a frustrated shake of her head. "All right, but if I can't find you, I'm leaving your ass."

He knew she wouldn't since he was now her way home, but Lev didn't tell her that. "Fair enough."

When he reached the marina, the sky was just starting to turn a faint, pale blue far on the horizon. It was a nudge to remind them that they needed to get moving.

But he didn't release her hand, and she didn't let go of his. They sat staring out the windshield, neither saying what was on their mind. Lev knew there was a chance that she'd be caught getting to her boat. He didn't like not being there to watch her back.

Reyna was aware something could happen while Lev was hiding the car or stealing the phone and she wouldn't realize it until she went looking for him.

"Don't go up and down the coast," he warned her. "If you don't find me, keep going. I'll find a way to get to Norway."

"If that's the case, we need to pick a city."

He waited until she unfolded her map and spread it open to Norway. Lev fisted the hand that had held hers to try and remember what it had felt like to feel her. He leaned over and looked at the map.

Lev spotted a little piece of land jutting out from Bergen called Fjell. "There," he said. "We'll meet at the airfield, there."

Reyna folded up the map and handed it to him. "I have another on the boat. Keep this one."

"I won't need it," he assured her.

Her brown eyes were steadfast as she held his. "I know. Be careful."

"You, too."

Then, to his surprise, she leaned over and pressed her lips against his briefly. It barely registered before she was out of the car, her pack looped over one shoulder, and the bag of food in her hand. Lev watched her through the passenger window as she walked away.

He didn't know why he didn't drive off. It would be the right thing to do, but he couldn't. Reyna walked about twenty steps before she turned and looked back at him. She paused for a moment. He wished he could see her face, but he knew her gaze was on him.

Lev didn't leave until she continued walking. He exited the marina, looking for signs of anyone. The problem was that several people milled about. Any of them could be a Saint.

"Stop," he ordered himself.

If he continued thinking like that, he wouldn't be able to complete his part of the plan. Lev cleared his throat and adjusted in his seat.

Once clear of the marina, he headed east, staying as close to the coast as he could. He went four miles and was about to pull over to hide the car when something told him to keep going. It was another six miles before he found the derelict building.

He pulled up to it and quickly looked around. That's when he found the roll-up door in the back. He hastily returned to the car and drove it to the rear of the building. From there, he made his way inside and used the chains to roll up the door.

Lev strained against the rusted chain that obviously hadn't been used in years. When he finally got it to move half a foot, the sound was so loud, he was surprised that someone didn't come running to investigate.

If he thought moving it once would then make it easier, he was dead wrong. He wasted more time getting the door lifted inch by inch than he wanted. Finally, he had it raised enough that he could drive the car in.

Except when he did, he scraped the roof, but he didn't stop. He pulled through and shut off the engine, grabbing his pack and the map. Then he shut the rolling door, which proved an easier feat than opening it.

From there, he slung on his backpack and began jogging to the coast. He found several vehicles in a parking lot. After a look around to see if anyone was near, he started peeking into windows to see if someone had forgotten their phone.

Just when he didn't think he'd get lucky, he found one. The cell phone was on the floorboard. He'd nearly missed it, in fact. He found a good-sized rock and busted the window to unlock the door.

He wrapped his hand around the rose gold glitter case and stuffed it into his pack. Then he raised his gaze to the boats nearby. All he could do now was hope that he hadn't taken too much time hiding the car so he'd missed Reyna.

There was a little money left, but not enough to buy himself a way across the sea to Norway. He found a pier that jutted out into the sea and walked to the end of it.

The sun was rising in the east, but his gaze was pointed west. He hadn't asked Reyna what type of boat she had. It wouldn't have mattered anyway. He knew nothing about them. It wasn't as if he came in contact with many, even with working Sergei's business on the docks. The vessels they dealt with were cargo ships.

The minutes ticked by. Five. Ten. Twenty. Thirty.

Lev was thinking about ways he could get across the sea when he spotted a boat with black detailing coming to a stop. His heart skipped a beat when he spotted Reyna's caramel- colored locks flying in the wind as she came to the railing.

She smiled and waved. Lev lifted his hand and was about to jump into the water to swim to her when she ducked back inside. To his surprise, she pulled the boat up alongside the dock.

"Hurry," she shouted over the engine.

He heard the boat scrape something as he jumped the three feet separating them. His hands gripped the railing as he got his footing and pulled himself over. All the while, Reyna reversed and then took them farther out to sea.

Once he was on the boat, he made his way into the helm and stood beside her until they were in open waters. Then she turned to him.

Lev dropped his pack and pulled her into his arms.

14

Kiev

The click of Lorraine's heels on the floor beat in time with her racing heart. It wasn't odd to get called into her superior's office.

But this time, she knew it wasn't for a new assignment or praise for a job well done. This was about her complete failure to capture Lev or Reyna.

Lorraine approached Lester's door. His assistant looked up from his computer screen, but there was no welcoming smile in his eyes. Still, she nodded her head in greeting. She didn't know his name and didn't bother learning it. Lester went through assistants quicker than any other person in his station.

"He's ready," the assistant stated before returning to his work.

Lorraine squared her shoulders and went to the office door. She rapped twice on it before she heard Lester's booming voice telling her to enter. She walked in and closed the door behind her as she met her boss's gaze.

Lester Barros had the lined, weathered face of

someone who had spent countless hours in the sun. His years moving around the Middle East from one desert to another had taken a toll on him physically.

But she didn't know anyone tougher, even though he walked with a slight limp from an IED explosion.

"You sent for me, sir?" she said.

Lester tossed down the pen he'd been using and pushed back his chair. He said nothing as he stood and walked to the windows overlooking the city. With his hands clasped behind his back, he let out a sigh.

She noted the neat stack of files on his desktop, one folder opened. Lorraine took a slight step forward to get a better look, but she still couldn't make it out. And she knew better than to push her luck.

Lester had removed his suit jacket, and it now hung on a hook near the door. But his tie was still cinched tightly around his neck, which meant he wasn't too stressed yet. He was tall and thin, with a head of thick, salt-and-pepper hair that held just a hint of a wave to it. Lester wore it combed back, but there was always a section over his left eye that curled onto his forehead.

She'd learned six years ago when they had a drink together that he'd come to the Saints via the Secret Service after several tours as a Marine Force Recon. Anyone stupid enough to underestimate him soon realized their mistake.

He might be at a desk now, but that didn't mean he wasn't as sharp as he had been when he had her job.

"What happened?"

Lorraine mentally steadied herself. She'd known this question was coming. "I've been asking myself that since I learned that Reyna Harris might very well be a double agent."

"She was fully vetted."

"I'm aware, but there's no denying something isn't right with her."

"She's done an exceptional job. Every mission she's sent on, she completes quickly, cleanly, and effortlessly."

Lorraine hated that Lester kept his back to her. That wasn't a good sign. It meant that he was still undecided as to what to do with her. She needed to turn his mind to her way of thinking. And this was her only opportunity.

"Reyna came under suspicion when I saw her and Lev Ivanski driving away together."

Lester's shoulders raised as he took a deep breath. "I, too, saw the footage. She had him at gunpoint."

"True. However, when I went to get Ivanski from her, she wasn't at her flat."

Lester turned on his heel and faced her before leaning his hips back against the window. "Why didn't you wait for her to bring him to you?" Before Lorraine could respond, he continued. "Because you wanted credit for the capture of Ivanski. I'm sure you hoped you could have a few hours with him to learn about the Loughmans before having to turn Lev over to me."

"You've never questioned my methods before."

"Your drive to be the best has made you many enemies. You've remained at your post because I fought to keep you there."

Lorraine was taken aback by the news. "What?" she murmured.

Lester lifted one shoulder in a shrug. "There was

no need to tell you. I put my neck on the line for you, but you've never let me down before."

"I pinged Reyna's phone. She was supposed to be at her flat," Lorraine stated, knowing she was running out of time. "It's because I knew she was up to something that I was able to get a trace on her when I called. She'd taken Lev out of the city."

He lifted a bushy brow. "How many times have you done that?"

She opened her mouth to respond but found no words.

"Exactly," he said. "Many, many times. Reyna had Lev. We *need* him to get info on the Loughmans. Instead, she must have figured out that you were questioning her loyalties and ran."

"They're working together now."

He snorted. "Your actions might have effectively turned one of our best—possibly *the* best—operatives away from us."

"I don't believe she was ever ours. She came into this building and went down to archives."

Fury contorted Lester's face as he pushed away from the window and stalked to her. "How do you know this?"

It took all of Lorraine's will not to back up a step. She'd seen that look come over his face once in the past—right before he slit an enemy's throat.

Lorraine swallowed, the sound loud to her ears. "I followed her movements for a few days. Her coming here was the only thing out of the ordinary."

"Did you ever think she was sent for?"

"Was she?"

"I'm the one asking the questions," Lester said in a low, deadly voice that brooked no argument.

Lorraine glanced at the floor. "I wasn't thinking about the possibility that she'd been sent for. Not when I saw that she'd gone into the archives, and the feed was corrupted so I couldn't see what she did."

"When you weren't able to capture Reyna or Lev, you then decided to ignore all common sense and contact the elders to see if one of them would talk to you."

"It was a bold move, I agree, but it was ne—"

"If you want to be standing when you leave this office, you'll shut your mouth right now."

She'd never heard such a cold tone from him before. Lorraine suppressed the shiver that ran through her as she realized she had managed to take her one ally and sever that bond.

Lester glared at her, disappointment and anger tightening his visage. "I would expect something so impertinent from a new recruit, but not you."

"I've given my loyalty and my life to the Saints. I'm simply trying to ensure that nothing can hurt us."

"You've not given your life. Yet," Lester threatened. He pivoted and returned to his desk. After sinking into his chair, he rested his forearms on the wooden surface.

Lorraine raised her chin defiantly. "If I must give my life, I'll gladly do it. I've done nothing but serve. I may have overstepped bounds—"

"May?" Lester asked with raised brows.

"I overstepped bounds," she corrected, only a tinge of irritation coming through in her voice. "But I did it to help this organization."

Lester snorted and shook his head. "Reyna has been on your team for five years. You've always had great things to say about her, even when you were jealous of how well she did. Why would you question her now?"

"She's never lied to me before."

Lester held Lorraine's gaze for a long minute before he leaned back. "As you well know, operatives are trained to lie. It's what they do."

"I never lied to you. I expect the same from those on my team."

He nodded and tapped a finger on the desk. "That one lie had you digging into her life?"

"Yes. I know the reach and strength of the Saints. One person couldn't do us harm, but I don't want to be the one responsible for that individual. Reyna was vetted, yes, but she was under my watch. It falls to me."

"And me," Lester added with a sigh. "I spoke with the elders. None of them requested Reyna."

Lorraine bit her tongue to keep from smiling. Lester wouldn't approve of her showing any type of victory now. "Does that mean I can go after her?"

"Yes. Wait," Lester said when she started to leave. "The elders want her and Lev alive and brought back here."

Some of Lorraine's excitement dulled. She'd been dreaming of taking Reyna out ever since she realized that she was a double agent. "I'll do my best."

"Let me put it this way, Lorraine. If either Lev or Reyna is killed, don't come back. Make it clear to your team that they are to be detained only. *And*," he continued, "no torture. Lev's and Reyna's questioning will be handled by the elders."

As long as Lorraine had been with the Saints, she'd never heard of the elders doing such a thing. "Of course."

"Understand that if either of them is killed, tortured, or questioned, you'll be the next one hunted. As will everyone on your team."

She nodded. "I understand completely."

"Good. Don't let me down."

"I won't."

Lorraine left Lester's office with her mind already planning how to get Reyna and Lev. She was so deep in thought that she didn't realize that someone was in the elevator with her until she heard Anatoli's voice.

"You scraped by on this one," he stated. "By the skin of your teeth."

She decided it was best to ignore him. Engaging him would only make her angry, and she was in too good of a mood to let anyone—especially him—dampen it.

"You underestimated them once. Don't do it again," Lester cautioned.

She didn't heed her own advice as she turned her head to look at him. "Have you forgotten how good I am? I can handle this."

"Everyone comes up against their match eventually, Lori. This could be yours."

There was no teasing in his blue eyes, only concern. His voice held a note of worry that Lorraine hadn't heard since they were lovers. It brought her up short. Were Lev and Reyna her match? No, that wasn't possible. It would take someone like Lester, someone who had been through it all and came out stronger, cleverer, to best her.

"Reyna knows we're closing in. She knows our strategies, so she knows what we're capable of," Lorraine said. "As for Lev, he's too stupid to realize what he's landed in. But he's about to. I've never failed on a mission before. I won't do it now."

"Let me come with you."

She barked in laughter as the elevator chimed when it reached her floor. Lorraine stepped out of the car and said, "I don't need you to do my job. I never did."

Anatoli put his hand on the door to stop it from closing. "How about someone you trust watching your back?"

"You?" she asked and shook her head. "No, thanks."

He moved out of the elevator, and the doors closed behind him. "You're going to need all the help you can get."

"I've got a great team. Go back to yours," Lorraine told him and walked to her office.

There, she looked at a map of Poland and the surrounding countries pulled up on a giant screen. She used her hands to turn, zoom, and maneuver the image to look at it from all angles.

"You're going to the sea," she murmured. Lorraine leaned over and punched a button on her desk phone to ring her assistant. "Get men ready. I want twenty of them stationed along the Kattegat strait."

Lorraine smiled as she realized how easy it would be to grab Lev and Reyna.

15

Reyna didn't think anything could fell Lev Ivanski. But one look at the greenish tint of his skin said otherwise.

"You didn't tell me you got seasick," she admonished.

He shrugged. "It wouldn't have done any good."

"We'll only be on the water for about six hours. Better than weeks at sea." She winced when he groaned and clutched his stomach. "Keep your eyes on the horizon."

"I can do that."

She hurriedly went for the stash of ginger she always kept with her. "Chew this," she ordered as she handed him two tablets.

"Gum?" he asked with a frown. "That doesn't sound good."

"It's ginger, which is a natural herb for calming nausea and motion sickness."

He took them and began to chew.

"I know we need to keep hidden, but fresh air does wonders. Open the window there and keep your face beside it," Reyna told Lev as she once more took the wheel to navigate.

Ten minutes later, she glanced Lev's way to find his color returning.

"This gum is amazing," he said.

She chuckled. "I always keep some with me. You never know when you might get an upset stomach. Always calms mine when it happens."

"I just might survive the sea."

They shared a grin.

At least she could smile now. For a bit, she'd been worried that she wouldn't find Lev. Since she hadn't known how long it would take him to hide the car and find a phone, she had driven slower than she wanted. But she was glad that she had. Otherwise, she wouldn't have seen him.

"I think I can make that call now that my stomach is settled." He bent to grab the phone from his pack and dialed.

Reyna kept her attention on the water, but she was already thinking about how they could get to the States if Mia couldn't fly down to get them. To have anyone leave the US put their lives in danger.

"Hang up," she told him.

His dark brows snapped together as his blue eyes fastened on her. "Why? What's wrong?"

"The Saints are already going after your friends. We shouldn't separate them. Besides, we're pretty resilient. We'll find our way home."

"Reyna," he began. But his attention shifted, and he said into the phone, "Callie, it's Lev."

Reyna could hear a voice, but she couldn't make out the words. Lev's gaze lowered to the floor, and she looked back out the window. The sunrise was spectacular. Yellow, orange, and red streaked the sky in a magnificent display.

"Hey," Lev said as he came up beside her. "Say hello to Callie."

Reyna looked down to see that he had put the cell phone on speaker. With no other choice, Reyna said, "Hi, Callie."

"Hey. It's nice to get to talk to you," Callie said.

Reyna smiled when she heard the Texas twang.

"Callie is the one who deep dives on others," Lev explained.

In other words, Lev was telling her that Callie had given her background a thorough search. Probably as thorough as the Saints had.

Reyna nodded at Lev to let him know that she'd expected it.

"You have an impressive history," Callie said.

"Thanks," Reyna replied. "I know none of you have any reason to trust me, b—"

"Lev trusts you," Callie interrupted. "That means we will, as well. Until you give us a reason not to."

The warning was loud and clear. "Understood."

"Great. Let's move on," Callie stated. "Where are y'all?"

"In the Baltic," Reyna explained.

Then Lev said, "As soon as Reyna told me there was only one way out, I knew the Saints would be waiting for us."

"Yep. They sure will be," Callie agreed.

"I came up with a plan, and Reyna agreed. We're headed to Sweden, where we'll cross into Norway."

Callie said, "Ahhh. I see. And you're going to get another boat then?"

Reyna met Lev's gaze and nodded. It was the

easiest thing to do. It wouldn't be simple to steal a boat, but it would keep Lev's friends away from the Saints for at least that much longer.

"That's one option," Lev said. "I wondered if Mia would be up for making a trip, though."

"You know she would," Callie replied.

"There's just the matter of a plane."

Callie snorted. "Yep. That small matter."

"Sergei can help with that. I'll call him. I should check in with him anyway."

Reyna closed her eyes as she recalled the things she had done to those who had stood against the Saints. She didn't want that happening to Lev or any of his friends, and if anyone came for them, that's exactly what would happen.

"We'll find a boat in Norway," Reyna said as she opened her eyes and looked at the sea. She ignored the penetrating look Lev leveled at her.

Callie hesitated before she said, "Umm, it's going to be dangerous either way."

"Sending Mia here is the most dangerous," Reyna said.

Lev quickly added, "And letting the Saints catch up to us isn't?"

Reyna sighed and looked at Lev. "I know what the Saints do to people like Mia. I don't care how tough a person is, everyone has a breaking point. They'll do unspeakably horrible things to Mia and anyone who comes with her."

"You make it sound as if she'll get caught," Lev said.

Reyna shrugged. "There's a good chance she will. They'll be on the lookout for any private planes leaving the States and headed this way. Even if she doesn't call in her flight plan, they'll pick her up on radar and track her. When she lands, they'll grab her and us."

"She's right, Lev," Callie said. "But even so, I know Mia would come for you. She and Cullen both owe you."

Lev blew out a long breath, his face tight. "No. Don't say anything to Mia. Reyna's right. We'll be fine."

Callie issued a loud, sarcastic snort. "How about we stop with the bullshit. We all know the Saints are coming. It doesn't matter if we're together or on opposite sides of the world. We're fighting. That's what matters. And we have each other's backs."

Reyna couldn't help but smile. Callie was right. It was easy to forget that Lev wasn't on his own. And—for now, at least—neither was Reyna. She was so used to doing things for herself *by* herself that she had to stop and remind herself that she didn't have to do it all anymore.

"I don't keep secrets from the group." Callie mumbled something incoherent. "Okay, so I only keep small things from them. Like eating Owen's lemon cake. That thing was just too damn good. My point is that I'm going to fill the others in. I won't tell them that you thought about asking Mia to fly, but don't be surprised if she comes up with it on her own."

The tension was gone from Lev's face. He was calm once more. "Cullen won't let her do it."

"She's a combat pilot. She doesn't need Cullen's permission to do anything," Callie stated, a hard edge to her voice.

Reyna couldn't wait to meet both Callie and Mia.

They sounded amazing. But first, she and Lev had to get to Sweden, then across it into Norway.

"Also," Callie said hesitantly. "There's a little matter of Maks."

"Maks?" Reyna asked Lev with a frown.

It was Callie who answered. "He's ex-Delta Force. He served on Wyatt's team but left to join the CIA. The Saints tried to recruit him, but he disappeared. Which was answer enough for them."

Reyna nodded as she listened. "He's exactly the type of person the Saints would want. I'm surprised he got away without them forcing him to make a decision."

"You don't know Maks," Lev said dryly.

Callie laughed over the line. "Lev's right. Maks is...well, let's just say he told us he was going out. I put a tracker on him, and Wyatt put one in his pack, but Maks found both. The last I had him was in Turkey."

"He's a ghost," Lev said.

Reyna whistled softly as she looked back at the water. "That's an impressive skill."

"He might be near y'all," Callie said. "I could try to get ahold of him."

Lev shook his head, even though Callie couldn't see it. "If Maks left, it's because he has something he needs to do. Let him see it through."

"Lev," Callie began.

"I knew what I was getting into when I agreed to this mission," he cut her off. "I knew the risks. So did Reyna when she decided to infiltrate the Saints. We've gotten this far. We'll figure something out. I'll be in touch when I can."

"Be safe," Callie said before the line went dead.

Lev then called Sergei. The call was quick, only a few words exchanged between the two before Lev tossed the phone out the window into the water.

Minutes ticked by without Lev saying anything. Reyna finally couldn't take it anymore. She said, "I'm sorry. I want to go home, too. I'm just worried the Saints would grab Mia."

"There's nothing to be sorry for. You were right. Cullen would've flown with Mia. It would be a big coup for the Saints to get a Loughman. That can't happen. Besides, they're better together."

"You make it sound like you aren't one of them."

Lev shrugged. "In many ways, I'm not. I didn't want to be a part of this, but I am now. And glad of it. But I'm not blood. That family is...tight."

"We'll make it back," Reyna promised.

Finally, he turned his gaze to her. "I know."

She didn't mention that he no longer looked seasick. It was better that his mind was on other things than a nauseated stomach.

"Where are you headed exactly?" Lev asked as he looked down at a coastal map of Sweden.

"The closest port." She pointed to the bottom tip of Sweden.

Lev twisted his lips. "I'm not keen on remaining out on the water any longer than I have to, but does that put us too close to the Kattegat strait?"

"Closer than I'd like. I figured we needed off the water quickly. Are you suggesting we go farther north?"

"I am," he said. "What do you think?"

"I think any distance we put between us and them is a win. Only so much time will pass before they realize we aren't coming. Then Lorraine will look at different locations we could go. She'll come to Sweden."

Lev smiled as he crossed his arms over his chest. "Unless she begins to second-guess herself and wonder if we continued over land instead of coming to the sea."

"Now that would be nice. Most likely, Lorraine will split her team and send half in either direction. She is nothing if not persistent. She's never failed. She hand-picks each member of her team."

"So, you know how she thinks."

Reyna shrugged. "She's thorough. The fact that we got away will leave a rather nasty taste in her mouth. She'll come at us with everything she has now. We're going to have to be even more careful."

"I'm not worried. Are you?"

Reyna flashed Lev a smile, surprised when the truth filled her. "Not at all."

"We have each other. Like we told Callie, we've gotten this far. We'll keep going until we can't go anymore."

"Sounds like my kind of plan."

The corners of his eyes crinkled as he grinned. "I'm glad you didn't shoot me at the theatre."

"I thought about it."

"I know. I saw your finger on the trigger. What stopped you?"

She couldn't tell him the truth, that there was something in his eyes that had called to her. Instead, she said, "I followed my gut."

16

G etting to the coast of Sweden was thankfully uneventful. Lev's stomach had settled considerably with the ginger gum, along with taking his mind off being on the water. He remained next to the open window to stave off the worst of the nausea.

Even though the air coming off the water was chilly, and he saw Reyna shiver a couple of times, she never once complained. They each kept a lookout for any vessels that appeared to be following them or coming too close.

When they finally sailed into the marina just south of Simpevarp, it was nearing dusk. Lev made his way out onto the deck of the boat and looked around. Reyna navigated the water and boat traffic expertly to pull them up to a dock.

Lev jumped over the side, landing on the deck to tie off the boat. Reyna was standing beside him with both of their packs when he finished securing the last line. She flashed him a smile, and he was glad to see her wearing the hat again.

"Ready?" she asked.

He stood and let his gaze scan the area. "Let's put some distance between us and the marina."

"Agreed."

They casually set out at an easy pace. He spotted the first camera quickly.

"We're being watched," he told her.

She adjusted her backpack and tucked her chin. "I've spotted four already."

"We won't be taking a car here."

"We need to stretch our legs anyway."

They shared a grin as they left the marina and entered the parking area. In minutes, they were near a busy street. Several taxis drove past, but neither of them flagged one down.

Lev spotted a large house near the shore. It suddenly gave him an idea. "We can't chance a hotel."

"I know," she replied as she turned her head to him. "But you need to sleep."

He'd planned to rest on the boat, but he knew if he lay down, things would've been worse for him with the seasickness. "True, and I'm not keen on sleeping on the ground again."

"You sound as if you have a plan?"

He tilted his head toward the house.

Reyna's eyes widened. "You want to break into someone's house?"

"It's just for a few hours. Think about a shower, hot food, and a bed."

"I hope you aren't expecting me to cook."

He laughed. "I can handle the food."

"Really?" she asked, her brows shooting up in her forehead.

"You don't think I can?" he teased.

"I'm beginning to believe there isn't anything you can't do."

That made him smile and feel something...warm deep inside. The place very near where his heart used to be. "Come on. There seems to be several nice houses."

"Why those? They'll have alarm systems we'll need to bypass. Let's choose something less difficult."

"It won't hurt to look."

"I don't know about this," she said, but she still followed him.

They kept out of sight of cars as they made their way to the row of houses. There was one that didn't appear to be occupied. Lev took the left side as Reyna moved to the right to investigate and see if it looked like anyone was home. They met at the back of the house.

"There're no dishes in the sink," she said. "Either those living here are really neat, or they're gone."

"Or they have a maid," he said.

She shrugged. "I'm willing to try. A hot shower is sounding pretty nice."

"So does a hot meal and a bed. I did find a security system. It should be easy to bypass, though."

"Another surprise," Reyna said with a quick smile.

She kept a lookout while Lev found the outside electrical box. He used her mini flashlight to find the wires he needed to disable the system but not sever it altogether. Because doing that would alert the fail-safes and set off the alarm.

He put away the flashlight and returned everything to the way it was. "Ready?"

"I call dibs on the shower first."

He grinned at her excitement. "I'm fairly certain there's more than one."

"Well, expect that I'll use all the hot water."

Lev chuckled as they walked to the back door. Reyna easily picked the lock. They hesitantly stepped inside. Lev searched for the alarm base to see if anything was flashing red. Everything looked good, so he gave her a thumbs up.

"Do a quick search before we make ourselves comfortable," she said.

He nodded and went upstairs as she searched the ground floor. He found five bedrooms. Three were kids' rooms, one looked like a guest suite, and then there was the master. Lev eyed the large shower before he pivoted and returned to Reyna.

"I found this," she said when he walked into the kitchen.

He looked at the calendar her flashlight had highlighted. There, in bold, neat letters across two weeks was the word *VACATION*.

"They won't be back for another week," she said and waggled her brows.

"You're going to love the master bath. Last door on the right."

She started to walk off but hesitated.

"What is it?" he asked.

She glanced down at her clothes. "I don't want to be clean and get back into dirty clothes."

"See if there's anything here you can wear."

"I'd rather wash mine."

He had to admit, it was a good idea, even as he thought about her walking around the house naked. Lev inwardly shook himself. "We'll have plenty of time."

"Good. Strip."

He blinked. "What?"

"Get out of your clothes. I'll start a load while we both take showers."

For a second, Lev couldn't move. He couldn't stop thinking about her naked. In the water.

With his hands on her.

"You okay?" she asked with a frown.

He nodded quickly and removed his boots. "Yeah."

Lev didn't say anything else as he removed each item of clothing until he stood naked before her. She held his gaze before she too removed her clothes.

His gaze raked over her pale form. The gown she'd worn to the theatre had shown her incredible figure, but seeing her bared before him now made his blood heat.

She was stunningly beautiful. Every muscle toned, but she still had the curves of a woman. Her caramel-colored locks were in disarray from the cap, but he quite liked the tousled look. Her breasts were small and firm. It was the sight of her pink-tipped nipples that hardened beneath his gaze that had the blood rushing to his cock.

Then his eyes lowered to the juncture of her thighs. His mouth went dry when he saw that she was completely free of hair.

Reyna gathered the clothes and walked to the washing machine. Once the cycle was set, she moved past him to the stairs. But on the second step, she stopped and looked back at him over her shoulder.

The silent question in her eyes propelled him forward. He reached her, and they ascended the rest of the steps together. No words were spoken as they made their way into the master bathroom.

Lev turned on the water while she retrieved towels. It wasn't long before steam began to fill the room. Reyna was the first beneath the stream, but she quickly reached out and grabbed his hand to pull him in.

He shut the door behind him. He couldn't take his gaze from Reyna as she leaned her head back and wet her hair. His eyes followed her hands as they ran over her locks. He followed the rivulets of water as they ran down her chest to her nipples and then dropped to the tile.

Unable to help himself, he reached up and cupped her breast. He learned the weight of it before he ran his thumb over her nipple.

Reyna gasped and grabbed his arm, her nails digging into his flesh. The pleasure on her face was all he needed to see to keep going.

He tweaked her other nipple, causing her to moan. Lev was so focused on her that he never saw her hand move until her fingers wrapped around his length. Then it was his turn to moan.

The feel of her hand moving up and down his shaft was amazing. He kept one hand teasing her sensitive nipples before he slid his other hand down to her sex. He dipped a finger inside her to find her wet to his touch.

His cock jumped, eager to be inside her. He spun them both so his back was to the water and hers was to his chest and began to slowly run his finger around her clit.

Her moan of ecstasy was music to his ears. She gripped the sides of his legs, her hips moving in time with his finger. He moved faster and faster until she had to brace her hands against the tile.

To his surprise, she reached around and once more took hold of his cock. Then she arched her back, maneuvering him so that the head of his arousal brushed against her sex.

His hips pushed forward of their own accord, and he slid into her. Lev closed his eyes at the feel of her slick heat wrapped around him. It felt so good, he wasn't sure he ever wanted to move.

But his body took over once more. He began to thrust, slowly at first, and all the while, he continued to run his finger around her clit.

Her cries became louder. A heartbeat later, her body tensed as her orgasm ripped through her. Lev drove hard and deep, loving the feel of her clamping around him. He didn't stop circling her clit until her head fell forward.

Lev then clasped his hands on her hips and began to plunge inside her. She pressed her hips back, meeting each of his thrusts. It wasn't long before he, too, started to climax. He pulled out, spilling his seed onto her back.

They stood together, each breathing heavily beneath the stream of hot water. Lev moved aside and let the spray rinse off Reyna's back.

She turned then and wrapped her arms around his neck. "That's the first time I've had sex with a man before he kissed me."

Lev looked down at her lips. How had he forgotten to kiss her? Then he glanced at her breasts. That's how. But he would make up for it now.

"I can fix that," he told her.

He bent his head and captured her lips. He

moved his mouth over hers slowly. Then he slid his tongue along the seam. The moment she parted for him, he slipped his tongue inside to find hers.

Reyna sighed as she pressed her body against his, her arms tightening around his neck. Once he'd tasted her, he couldn't stop. The kiss continued, burning hotter and more fiery with every heartbeat.

Until he was hard for her again.

She was the one who tore her lips from his. Her brown eyes had a dreamy cast to them as she touched his mouth with her finger. "That was... Kiss me like that again."

"Then come here," he ordered.

She shook her head. "If you kiss me again, I'm going to want you."

He grinned. "And what's wrong with that?"

"Because I want to scrub my body and yours so I can have my way with you later."

Lev wasn't going to argue with that. He grabbed a bar of soap. "Get to washing."

She laughed and took the soap.

17

A ll Reyna had wanted was a shower.

Until she'd seen Lev naked. Then, all she wanted was him. And he hadn't disappointed. Her body was still quivering from the toe-curling orgasm he'd given her.

Now, she and Lev were quickly washing their hair and bodies, alternating using the water all while doing their best not to touch each other. Which, of course, meant they each kept bumping into the other.

Though, half of her times were on purpose. She just couldn't stop touching him. And once she felt him, she couldn't seem to let go. He was like a magnet, drawing her to him.

Somehow, they managed to get clean and the soap rinsed off in a relatively short amount of time. The moment the water had been turned off, she reached for one of the towels. Reyna barely started to dry off before she was lifted off her feet and carried to the bed.

She wound her arms around Lev and gazed into his blue eyes. Water dripped from his hair onto her face, but she didn't care. The instant their lips met, the worry plaguing her, the Saints, and the entire outside world fell away.

It had been far too long since she'd felt the warmth and weight of a man's body. She likened it to being woken from sleepwalking. Everywhere Lev touched, the nerve endings came alive.

Her eyes rolled back in her head as he skimmed his hands up her legs, starting at her ankles and moving all the way to her hips. She felt the bed give as he placed his hands on either side of her head. She opened her eyes and smiled up at him.

She placed her hands on his trim waist and moved her palms down over the firm cheeks of his butt, then moved upward to his back, feeling the dampness of his skin. She slowly slid a finger along his spine up to his shoulder blades. Unable to resist, she caressed over his broad shoulders and firm biceps then back to his impeccable chest. He didn't move a muscle as she let her fingers trail down his washboard stomach to his thick cock that strained between them. She pumped her hand on him slowly a few times.

His arousal had already been inside her. She knew how it felt to have him sliding in and out of her, bringing her unimaginable pleasure. His fingers had known just where and how to touch both her sex and her breasts to bring her to the brink of climax in quick order.

She wanted him to feel that same kind of pleasure. She wanted him to squirm for release the way she had. Her fingers wrapped around his rod.

And she knew just how to do it.

Reyna pushed at his shoulder with her free hand. Lev rolled onto his back, his gaze never leaving her face. She rose up on her elbow and bent to kiss his chest. She flicked her tongue over his nipples and felt his quick intake of breath.

She continued kissing down his stomach until she reached his cock. There, she parted her lips and took his length into her mouth. She had only just settled in when she felt his hands on her, pulling her. Reyna lifted her head, and in the next breath, Lev had her turned around and straddling his face.

A sigh escaped when he licked her clit. There was a smile on her lips when she returned her attention to his rod. It was difficult to keep her focus on him when he made her feel so good.

She wanted to make him come with her mouth, but when he flipped her onto her back and entered her with one thrust, it no longer mattered. Their gazes met as his hips pistoned, him moving in and out of her, filling her again and again.

Suddenly, he leaned down and kissed her. A kiss that scorched her all the way to her bones. She'd never felt another so sizzling, so...passionate. It felt as if she had finally found something she hadn't even known she was looking for. Lev ended the kiss by sucking on her bottom lip.

The climax came out of nowhere. It slammed into Reyna and swept her away. The cry of pleasure locked inside while her body convulsed, the orgasm prolonged with every thrust of Lev's cock.

Finally, she began to come down from the intensity of it. She looked to see their bodies meeting before she raised her gaze to his face. There was something in his eyes, something she hadn't seen before. It was almost like a...silent promise.

Once more, Lev pulled out of her as he climaxed. This time, he spilled on her stomach. Seeing the ecstasy on his face, hearing his shout of pleasure made her smile in contentment.

"Fuck. That was amazing," he said as he looked at her with a crooked grin.

"It really was," she replied.

She tried to get up to grab a towel, but Lev held her in place with one hand. Then, without a word, he rose and walked into the bathroom only to return a moment later with their towels. He handed one to her while he used the other to wipe himself.

Reyna cleaned off her stomach and then dropped the towel onto the floor as she looked at the ceiling. Lev climbed into bed beside her. She immediately rolled toward him to lay her cheek on his chest.

He put one arm around her and the other behind his head. "What are you thinking about?"

"That this is the first time I've felt this good in many, many years."

"I'll be happy to repeat that anytime."

She lifted her face to his and smiled widely. "Then I'll want to book you every night."

"Consider it done."

But thinking about the future made her thoughts turn to their current predicament and the Saints.

"Don't," Lev said, his face serious. "Don't let the world intrude."

"It already has."

He shifted onto his side to face her and shook his head. "You have the power to control that. Give yourself tonight. Give *us* tonight."

"You're right."

"I'm always right," he retorted with a wink.

She chuckled. "Well, none of this would've

happened if I hadn't taken off my clothes or stopped on the stairs."

"Oh, I beg to differ. It's all I've been thinking about for some time."

"Is it?" She was intrigued now. "So, you would've done something tonight?"

"Without a doubt."

"Hmmmm. Good."

He kissed the tip of her nose. "As much as I want to lay here, I think we should get some food."

"Agreed." Though she intended for them to return to bed immediately after.

Lev was the first to get up. Reyna picked up the towel only to find Lev holding out a pink-and-white-striped robe. She gladly put it on while he pulled on a pair of plaid lounge pants.

Reyna combed out her hair while Lev went downstairs. Then she gathered their towels and brought them down with her. She found him in the kitchen with various ingredients laid out.

"I'd offer to help, but I'll mess things up. It's better if I stay out of the way," she said.

He laughed and looked at her over his shoulder. "We'll see about that."

"I have many skills, but cooking isn't one of them."

"My mother wanted to make sure I knew how to cook, so she always had me in the kitchen with her. I liked it, actually."

Reyna walked to the island and took one of the bar chairs. "When did you first learn?"

"I was seven when she first had me in the kitchen with her. At least, that's when she was asking me to help her. I got her ingredients, measuring cups, and the like. She had a chair pulled up to the counter that I stood on so I could see." He paused in the chopping to rummage in the cupboards to look for a pan. When he had it, he put it on the stove. "Everything just developed from there."

"My mom had me in the kitchen as well, but I hated it."

"There were certainly times I fought being in there with her. I would have rather been with my friends or doing anything else, but eventually, I realized that I had to do it, so I might as well make it fun."

Reyna leaned her forearms on the island and smiled as she pictured a young Lev in the kitchen. "Were you any good at it?"

"My mom said I was a natural. She actually pushed me to go to culinary school. It was something I considered. I was always coming up with different dishes to try."

She looked around at what little he'd pulled from the pantry and fridge. "Let me guess, you would see what your mother had, and then just come up with something based on what was there."

He paused and turned to look at her. "Yeah."

"Exactly what you're doing now."

His lips turned up in a grin. "Yeah."

"Then don't let me stop you. I'm famished."

His laugh filled the kitchen as he returned to whatever it was he was doing. And for just a moment in time, Reyna could pretend that this was their home, that it was just a regular night with him cooking and her sitting there as they shared details about their day.

Yet it was all a fantasy. This wasn't their home,

and this wasn't a normal night. They were running for their lives, staying away from anyone for fear that they might be a Saint.

And just like that, the world intruded.

Reyna squeezed her eyes closed and took a deep breath. As she let it out, she also released thoughts of the Saints. Lev was right. This was their night, and she had power over what she let into her mind.

When she opened her eyes, he was standing on the opposite side of the island, looking at her. She smiled. "I'm good."

"We're going to be okay."

"I know." She'd said it because it was almost expected, but when the words came out, she realized that they were the truth.

Reyna spotted a bottle of wine and rose to get it. It took a few tries before she found the opener, but she got the cork out and the alcohol poured into two glasses.

"Perfect," Lev said as he accepted the wine and gave her a quick kiss.

She stood beside him as he put noodles into a pot to boil. In another pan, he had onions and garlic sautéing in olive oil. Her stomach rumbled at the delicious smell. But her mouth began to water when he added crushed tomatoes and some of the red wine she'd just opened to make his own red sauce.

In short order, the pasta was ready. To make sure no one was alerted to their presence, they turned off the lights and lit a few candles. They sat at the bar, eating right out of the pan after he'd combined the pasta and sauce with the bottle of wine between them.

Reyna told him about her first days at the CIA

and going through the selection process. He shared stories of medical school and some of the classes he had taken.

It was the most romantic, incredible night of Reyna's life.

They laughed, they joked. They spoke from the heart. Because each knew that it could be their last few hours. Neither knew what tomorrow would bring.

Reyna was reminded of something she'd once read that said to live each day as if it were your last. Many said they did that, but she knew it was a lie. Only people in her and Lev's shoes truly understood how fleeting life was.

She went to take another bite and realized she had eaten the entire thing. The pasta was finished, and the wine was gone. It saddened her somehow.

Lev was staring at her again. He reached over and took her hand. It was as if he could read her thoughts.

"I'll get the dishes," she said.

He took the pan. "We'll do it together."

There was no more talk as they cleaned every dish, wiping it dry and returning it to its place. Then they wiped down the stove and counter and put the empty wine bottle into the garbage. Then Lev blew out the candles.

Reyna transferred their clothes to the dryer and put in the towels. She walked through the house to find Lev. She found him in the master bedroom near the windows, looking out at the sea.

"If you could live anywhere, where would you go?" he asked.

Reyna came up behind him and wrapped her arms around his waist as she rested her cheek against his back. "I've lived in so many places, but it's been a really long while since I've had a place that I considered home. I don't think it's the place, though. I think it's being with someone who makes it feel like a home. Why?"

"Because I've been thinking about it for a few days now."

"And?" she pushed.

He turned and wrapped his arms around her. "I want one."

"Me, too."

18

"What do you mean, you haven't found them?"

Lorraine glared at a member of her team. She didn't even bother hiding the fact that she was furious. None of them realized—or cared—that her life hung in the balance.

None of the elders accepted failure to any degree. The fact that she was still alive despite losing Reyna and Lev was only because she had been successful up until that point. But everything hinged on her finding them now.

And if she didn't...there wasn't a person in the organization that could save her.

"We've stopped and searched every boat going through the strait over the last ten hours," the young woman explained. "They're not here."

Lorraine wanted to rail at the woman, but she turned on her heel and walked away instead. That's when she spotted Anatoli. It galled her that after refusing to allow him to come, the elders had ordered Anatoli to do just that.

Did that mean they didn't trust her? Or was Anatoli there to watch her? Fine. Let him stay. It was better to keep enemies closer anyway. He moved out of the way as she neared and then followed her back to her vehicle without saying a word.

She got behind the wheel and grabbed hold of it to squeeze. If only it were Reyna's neck her hands were around. Lorraine closed her eyes and tried to shake off the feeling that a blade was headed straight for her heart.

"There's still a chance that they'll come through the strait," Anatoli said.

She'd been so lost in thought that she hadn't heard him get into the car. There was nothing to say, so she didn't respond to him.

"Lori, it's going to be all right."

Her eyes snapped open as she turned her head to give him her nastiest scowl. "All right? It's not going to be anything close to that if I don't find at least one of them."

He smiled, unfazed by her fury as he leaned an elbow on the passenger door and braced his hand against the side of his head. "It's quicker for them to travel by boat. I believe they'll come through the strait, but they also know you'll be watching it. If I was them, I'd wait a few days before striking out."

"And if I was in their place, I'd set out as quickly as I could."

Anatoli shrugged one shoulder. "What will it hurt to keep a contingent of your team here to continue searching the vessels?"

It was the smart thing to do, and she'd decided on that earlier. But her mind was already thinking ahead. She pulled out her tablet from her purse and opened it to the map of the surrounding countries.

Anatoli leaned over to look at it and made a line

from Kiev to the Baltic Sea through Poland with his finger. "The quickest route is by water."

"But it isn't their only way," Lorraine stated while her gaze moved to Germany. "If they could reach the North Sea via Germany, then they could bypass the strait altogether."

"That's a lot of land to cover. Not to mention the borders."

She fought not to roll her eyes. "We've both seen how easily they cross borders. Even ones we're patrolling."

"Then send a team to Germany. They can reach it by air in a few hours."

She lifted her phone and punched in a number. "I don't have to send a team. I have one there already. They'll spread out and search the marinas."

"Have them stop any boat that looks suspicious," he added.

Lorraine finished sending the directive via text, but she couldn't shake the feeling that she wasn't anywhere near to catching Lev and Reyna.

"I know that look," Anatoli said. "You're still not happy."

"Because they could get away."

He sat back and twisted his lips. "Then put all your teams on alert across Europe. I'll do the same with mine. With that many searching for them, Reyna and Lev will be found."

Lorraine didn't want to accept help. She wanted to tell Anatoli to kiss off, but she wasn't that stupid. "Thanks for the offer."

Both of them began sending alerts to their teams. Lorraine finished and went back to looking at the map on her tablet. The only other direction for the couple to go was north, and that was the exact opposite way they needed to go.

"What?" Anatoli urged when he saw her staring.

"What is the one direction we wouldn't look for them?"

Anatoli frowned and pointed north. "Why?"

"What if they went that way?"

"Why would they? It would take them away from where they want to go."

Lorraine sighed loudly. "Because we wouldn't look there."

Anatoli shook his head. "North, no. Norway? Now that, I can see."

Shit. That hadn't even entered her mind. "Of course. Norway."

Lorraine quickly sent out messages to the Swedish and Norwegian teams. This time when she set down her phone, she smiled because she finally felt as if she were closing in on the couple.

Anatoli shot her a grin. "I told you everything would be all right."

"I won't believe that until I have both of them in custody."

Anatoli made a sound in the back of his throat. "They could've split up."

"Up until now, they've worked together. Why would they do that?"

"You assume they're allies. What if they aren't? What if they had to work together to get out of Ukraine, but now that they accomplished that, they went their separate ways?"

"And since we're looking for a couple, we'd pass right by them."

Anatoli nodded. "If I wanted to live, I'd set out on my own."

She gave a bark of laughter. "No, you wouldn't."

His blue eyes turned deadly as they slid to her. "You remember the young man I was. I'm not the same anymore. I learned from the best."

Lorraine knew he referred to her. She looked out the windshield and tried not to let his comment hurt her, but it did. The Anatoli she'd fallen in love with had been a good, honest man who would do anything for those he loved.

Her mistake was thinking that he was *still* that man. She believed he'd offered to help her because he might still have feelings for her. Now, she realized she might have underestimated him.

He'd acted as though her leaving had hurt him but that he was over it. Could it be that he wasn't over it? Or worse, that he was and no longer had any sort of feelings for her? In which case, she needed to watch her back.

She hadn't wanted him to come, but she hadn't once thought that he would try to hinder her or take credit for anything. That wasn't Anatoli's way.

Or it hadn't been the way of the man he'd once been. Perhaps she needed to reevaluate some things. Lorraine had made a critical error with Reyna. She couldn't afford to do the same with Anatoli.

"If you're here to try and ensure that I screw this up, then leave now. Or I'll kill you," Lorraine said.

He laughed softly. "You still don't trust anyone."

"And you've given me ample reason not to trust you."

Anatoli blew out a long breath. "Don't pretend you ever did."

"I did. Once." She couldn't help but glance at him.

He had his head turned away from her so she couldn't see his face. "Let's get this straight right now," he said. "I'm here because I was ordered to be. If you fail, then I fail. I'm not ready for my life to end."

Before she could reply, he opened the door and got out. He didn't slam it closed in a fit of rage as she would have. Instead, he softly shut it and walked back to the docks to talk to his team.

Lorraine watched him. The team members were quick to give reports and even smiled at Anatoli. But that was his way. He was easygoing and yet commanded respect effortlessly.

It wasn't the same with her. She had to fight for everything she had. Including respect. She liked that the people working for her feared her. That kept them in line. She didn't want them smiling at her and talking to her like a friend. Because friends found it easy to betray.

Those who feared, stayed in line.

Despite knowing that, Lorraine was still jealous of how easily Anatoli fit into his role. He didn't fight for anything. He set his gaze on something and conquered it. Whatever it was. A target, a position within the Saints...even her. It all fell into line so smoothly and naturally landed in his lap.

Lorraine heard his laughter, even from the distance. It brought her back to twenty years before when he used to tell her jokes just to make her smile. Usually, it was his laughter that did the trick, not his stupid jokes.

He had the best laugh, though. It was full and

boisterous, the kind that made you want to be a part of it, a part of *him*. His eyes would crinkle at the corners, and he'd hold her tighter. Just thinking about it made her smile.

With him, Lorraine felt comfortable. Safe, even. It was the reason she'd left since it had felt as if the world were passing by without her. But there were those rare times when she thought about what life could have been.

Especially around her birthday. Her parents had never made a big deal about the day of her birth. Anatoli, however, had gone all out. Every year, there was a cake, balloons, flowers, and presents. It wasn't the size of the gifts that mattered, but the thought that he'd put into them.

She lifted her hand to her chest and felt the gold *L* pendant beneath her clothing. It had been his first gift to her, and she was never without it. He didn't know that, though—and he never would.

While many women took time off to have children, Lorraine had never felt her biological clock. She didn't care that she went home to an empty house since she always had so much work. She didn't care that she spent holidays alone because that meant she didn't have to deal with anyone's bullshit.

But all of that was a lie she told herself.

Because if she let the perfectly crafted world she'd created crumble, she'd never be able to resurrect it. She'd chosen the path she was on, and she was proud of it. So what if she got lonely at times? It always passed.

The only reason she was having trouble now was because Anatoli was with her. His presence brought all the things she refused to think about to the forefront of her mind when she should be focusing on Reyna and Lev.

"Damn you for that," she said.

Suddenly, he turned and looked at her over his shoulder. Their gazes met, but he didn't walk to her. He turned back to his men and continued talking.

Lorraine knew it would be pointless to leave. He'd just find her again. He might be there to watch her, but it also gave her a chance to observe him. If there was even a remote chance that he might try to take credit for the capture of Lev and Reyna, she was going to make sure the elders knew the truth.

She started the car and put it in reverse. Let him stay out here. She was going back to the hotel to wait for word from her team. There were choppers on standby to take her wherever she needed to go in case the couple did head in one of the other directions.

As Lorraine drove, she thought over everything. Reyna and Lev had been decisive about their every move. If they were going by boat through the Kattegat strait, the Saints would've found them.

They'd headed in another direction. The problem was figuring out which one. She had her teams stretched thin in search of them. That could make it easy for the couple to slip through. Then again, her team wasn't the best for nothing.

She pressed a button on her phone and called her assistant. "Check all outgoing private plane routes from the States to Europe."

"All of Europe?" the woman asked in surprise.

"Yes, all. I especially want details regarding any planes flying into Germany or Norway."

"Yes, ma'am. I'll get right on that."

Lorraine disconnected the call. The Loughmans factored into this since Lev was with them. They'd gone to great lengths for their friends in the past. They could again. And if they did, Lorraine would be prepared for it.

19

The house looked just as they'd found it by the time dawn broke. Lev reactivated the alarm before he and Reyna set out. Dawn had yet to break when they started walking.

The air coming off the water was cool, and Lev would have preferred staying in the warm bed with Reyna to being back out in the weather. But neither wanted to chance remaining and being found by the Saints.

Of course, the Saints could find them at any time. But it was harder to do when they were on the move versus sitting in one place, waiting to be located.

Lev took Reyna's hand in his. She looked his way and smiled. The few blissful hours he'd had last night were the best of his life. And he wasn't just talking about the sex.

Holding Reyna, talking to her, listening to her, had formed a bond he'd never had before. One that had begun when they fought to stay alive together. Now, he was closer to her than he'd been to any other human in his life. It was shocking to feel so...connected to another.

And yet, it felt right at the same time.

He hadn't wanted to sleep, but his body hadn't given him a choice. Besides, he needed to be rested and focused for the day ahead. He hated that he'd lost those hours in sleep when they could have been spent talking to Reyna or enjoying holding her.

Oddly enough, he'd slept peacefully. He wished he could say that it was because they were in a house where the Saints couldn't easily find them, but he knew the reason—Reyna.

"You okay?" she asked.

He nodded. "Better than okay."

"Me, too."

To anyone who looked at them, they appeared to be a normal couple starting their day. If only things were that simple. Lev found himself envying Cullen and his brothers the ease with which they could be with their women.

Sure, the Saints were after the Loughmans, but they weren't running for their lives. The entire lot of them were on their ranch in Texas where they could see the Saints coming at them from miles away.

That wasn't the only reason Lev was jealous—an emotion he detested with every fiber of his being. Cullen had a home with Mia. They had a life together.

The same couldn't be said for him and Reyna. Even if they were together, with the Saints breathing down their necks, every minute was a gift. And they spent it trying to make it to the next hour.

"You look worried," Reyna said.

He met her dark brown eyes and forced a smile. "Just thinking."

"I know the feeling. It's going to take about four

hours to cross Sweden. Then another three or more to get through Norway. I know where to cross into Norway where the few checks the border patrol does won't affect us."

"That's good news. I think we should steal a car here and then another across the border."

She nodded. "Agreed. Better to keep everyone on their toes. We should also get another phone."

"Not until we need it. I don't like holding onto them longer than we need to."

Suddenly, she smiled at him.

He frowned, worried about what had brought on the grin. "What?"

"I haven't held anyone's hand in ages. I like it."

That had him smiling like an idiot. "I can't remember the last time I held anyone's hand either. I think it might have been my mom's."

"Not a girlfriend's?"

He thought for a moment and shrugged. "Maybe. I'm sure I probably did, but it's been a while."

She snorted and shook her head, causing her hair to move against her back. "We should be planning for attacks and where to go next instead of talking about holding hands."

"I'd rather be talking like we are. The other will always be there."

She leaned her head against his arm for a moment. "It's easy to pretend that the part of our lives that has us going across Sweden is just a dream."

"We're here. Alive and together. That's enough for me. For now, at least."

"For now?" Reyna asked teasingly as she gazed up at him.

He nodded and looked ahead. "I'm not the kind

of man who gives up easily. If the Saints want to catch us, they'll have to come at us with everything."

"You're looking ahead," she said softly.

"To life in the States? I sure am."

She lowered her eyes to the ground. "I've not dared allow myself to think like that."

"Why not?"

"It's dangerous. You can lose focus on what's important."

"Life is important."

She tightened her fingers on his. "I'm coming to realize that. When you think about the future, what do you think about?"

"Walking down a street just like this while holding your hand. Except I'm not worried about the Saints. I'm more concerned about finding the perfect restaurant to take you to."

He spotted her soft smile. His words pleased her, which made him happy. It was such an epiphany that he nearly stumbled on the sidewalk. As long as Reyna was happy, then Lev was, as well.

Could it be that simple? That...straightforward?

"I'm not picky about food," Reyna told him. "I should warn you that every so often I want a reason to get dressed up and be taken out to the symphony or theatre."

"Or a ballet?" he asked with a grin.

She busted out laughing and met his gaze. "I actually like the ballet. So, yes. Though I don't think I'll ever look at another without thinking of you."

He loved hearing her laugh. It was soft and easy, as if the sound couldn't wait to be released and touch everyone near. "I think I can handle such a request. How are you with gifts?"

"Meaning?" she asked with a frown.

"Are you the type that finds the perfect gift for someone easily? Or do you struggle?"

She shook her head as she chuckled. "I'm the type who sends gift cards."

"Oh. Then I'm not sure this can work," Lev teased.

She feigned shock, her eyes widening. "You mean, you buy gifts? Actual gifts?"

"Absolutely. I put in a lot of thought when I purchase something for someone."

Reyna halted and faced him. He was a half-step behind her, but he stopped and looked her way. "What?" he asked.

"I'm having fun."

He raised a brow, skeptical. "By the frown on your face, I wouldn't agree."

"I'm frowning because I'm having fun."

"I don't understand."

She smiled sadly. "I don't want to have fun with you. I don't want to wish we could return to the house and continue on with our lives as if nothing over the past few days has happened. I don't want to dream of a life with you. But I am."

"And it scares you," he guessed.

Her head bobbed up and down. "It terrifies me. I've lost one man in my life. I can't l—"

"Don't say it," Lev said over her. "We've a long road ahead of us. Anything can happen, both good and bad. We have each other. That's not something the Saints have."

He pulled her into his arms and held her as he closed his eyes. He too wanted a life with her. They had been thrown together by Fate, but it would be their skills that kept them alive. It was a long shot, he knew, but one he was very willing to take.

They remained there for another few minutes before they once more linked hands and continued walking. Thirty minutes later, they found a car. This time, Reyna got behind the wheel while he navigated.

The miles quickly fell away behind them, but neither spoke of the future again. Or their feelings for each other. Lev wasn't even sure how to put his into words. He knew he wanted Reyna by his side. And for now, that was good enough for him.

Dover Port, Maryland

Sergei was glad he'd gotten to talk to Lev for a few minutes yesterday. He missed his *Brigadier*, but not because Lev was good at his job. He wished Lev were here because he was the son Sergei never had.

He leaned back in his office chair and looked over to the corner where Lev usually stood. Sergei would've given up his position years ago if Lev had taken over, but Lev had been adamant about not wanting it. Sergei had hoped the years would change Lev's mind.

Perhaps it was time to broach the subject again when Lev returned. Sergei was getting tired. Besides, Lev took on so much of the duties, he was all but the boss anyway—though Lev didn't know it. Sergei had been sneaky in how he'd gotten Lev to begin taking on more duties.

Sergei downed his shot of vodka and looked at his phone where he had a picture of him and Lev together. It was a rare instance when Lev was smiling. The same photo was framed in Sergei's house.

He frowned as he worried about Lev's return to the States. He knew from his communications with Mia and the Loughmans that things had not gone well for Lev despite Lev telling him that everything was fine. The Loughmans were worried about Lev, but Sergei wasn't.

None of them knew his *Brigadier* like he did. If anyone could get out of Europe and away from the Saints, it was Lev. He had what his father never did—drive. An inner force that had Lev reaching for the stars—and knowing he could obtain them if he worked hard enough.

Lev didn't know the meaning of *quit*. While he navigated life in the gray area, he was innately noble and fair. It's why he commanded respect quickly and easily. And why he was the only one who could take over Sergei's business.

There was a knock on Sergei's office door. He bid the person to enter.

One of the *Byki*, the bodyguards, poked his head around the door. "Your car is ready to take you home."

"I'll be right there. Did Alexi get our cut from the most recent arrival to the docks this afternoon?"

The man grinned, showing a missing front tooth. "He did. It's in our warehouse and being distributed between our men."

Sergei pushed himself up and walked around the desk. "That's good news."

"Any word on when Lev might return?"

"Soon," Sergei replied with a grin.

The man gave a nod. "It's not the same without him."

"No, it isn't."

Sergei reached the door, and they walked out together. He nodded to the others who worked for him. He knew all their names, but it was getting harder and harder to remember them each time. Age had a way of affecting minds that way.

He walked out of the building and drew in a breath as he looked at the moon. It was three in the morning halfway around the world. He wondered what Lev was doing.

"Be safe, my son," he murmured.

Sergei got into the back of the Mercedes-Benz S-Class sedan. The *Byki* shut the door and turned to walk away.

"Ready, sir?" his driver asked.

"Take me home, Teddy."

The moment Teddy pushed the ignition button, Sergei heard the click. His last thought before the car blew up was that he hadn't gotten to tell Lev everything.

Wyatt was talking to his father when he glanced into the control room and saw Callie's face go white. He rushed to her as she slowly turned in her chair to face him.

"What is it?" he asked. "Are you feeling unwell?"

Tears glistened for a heartbeat before one fell down her cheek. "I just got a call from one of Sergei's men. Sergei's car blew up. He's...dead."

Wyatt had wondered when the Saints would strike back. It looked like they had. And against an old man.

"I feel sorry for the Saints now," Orrin said.

Wyatt nodded, knowing that his father was right. Because when Lev found out about Sergei, he was going to stop running from the Saints and go right for them.

20

"I'd like to come back one day and actually enjoy what I'm seeing," Lev said as he looked out the window at the Swedish scenery.

Reyna nodded in agreement. "I've only been to Stockholm, but I really liked it. I've always wanted to see more of Sweden."

Lev's head swiveled to her. "Well, we're certainly getting to do that."

They'd decided to stay off the main highways and instead took the back roads to avoid cameras. Reyna had seen something she would've liked to stop and look at several times, but this wasn't a holiday.

"Does it count when you don't get out and experience anything?" she asked with a smile.

One side of Lev's mouth tilted in a grin. "I think it does. We're still seeing the beautiful countryside."

It suddenly hit her then that she might never get to see Sweden again. If things went sideways—and there was a good chance it could—then this was the only time she might be here.

Reyna pulled off the road onto the grass and shut off the car. Lev climbed out without a word. She quickly followed and walked around the vehicle to stand with him.

"Good choice," he said.

"It's beautiful here."

He wrapped an arm around her shoulders and pulled her against him. "I'm glad I'm experiencing it with you."

She wound her arm around his waist and leaned against him. "There's no one I'd rather be with."

The day was gorgeous. Thick, puffy clouds drifted lazily across the bright blue sky, a subtle wind stirred the air, and she had a man who had snuck into her life unexpectedly. Birds sang, lulling them in the quiet. Reyna closed her eyes, grateful that the road wasn't filled with passing cars.

"Gun!" Lev suddenly said as he jerked her to the side, causing her eyes to snap open.

Almost immediately, she heard the retort of the weapon. They fell to the ground as more shots rang out.

"Get in the back and get down," Lev said as they crawled around to the other side of the car while bullets slammed into the dirt and the vehicle.

Reyna winced when debris from the ground sprayed up into her eyes. She felt something pull at her side, but she ignored it as she hurried to find cover. Lev opened the driver's side door as well as the back seat door behind him.

"Ready?" he asked.

She nodded, and they both dove into the vehicle. Reyna got the door closed behind her just as the window shattered on the side opposite her. She pulled out her gun from the pack and rose up enough to fire out the opening in the direction of the shooter while Lev started the car and sped off.

The tires squealed from the acceleration while trees cut off her view of the shooter. Reyna lowered her weapon, wincing from pain that suddenly lashed through her. She looked down to find her left side coated in blood.

"We're free of them for now," Lev said as he looked at her through the rearview mirror. "We'll need to change cars."

"Yeah." She pressed her hand against the wound and gritted her teeth to stop the moan of pain. When she looked up, Lev was staring at her in the mirror with narrowed eyes.

"You good?"

She licked her lips. "Not really."

He briefly turned in the seat to look at her. "Fuck, Reyna. That looks bad."

It hurt like hell, but she was going to keep that part to herself.

"I need to see to that before we do anything."

She shook her head. "We need to ditch this car. Otherwise, they'll find us."

A muscle in his jaw jumped. The engine revved as he pressed the accelerator. Reyna wanted to lay down, but she knew any movement would cause more blood loss. Not to mention she needed to conserve her energy for when it came time to hide the car and get to safety.

"Hold on," Lev said as he met her gaze in the mirror again, "Do you hear me? You hold on."

She forced a smile. "You can't get rid of me that easily."

Then she closed her eyes to concentrate on not

passing out as the pain escalated. She didn't know how much time had passed when Lev pulled to a stop. She was in and out of consciousness the whole time.

She looked out the front window of the car and found that they were parked at a lake. The back door opened, and Lev retrieved the two packs and rifles, setting them aside before reaching for her.

He said nothing as he helped her out of the car and then over to a tree so she had something to lean against. Reyna felt her energy draining with every drop of blood that fell from her wound. She didn't know how long she could stay on her feet, but she'd fight for every second. Not because she thought Lev might abandon her, but because she didn't want him to have to carry her.

She watched as he put the car in neutral and pushed it into the water. He didn't wait to see it submerge before he was jogging back to her.

"How are you doing?" he asked.

"I'm fine."

He quirked a black brow, telling her with one look that he didn't believe a word she said. "I spotted a cabin through the trees."

"We don't have time for such things."

"If I don't see to your injury, you're going to bleed out."

There was no other choice, and she knew it. Lev put both packs on and moved to her wounded side. He pressed her against him while wrapping an arm around her. Reyna looped her arm around his shoulder and ground her teeth together from the agony of their first step.

They moved quickly, but even so, she felt the

blood run down her leg and into her boot. It took everything she could do just to remain on her feet. The darkness began to creep in at the edges of her vision. She fought it, but it was too strong.

Reyna pitched forward as her body went limp. Lev managed to stop her fall, but he lost his balance in the process. One of the packs fell as he knelt on the ground and turned her so he could see her face. A sigh of relief escaped when he found that she was unconscious and not dead. But time wasn't on their side.

He didn't know how the Saints had found them, and it didn't matter. Lev needed to see to Reyna's wound, but they'd have to be on the move after that. She was no stranger to such things. That didn't make it any easier for him. Not when he knew she needed time to recover instead of being moved and likely busting her stitches.

Lev slung the dropped bag over his shoulder again, then gathered Reyna in his arms and climbed to his feet. The cabin was just up ahead.

Working his way through the trees, he finally reached the small structure. He had to set Reyna and the packs down when he found the lock on the door. It would be easy to shoot the damn thing off, but he didn't want to alert anyone to their presence, so he used the butt of his handgun to break the lock.

He then threw open the door and looked inside. When he found the bed bare, he hurried to it and lifted the mattress to make sure there were no critters. Next, he brought Reyna inside and laid her down.

After retrieving the packs, he shut the door and returned to her. He cut open her shirts with his knife to reveal the wound and used the clothing to try and staunch the blood that poured from her at an alarming rate. It was as bad as he thought. There was no first-aid kit in his pack, but there might be in hers.

Thankfully, there was. He pulled it out and opened it. After he'd made sure that he had everything he needed, he searched through the two cupboards in the cabin and found a bottle of vodka.

Lev took a long drink and brought the bottle as well as a chair from the table to the bed. He set the bottle near his feet after he'd lowered himself onto the chair. Reyna's face was pale, and beads of sweat dotted her forehead.

The streaks of bright red blood against the pale flesh of her abdomen caused Lev a moment of panic. It wasn't his first bullet wound, and he doubted it would be his last. But this wasn't just anyone he was working on. This was Reyna.

"Don't you die on me," he told her.

Lev got out everything he would need from the first-aid kit and then set it out in the order he would need it. He found a bowl and doused the needle with vodka.

Once the latex gloves were on, he rolled Reyna to her side to see if there was an exit wound. He hoped he didn't have to go digging around inside her to retrieve the slug. Luck seemed to be on their side because it appeared the bullet had gone straight through.

The fact that no major organs seemed to be hit was very good news. It meant that there was less chance of internal bleeding. Lev worked fast, using the Quickclot to stop the bleeding before he stitched both the entrance and exit wounds. He covered the injuries with gauze before reaching for the tape to hold it in place. He used his teeth to rip the tape instead of using the medical shears to cut it.

His hands didn't start shaking until he finished. He looked down at the blood covering the gloves and hastily jerked them off before tossing them aside. Lev scrubbed his hands over his face before raking them through his hair.

He checked Reyna's pulse. It was steady if still a little fast. Her forehead felt cool to the touch, which was good. He rose and searched until he found a sealed bag with a blanket inside. Lev pulled it out and covered her.

Then he went to the windows and peeked through the slats to see if he spotted anyone. They were close to the Norwegian border, and there was plenty of daylight left, but Reyna wasn't going anywhere on foot. If need be, they would stay in the cabin for the night.

Which just might happen if Reyna didn't regain consciousness. She'd lost a lot of blood. In fact, Lev was surprised that she hadn't passed out sooner. It was going to take her some time to build her strength back up.

After another round past the three windows, Lev returned to Reyna. He placed his hand on her brow first, then he took her hand to check her pulse. Her fingers curled around his.

His gaze snapped to her face to see her eyes open just enough to look at him. He smiled. "Hey, there. It's going to be okay."

The ghost of a smile pulled at her lips before she

squeezed his hand once more. Then she was unconscious again.

Lev couldn't release her hand. He'd gone into medicine because he liked the idea of helping people. Even though he hadn't finished his medical training, he used what he'd learned often. But this was the first time he'd ever sat by someone's bed, praying that they lived.

For the next few hours, Lev alternated between checking the area through the windows and staying by Reyna's side. She didn't awaken again, though.

He ate a bag of cashews and studied the map he'd laid out on the floor. Since he hadn't opened the shutters, there was little light coming in. He used Reyna's flashlight to find their location on the map and see what the best route to get them across the border would be.

His goal had been the southernmost part of Norway to get a boat, but now he just wanted to get to the coast. It didn't matter how long they were on the water, as long as they got to it.

The snap of a twig outside jerked his head up. He shut off the flashlight and quickly folded the map before he reached for his weapon. Lev rose and silently walked to the window closest to him. He looked out and saw a man coming toward him with a rifle trained at the door.

Lev looked out the other two windows and saw two more men. There was a chance there was a fourth, as well. He glanced at the bed. The wood of the cabin was thick, but not thick enough to stop a bullet.

He removed the blanket from Reyna and laid it on the ground then gathered her in his arms. He lowered her to the quilt and then scooted her under the bed.

Lev had both of his guns in their holsters but grabbed a rifle. He straightened and turned toward the door. He threw it open and shot the first man in the middle of the forehead.

Immediately, shots rang out through the cabin as bullets slammed into the wood. Lev dove outside and rolled. He came to his knees while dodging bullets and then turned his weapon on the shooter to his right. He pulled the trigger.

Two down.

A bullet landed within millimeters of his leg. Lev dove to the side as more shots bombarded him. He felt the wind as one zinged past his head. He fired two shots, killing the third shooter.

Lev jumped to his feet and made his way around the cabin looking for more men.

21

There were more. Lev knew it, but as he slowly walked around the cabin, he didn't find anyone. Then he realized where they were.

He hurried back to the front of the structure as quietly as a ghost and checked the remaining bullets in the rifle. There was only one, so he set it aside and grabbed for his pistols. Ducking beneath one of the windows, he heard the faint thud of a standard-issue military boot on the wood. Without a doubt, he knew they were after Reyna. He never should have left her alone.

Lev flattened his back against the cabin and listened. He picked up two distinct sets of footsteps. They were quick and efficient. Lev didn't like waiting for them to appear, but he couldn't chance walking in and firing, only to hit Reyna.

He could stay where he was and take his chances when they exited the cabin. But anyone with training would suspect that he'd be right where he was. He might get a shot off, but they'd gun him down quickly.

And if he were going to take Reyna back from

them as well as survive, he needed to come up with a better plan.

Lev's gaze moved to the forest. The coming twilight made it easy for him to hide. No doubt the men had night vision goggles, but it wasn't dark enough for them yet. He pushed away from the cabin and darted to the side until he was safely behind a tree.

Methodically and carefully, he moved from one tree to the next until he was in front of the house. No sooner had he reached his destination than a man in solid black gear appeared, his rifle trained at the spot where Lev had been.

The shooter quickly switched sides and looked around for Lev before he motioned to his comrade inside the cabin. The second man appeared. He was in the same gear and had Reyna slung over his shoulders in a fireman's carry.

Lev's jaw clenched when he saw blood staining her bandage and spreading rapidly. The men had their guns lifted and moved them right to left and back again, looking for Lev as they jumped from the porch and started running.

Without hesitation, Lev lifted his gun and shot the first man. He went down without a sound and didn't move again. The second soldier ran faster, even carrying Reyna. Lev sighted down his gun and fired.

The man let out a strangled cry that was cut short as he toppled to the ground. Reyna fell from his shoulders and rolled, unmoving, a few feet away. Lev kept his gaze on the downed man as he stalked toward him, gun aimed and ready to fire.

He reached the soldier only to have a rifle raised at him. Lev kicked the weapon, and the bullet went wide, striking a tree. Lev hadn't felt such fury in many years—not since he'd gone after those who killed his mother.

The man smiled up at him. "You won't kill me."

Lev heard the Swedish accent. It confirmed that the Saints had suspected their choice of direction and had men waiting. It was a setback, but one Lev could work with. But first, he had to get Reyna and get out.

"Why not?" Lev asked.

The soldier laughed, though lines of strain formed around his mouth from the bullet in his thigh. "I have information you'll want."

"Then give it to me."

"Give me some incentive."

Lev had come up against all sorts of men while working for Sergei. He also knew that those working for the Saints didn't switch sides for fear of death.

The man had his hand over his wound as blood seeped between his fingers. "I have a wife. A newborn son."

"Then you chose the wrong side," Lev told him.

"Let me live," the man begged, the smile now gone.

Lev kept his gun aimed. "Give me the information."

The soldier lunged forward with his bloodied hand to grab a gun holstered on his calf. Lev fired two quick shots into the Saint's heart, killing him instantly.

Without another look, Lev rushed to Reyna. She had abrasions on her arms and chest from falling with nothing but her bra on, but his bandages held. He carefully lifted her and hurried back to the cabin where he worked quickly to restitch one of her wounds and then bandage her again.

Lev couldn't take her out without some kind of shirt. He looked in her pack and found a black, long-sleeved tee that he put on her. Then he consolidated everything into one bag before he gathered the weapons and ammunition from the dead men.

By the time he returned, Reyna's eyes were open. He smiled as he acknowledged the relief that surged through him so rapidly that he was suddenly lightheaded.

"Hey," he said.

She smiled lethargically. "Hey."

"How do you feel?" he asked as he walked to the bed and sat on the edge.

She licked her lips and swallowed. "Thirsty."

Lev got a bottle of water and helped her lift her head so she could drink her fill. It was a good sign that she was awake and wanting a drink.

Her gaze moved past him to the dead bodies. "I missed the action."

"It was nothing."

"It was recent," she said with a lift of a brow. "We need to move, don't we?"

He wished he could tell her no, but he couldn't. "Yes."

"It's getting dark, we don't know the territory, and I'm wounded. We won't get far."

"We'll be fine."

"You should leave me."

He looked askance at her. "No."

"I'm only going to slow you down."

"I got you here and tended, didn't I?" he argued. "I took care of the men."

Her hand moved to rest on his leg. "Thank you for all of that. However, the truth is that they know where we are. You've wasted too much time already. I'd leave you behind."

"No, you wouldn't." He'd come to know Reyna, and he knew without a doubt that she would've done for him what he did for her.

Her dark gaze moved away. "It won't do for both of us to get killed."

"The Saints don't want us dead."

Her brows snapped together as her gaze returned to him. "What?"

"In the attack, I went looking for more men. While I did, two came for you."

"What?" she asked in shock.

Lev nodded. "They had the chance to kill you, but took you instead."

"But they shot at us earlier. I was hit."

"Nevertheless, they were taking you."

She gritted her teeth and tried to sit up. Lev knew better than to try and dissuade her, so he helped her instead. Reyna was breathing hard, and her face was pale again, but she managed to stay sitting on her own power.

"You need the night to rest," he told her.

She shrugged one shoulder. "That's not an option. We go together now, or you leave on your own."

"I'm not leaving you."

"Then we go now."

Lev briefly thought about arguing with her, but she was right. They needed to get on the move. He rose and put the backpack on as well as the night vision goggles. Then he looped two of the rifle straps over his head while Reyna gradually moved her legs over the side of the bed.

She met his gaze when her feet were on the floor and smiled. "I can do this."

"Have you been shot before?"

She shook her head.

He had, so Lev knew exactly how painful it was. "You lost a lot of blood. The bullet went through the meaty part of your side, thankfully."

"In other words, I'm going to be weak."

"You need to rest to regain your strength."

"Something I'd gladly do if I was able, but I'm not. You continuing to tell me that doesn't help," she replied testily.

Lev knew she wasn't angry at him. She was frustrated with the situation and the fact that her body wouldn't do what she wanted it to. He'd been in that same position before, which was why he didn't take her words to heart.

Reyna blew out a breath and set her hands on either side of her hips. "I'm sorry."

"There's no need." He held out a palm to her.

She looked up at his hand. He could see that she wanted to refuse it, but thankfully, she accepted his offer. After she was on her feet, he shot her a smile.

"Where do we go?" she asked.

Lev walked to the open door and looked out. "I studied the map earlier. We're less than forty minutes from the border. There's a town five miles away. We can get a car there, or at least I'd planned on it before we were attacked."

"The Saints will be there," she said with a shake of her head. "We walk across the border just as we did in Poland."

Lev looked back at her. "It's a long walk."

"And they'll likely be searching the forest."

"We'll take as many breaks as you need."

She nodded and took the first tentative step toward him. She winced but took another. And another and another until she was even with him.

Reyna met his gaze. "I can do this. I don't want to fall into their hands, Lev. I can't."

"I won't let them touch you," he vowed.

She then took his hand and squeezed it before she stepped onto the porch. Before Lev followed her, he got the blanket. With her blood loss and the night temperatures, he didn't want to chance her getting chilled and catching a fever.

He flipped the goggles down to bathe the area in green light. The terrain wasn't easy for Reyna to traverse, but he was there to help her whenever she needed it. Many times, it was by sheer determination alone that she remained on her feet.

Their slow-going cost them three hours before they reached the border to Norway. Reyna was just about out of energy. She was breathing hard, and she favored her left side more and more. Lev needed to find a place she could rest.

He set her up against a tree with one of the rifles as he went to have a look around to see if any Saints were nearby. Lev crossed the border and slowed his steps. There was someone near, he knew it. He palmed his handgun and listened to the night, trying to pick up on the location and how many were out there when he heard something close.

Lev stepped around the tree and lifted his gun, only to come face-to-face with the business end of a rifle.

The old man had tufts of white hair and bushy white eyebrows. He said something in Norwegian that Lev couldn't understand.

"I'd love to answer whatever it is you just said," Lev replied, "but you'll need to repeat it in English."

"I said, what the hell are you doing on my land?" the old man stated angrily in heavily-accented English.

Lev lifted the goggles and held the old man's gaze in the dark. He could get off a shot as he dove to the side. There was a chance the old man might miss, but the way he held his rifle told Lev that the man used it often enough that his reflexes might be better than Lev thought.

"I don't have a choice," Lev said.

There was a good chance the man was a part of the Saints. He could lull Lev into believing that he wanted to help, only to call in the Saints as soon as he had both Lev and Reyna. And yet, Lev needed to get Reyna to safety.

The old man raised a brow. "There's always a choice, son. I've had men on my property for two days now, and I'm not going to have it anymore. If the authorities won't help, I'll do it myself."

"I'm not part of the others," Lev told him. Then, he made the decision to take a chance. "They're after me."

"And the woman with you."

Lev frowned.

The old man snorted as he lowered his gun. "I saw you two an hour ago. She's hurt."

"Yes."

"Then you best lower your gun and get her before the others find you."

Lev hesitated, his weapon still trained on the old man. If he made the wrong decision here, it could be the end of them.

The old man sighed. "Son, I'm too old for this. If you want my help, you have it. But you're going to have to trust me."

Trust. The very thing Lev had told Reyna she needed to do. That had worked out well. He only hoped this did, as well.

"Thank you," he said as he dropped his arm to his side.

"Reyna."

She lowered the rifle when she heard Lev's voice. He wasn't alone, however, and that worried her.

"It's okay," Lev said. "Helge is a friend. He wants to help."

Reyna trusted Lev, but she also knew how deep the Saints went into communities. It was the very young and the very old that people never expected, and yet that's exactly who the Saints sent after you.

Lev squatted beside her. He smiled in the darkness and put his hand over hers that held the gun. "Trust me."

"I do."

"Then let's get you to Helge's."

"If he's a Saint, it's a trap. If he isn't, then we're signing his death warrant."

Out of the darkness came a deep Norwegian voice, rusty with age. "It's a chance I'll take."

Lev gave her a nod.

What choice did she have, really? She was bleeding again. She'd felt it seep into the bandages. It wasn't a lot, but it was enough that it caused her to worry.

Reyna let Lev help her to her feet. The next instant, she had him on her bad side, and Helge was on her other. The Norwegian was bent slightly with age, but his gaze scanned the area as stealthily as an eagle.

The three were silent as they crossed the border. Reyna didn't brush Lev's hand away when he wrapped it around her to help support her. She was concentrating on putting one foot in front of the other, so she was surprised when Helge suddenly stopped and motioned them behind him.

Lev moved to a large boulder seconds before two armed men came into view. The three stood as still as the dead until the men passed. After, their pace quickened to Helge's.

They followed the Norwegian, who took them around boulders to the smoothest part of the mountain. Reyna was shaking from exertion by the time they finally reached Helge's house.

They entered through the back door with Helge closing and locking the door behind him. Lev led her into the kitchen where she sank gratefully into a chair before her legs gave out.

She lifted her shirt as Lev knelt beside her so he could get to the bandage. His lips flattened when he saw it stained with blood, but he didn't admonish her.

Reyna closed her eyes as he cut through the bandages with the first-aid supplies. She hadn't noticed the pain too much while they were dodging the Saints, but now that she was sitting down and relatively safe, it slammed into her.

"Good work," Helge said.

She opened her eyes to see him peering over Lev's shoulder at her injury.

Then Helge's blue gaze met hers. He gave her a nod. "How about some soup?"

"That sounds delicious," she replied as she realized how hungry she was.

He smiled and turned to the stove. Reyna closed her eyes once more. Lev's touch was light and quick. When he finished, she lowered her shirt but remained leaning back in the chair.

Lev's lips touched her forehead in a quick kiss that made her smile. She opened her eyes to look into his. Once more, she found herself thankful that luck had been on their side so they could make it this far.

"How much time did we lose while I was unconscious?" she asked.

He shrugged and took the chair beside her. "About four hours."

"We could be at the coast by now."

Helge snorted, his back to them as he stirred the soup in the large pot. "There are roadblocks everywhere. And you saw them in the forest. They don't care whose land they're on."

"Why are you helping us?" Lev asked.

Helge shifted to the side to face them. "I don't trust these people. They say they're part of my government and the police, but something isn't right. Why are they after you?"

Lev didn't reply. He looked at her, letting Reyna decide how much to tell the Norwegian.

She took a deep breath and released it. "They're called the Saints. They're a global organization that has infiltrated every government around the world. Their reach now extends to the military and other authorities, as well as common people such as yourself."

"You think I'm one of these...Saints?" Helge asked with a frown.

Reyna looked into his face lined with age. "I was undercover with them for five years. The Saints turn people you would never suspect."

"Like my grandson," Helge said. His gaze dropped to the floor as his eyes became unfocused with memories. Then he blinked and drew in a deep breath. "I didn't know the name of them, but I knew whatever he was involved in, no matter that it was for the government, wasn't good." He looked at Reyna then Lev and touched his chest over his heart. "I knew it here. I tried to tell him, but he wouldn't listen."

"Every person makes their own choices," Lev replied.

Helge sighed loudly. "I lost my grandson to them. I won't lose anyone else. Not even you two."

"They're after us," Reyna said. "They know I was spying."

Lev then said, "And I'm working with a group from the US who is fighting them."

"Good," Helge said with a smile. "People need to stand up for what they believe in. We don't need another world war."

He walked out of the kitchen then, leaving them alone. Reyna found her gaze sliding to Lev, who watched her.

"How are you feeling?" he asked.

She took stock of her body. "I've felt better, but I'll be fine with a bit of rest."

"You heard him. We'll have a hell of a time getting to the coast."

"We can't stay here, and we can't backtrack."

Lev rubbed his eyes with this thumb and forefinger. "Then I don't know what to do."

"Here," Helge said as he returned to the kitchen and handed clothes to her and Lev. Then he jerked his chin to Lev. "Go take a shower and change. It'll be another hour before the soup is ready."

Reyna nodded when Lev glanced her way. She had a handgun in the waist of her pants if Helge tried anything. Lev walked from the kitchen and disappeared around the corner.

"He cares a great deal for you."

Her head snapped to Helge. "We're in this together."

"Together, yes," he said with a nod. "But I see it in his eyes. Just as I see it in yours."

"What do you see?" She couldn't help but ask.

"A deep connection. There is love growing."

He said it as if he spoke about the weather, then turned back to stir the soup.

Reyna glanced in the direction that Lev had disappeared. "I loved once."

"You are again."

How could this stranger see what she couldn't? She knew she cared about Lev. That much was clear by how far she'd come with him. Then there was their night in Sweden.

When she glanced at Helge, he was grinning at her. "What?" she asked.

"You're blushing."

Her hands went to her cheeks that were indeed

warm. She lowered her arms. "He's amazing. I wouldn't be here without him."

"The two of you are a good team. I suspect, in all things. My wife and I were the same. The best day of my life was when I met her. The worst was when she passed."

"I'm sorry," Reyna said.

He grinned and shrugged. "I'm not. We'll be together again soon."

She realized that as much as she'd loved Arthur, she didn't feel that way about him. She could've had a good life with him. But when she thought of a future with Lev, she knew it wouldn't be good. It would be *great*.

Spectacular, actually.

"This may be the only time I have with Lev," she said.

Helge's lips twisted as he frowned. "Then I suggest you take every second you can. Everyone should do that with the ones they love because they're gone all too soon."

She was thinking about the Norwegian's statement when Lev returned. His hair was wet, but he had on clean clothes. The navy sweater was a little frayed around the edges, but the khaki pants were in excellent condition. And the fit was good, as well.

"The food smells delicious," Lev said.

Helge smiled and jerked his head to Reyna. "Take your woman and get her changed."

She laughed but took Lev's hand. They walked to the back room. As they did, she couldn't help but pray that Helge was indeed on their side and not with the Saints. She liked him, and she didn't want to have to kill him.

"I can remove the bandage if you want a shower," Lev said.

She shook her head. "As good as that sounds, I'm not sure I could stand up for it."

"You'll feel better after some food."

"I'm so hungry, I think I could eat the entire pot myself."

Lev laughed and reached for the hem of her shirt. Then he paused. "Your skin is chilled."

"A little."

"I think you should keep the tee shirt on and put the sweater on over it."

They put the cream sweater on together, and as soon as it was in place, she sighed. She'd had no idea how cold she was until then.

"I can't wait until I can remove your clothes instead of putting you in them," Lev said with a grin.

She laughed and lifted her face for a kiss. Their lips met and lingered before she pulled back. "I can't wait for that either."

Reyna swayed, but Lev easily caught her. "Whoa. Let's get you sitting down."

They returned to the kitchen to find three bowls of soup on the table, but Helge was nowhere to be found. He came back in a moment later with a bottle in one hand.

He lifted it up and said, "I thought we could have some *akevitt*."

Lev frowned as he glanced at her.

Reyna nodded to Helge and told Lev, "It's schnapps."

"I won't pass up that offer," Lev replied.

23

They just might make it. Lev didn't want to hope too hard because life had a way of kicking his feet out from under him when he became too cocky. But things were certainly looking up.

The schnapps was good. Or maybe it was the company. It could be because, for the first time in days, there seemed to be a light at the end of the tunnel. It was faint, but it was there.

Reyna smiled at him as she ate her second bowl of soup. She had only sipped her schnapps, preferring water instead. The warmth, food, and safety did her good, though he knew they couldn't remain with Helge too long. Already, they'd put him in danger. It didn't matter that he wanted to help them. Lev couldn't have the old man's death on his conscience.

Lev looked at the clock on the wall, tallying up the time they'd been at Helge's and figuring out when they should leave.

"Stay," the old man said. "You could both use the sleep."

Lev's gaze slid to Reyna. She needed the rest, that was for sure.

As if reading his mind, she shook her head before she looked at Helge. "We've already stayed longer than we should. The Saints will come looking for us."

"They've already searched," Helge argued.

Lev twisted his lips. "I know I'd come back and look again. Especially as vocal as you were about your dislike of them. I'd figure you'd be the one to find whoever I was hunting."

"And bring them back for food," Reyna added.

Helge poured more schnapps into his glass. "Let them come. I can hide you."

Reyna put her hand over his. "We appreciate that, but neither of us wants anything to happen to you."

Helge's aged eyes locked on Lev. "If you take her out there tonight, neither of you will make it. You know this."

"We might," Reyna said, not giving Lev time to respond.

Lev knew Helge had a point. However, he also knew how good Reyna was. If it were anyone else at his side, he might think twice. He very much wanted to stay and curl up in bed with Reyna beside him so she could sleep through the night. But it wasn't meant to be.

Helge made an irritated sound and shook his head. "It's the wrong decision."

"You need to be around to help others the Saints are after," Lev told him.

"Finish," Helge told Reyna. "You're going to need your strength."

Lev rose and retrieved his weapons. He checked each of them and loaded the magazines. Once that was done, he grabbed Reyna's and repeated the process.

Both took their guns and put them on their body. Lev stood the rifles in the corner so he could grab them easily if it were necessary.

"You're nearly out of bullets," Helge said.

Reyna yawned and said, "We'll make do."

He snorted and drained the alcohol in his glass before he got to his feet. "I have some. Let me get them."

Reyna looked Lev's way when the old man was gone. "I'm fine."

It was her way of telling Lev that it was time to go. He gave her a nod and grabbed his glass to finish off his schnapps when Helge stumbled into the room. His eyes were wide, and his hand clutched at his throat where red poured through his fingers to fall down his chest onto his shirt.

In the next heartbeat, Lev was on his feet, grabbing the rifles. Reyna rushed to Helge as he fell to the ground, but the old man was already dead.

She held out a hand, and Lev tossed her one of the rifles as she stood. He moved in front of her toward the entrance where Helge had come from. Reyna tapped his shoulder to let him know that she was ready. Then he leaned around the doorway.

Bullets pierced the wood by his head. Lev jerked back and pointed to the back door. Reyna took the lead, moving swiftly. No sooner had they gotten to the door and opened it than more bullets flew at them. Lev grabbed Reyna to pull her back before she got shot. He kicked the door closed as they put their backs to the wall.

"We're not getting out of here," he said.

She raised a brow. "I'm not going to wait for them to come for me."

"You want to run out there and be gunned down?"

"That's what's going to happen either way."

Lev glanced at the doorway he'd been in. "I'm not so sure."

"What are you talking about?"

"They obviously know we're here. Have for a while. Why haven't they busted through the door to contain us? I was in the shower. You were wounded."

Reyna thought about that for a moment and then jerked her chin at Helge. "Then why slit his throat?"

"Maybe he saw something he wasn't supposed to. Or heard something."

"They shot at us, Lev. I saw the bullets."

"They shot *toward* us," he corrected. "Not one of the rounds directed at me went past the doorway. They were in a cluster."

She looked at the wall where the holes from the bullets fired through the back door were and blew out a breath. "Another cluster. So, if they don't want to kill us, what *do* they want?"

"Information is my guess."

"If you're right, and they don't want to kill us, then they'll do anything to keep us in here until someone comes for us."

"And that someone will be Lorraine."

Reyna's lips turned down into a frown. "No doubt."

"I don't relish waiting for that to happen. If we're not going to wait here, then that means we need to leave."

"And take our chances that none of the bullets hits us."

He shrugged. "You have a better idea?"

"No," she said.

He glanced at her wound. "You up for this?"

"Even if I wasn't, I would still say yes."

Lev smiled. "I know."

Reyna blew out a loud breath. "I think we should go out different doors."

"No," he stated. "I'm not getting split up again."

"Because I'm wounded?" she asked tightly.

"That's part of it. The other part is that we're good together. If we split up, we give them an advantage."

She bit her lip and shrugged one shoulder. "I could argue and say that by splitting up we weaken them. Both opinions are valid. The truth is, I'd rather have you beside me. And it has nothing to do with me being injured."

"I know." He held her gaze, letting her make the decision of when they went.

"You ready?"

"Say the word."

She closed her eyes. "I'll be shooting to kill."

"As will I."

After another deep breath, Reyna's lids lifted. Her dark eyes met his. "We will get out of this."

"Absolutely."

Neither wanted to state the many and various incidents that could occur to sideline their plan. They needed to focus on living. It had gotten them this far.

"You take the lead," he told her.

He could see the argument beginning to form on her lips, but she nodded. With her injured and slower than usual, it would be better for him to watch her back. It also meant that he could get to her if her wound gave her trouble and didn't allow her to run.

"Even if we get past these men, there will be more," she said.

Lev shrugged. "There has always been that threat."

"Yes, but they found us."

"They've had us before."

She looked away. "I'm trying to tell you that I want you to get away if they get me."

"They won't get you."

"Lev—"

"Reyna," he stated. "I didn't leave you when you were shot and unconscious. I'm certainly not now."

Her gaze met his as she smiled sadly. "I could kiss you."

"No one is stopping you," he replied with a grin.

She laughed softly. As soon as she maneuvered toward the door, their conversation halted. Lev wanted to pull her into his arms for one last hug, but the time for romance was over. For now, at least.

Reyna looped the rifle over one shoulder and palmed her handguns. She looked back at him and smiled. Then said, "I've fallen hard for you, Lev Ivanski."

No sooner were the words out of her mouth than she threw open the door and rushed outside. Lev was right on her heels. Bullets flew all around them, and he heard someone yelling, "Cease fire!"

Reyna lifted her weapons and began shooting the same time he did. He didn't care that the Saints were being told not to kill them, because he knew what would happen if they captured him or Reyna.

He'd seen for himself the atrocities of the Saints, and he would do whatever he had to in order to keep that from happening to either him or Reyna.

Besides, he hadn't been able to digest her confession fully. And he wanted a chance to respond.

Lev winced when a bullet grazed his shoulder. Despite the orders of the soldiers to stop firing, they weren't listening. Lev saw one of the Saints turn his rifle on Reyna. Lev fired, putting his bullet dead center of the soldier's forehead.

The trees made it difficult for the Saints to get a lock on them as they put more distance between themselves and Helge's house. Lev had counted at least twenty Saints, and yet luck was once more on his and Reyna's side.

They weaved their way through the trees as they went down the mountain, slowing only when they had no choice. Lev eyed her injured side often to see if she was bleeding, but so far, everything looked good.

They didn't stop until the trees gave way to a road. Lev looked behind him to see if the Saints were coming. He caught movement about three hundred yards behind him. To linger meant capture and, ultimately, death.

"We need a car," Reyna said as she bent over to gulp in air.

Lev nodded and went to reach for the map. That's when he remembered that it was in his pack back at Helge's house. "Dammit."

"They know we're going to the coast," she said as she straightened. "They'll have Saints everywhere."

He looked back up the mountain. Whatever he'd

seen was gone now. "That's why they aren't chasing us."

"They're allowing us to think we got away. False sense of security."

Lev faced her and lifted his brows. "We have to get to the coast. I say we pick the city with the highest population. We'll blend in there more, which means, it'll be harder for them to find us."

"Like you said, we have to get to the coast."

"We're running out of land."

She nodded and looked up at the dark sky. "It doesn't matter where we go. Anyone who helps us will be killed."

Lev moved to stand before her and waited until her gaze met his. He smoothed her hair back from her face and pulled her into his arms. "If you thought you could make that confession back there and I would forget, you were wrong."

"I just wanted you to know in case I died."

"Then let me tell you that I've fallen for you, Reyna Harris. Hard. I know that when I'm with you, I feel as if I can do anything."

She lifted her face to his and kissed him. "Then let's go conquer the world."

He took her hand as they turned toward the road.

24

"What the hell do you mean, they're gone?" Lorraine demanded.

None of the soldiers would even meet her gaze. Fury burned within her. The men had cornered Lev and Reyna, and yet, somehow, they'd gotten away. She could barely fathom it.

She turned and saw Anatoli enter the house. At least he wasn't making some comment about her losing the couple again. He would later. Of that, she was sure. She had a small reprieve.

But she wasn't worried about what her ex-lover had to say. With every day, every hour that she didn't produce Reyna and Lev, her reputation within the Saints took a hit. She didn't care what those below her thought. It was Lester and the elders. Those were the ones who had the authority to order her death—or grant her life.

Lorraine knew that it would be pointless to yell at the soldiers. They'd been ordered not to shoot at Lev and Reyna, which gave them little options for containing them. She'd hoped that when she got the call that the men had found the couple that she would get to them before they made a run for it.

She hadn't been so lucky. In fact, she'd had nothing but *bad* luck since the moment Lev arrived in Kiev. If she were a suspicious person, she'd think someone had cursed her.

Lorraine sighed and looked around the yard. Bright lights were set up so she and Anatoli could see. The bullet holes that riddled the trees and ground proved that the men had fired upon Lev and Reyna, even though they had orders not to.

But with the couple wounding—and killing—at least two men, Lorraine didn't blame the soldiers for firing back. She certainly would have.

Things would be a lot simpler if the elders didn't want Lev and Reyna alive. Lorraine could set up a sniper and take them out easily. She'd be back in the office in a day instead of traipsing around after two people she wanted dead.

The sound of footsteps approaching pulled her attention from her thoughts. None of the soldiers would dare approach her, which meant it was Anatoli. And she wasn't in the mood for his comments.

"Two dead and seven wounded," he said when he reached her. He put his hands in his pockets and rocked back on his heels. "If that's what Lev and Reyna can do in the dark while running, I'm not sure I want to meet them head-on."

She rolled her eyes before she looked at him. "You afraid of them?"

He flattened his lips and shot her a dry look. "They're good, Lori. Even you have to admit that."

"I know how good Reyna is. I chose her,

remember?"

"And Lev?" Anatoli pushed.

Lorraine wanted to discount him, but she couldn't. "It's obvious Lev has some training. No US agency or military I spoke with admitted to training him, though."

"Some people have that kind of skill naturally. It's rare, but it does happen."

"I disagree. That kind of proficiency is only obtained by many years of intense training. Someone gave him the skills. I'll find out who one way or another."

Anatoli blew out a loud, exasperated breath. "What does it matter?"

"It always matters."

He faced her. "No. What matters is doing what you've been ordered to do. You've come close a few times, but your quarry continues to slip through your fingers. You would've had them this time had the soldiers not killed the old man."

"The men obviously felt they had no choice."

But she agreed with Anatoli. She couldn't believe they had possibly ruined the capture of Lev and Reyna simply because the old man had caught sight of one of them.

Anatoli rubbed a hand over his mouth and whiskered chin. "It's obvious where they're headed."

"The coast," she replied. "It's why I called those chasing them back. There's no need to waste the time and effort since I know where they're going."

He nodded as he looked into the darkness beyond the lights. "I would've kept men on them. It might have caused them to make a mistake."

"Yes, because that's worked to my advantage

since we began this."

Anatoli's blue eyes slid to hers. "We?"

"Do you have to be an ass about everything?"

"Up until now, you've said 'I.' I'm curious why you would suddenly include me."

God, she hated him. Really, what she hated was how he managed to catch her in such instances. "Fine. Since *I* began this. I would like to point out that you're here, which means you're on the hook for this, as well."

Anatoli chuckled. As he walked away, he said, "And you wonder why everyone thinks you're a bitch."

His words stung, but she wouldn't let it show. She didn't have her current position to make friends. So what if everyone thought she was heartless? It was that merciless, take-no-prisoners attitude that had gotten her where she was. She wouldn't apologize to anyone for that, nor would she change who she was.

Anatoli halted and turned on his heel to stalk back to her. He stopped in front of her, anger flashing in his eyes. "Everyone out here would stick their necks out for you if you showed them some respect. Instead, you treat them as if they're the dirt beneath your shoe."

"They do show me respect because of my position in the Saints. They know with one word that I could claim their life."

Anatoli shook his head, gazing at her with disgust. "We treat those not in the Saints like that, not our own."

"You don't," she reminded him. "I do things differently."

"And it's that approach that has you where you

are."

She barked with laughter. "What? Continuing to rise in the ranks?"

"Alone in the cold. Because that's what's going to happen if Lev and Reyna get away. No one is going to stand with you against the elders."

"Are you saying if we were still together that you would? Are you honestly telling me if I was nicer and complimented those around me that each and every one of those men would go before the elders and speak on my behalf?" Reyna snorted and rolled her eyes. "Bullshit."

"I would, yes."

Her head whipped back around to him. She hadn't really expected him to answer.

He lifted one shoulder in a shrug. "At least, I would have. You made your choices."

In other words, even he would forget that he knew her. Fine. If that's how he wanted it.

Lorraine inwardly shook her head. Of course, that was how he wanted it. She had left him without so much as a by your leave, and then for the next few years, went out of her way to ignore him. She'd climbed the Saints' ladder, doing whatever she needed to in order to get to the next level.

And she'd done it all with the knowledge that it might one day come back to haunt her. Although, she hadn't really thought that would actually come to pass. There was still a chance that it wouldn't. All she had to do was capture Reyna and Lev.

She lifted her chin and met Anatoli's gaze. "Yes, I did make my choices."

With that statement delivered, she turned and walked to the house. She put his words out of her mind as she looked over the bowls of food and the schnapps on the table. The old man held bullets clutched in one hand while the other was stained red with his blood.

If he were giving the couple ammunition, then they must be running low. And they had used a lot to escape the house. If only she knew for certain that they had used everything.

"Ma'am."

She swung her head around to find one of the soldiers holding up a backpack. Lorraine recognized it as one she'd seen Lev wearing. She walked to the man and took the bag from him to place it on the table so she could sort through it. Unfortunately, the only thing of use she found was a map. Everything else was food and water.

"What else did they leave behind?" she demanded.

It wasn't long before she saw the used bandages with dried blood as well as Lev's discarded clothes. There was nothing else for them there.

"Let's wrap this up and move on," she ordered. Her gaze landed on the sergeant. "Make it look like Reyna and Lev were intruders who murdered the old man."

Lorraine walked past Anatoli, uncaring if he agreed with her decision or not. The more people after her quarry, the better. Enough Saints were looking that Lev and Reyna should be found, but those not associated with the organization could be swayed to help them by seeing the lie about the murder. That would leave the couple nowhere to go.

She walked the scene again to make sure the bullet casings were picked up. The local authorities that would report this as a murder were part of the Saints and would disregard the number of bullet holes in the house and the trees.

When she made her way to the car, Anatoli was in the passenger seat with his head leaning back and his eyes closed. Still feeling ill-tempered from earlier, she slammed her door particularly hard when she got inside. The grin she wore slipped when he didn't even flinch.

"Norway has a long coastline," he said without opening his eyes.

She gripped the steering wheel tightly. "Our people are at every port. There is no other escape for them."

His head turned to her, and he opened one eye. "Death is an escape, Lori. Neither Lev nor Reyna seem the type to be taken as prisoners."

"They don't know we're not going to kill them," she replied.

"I spoke to the lieutenant of the soldiers. His men were shooting wide. They know."

Damn. She hadn't thought of that. "Then we'll have to make certain that neither Lev nor Reyna take their own lives."

Anatoli closed his eye and rolled his head back to its original position without responding.

Lorraine angrily grabbed at her seatbelt. As she went to fasten it, the tip of her finger got pinched in the mechanism. She hissed at the pain and shook out her hand. Unwittingly, her gaze lifted to Anatoli, but her ex-lover didn't seem to care that she was injured.

Just as it should be. He was an ex for a reason.

She started the engine and began the drive toward the coast.

25

Everything hurt. Despite her life as a spy, Reyna had never been shot. The closest she'd come was a graze on her arm. She wanted so badly to lay down, curl up, and sleep for a couple of months.

But she kept putting one foot in front of the other somehow. Actually, she knew how she was staying upright. It all had to do with Lev.

He grinned when he caught her looking at him. "I'm fine."

She glanced at the bandage she'd tied around his upper arm after she'd found it bleeding. Reyna was thankful that the bullet had missed him for the most part, rather than puncturing the arm. Otherwise, they'd be worse off than they were.

Lev's fingers tightened around hers. He'd taken her hand as they'd begun walking. The connection to him, the fact that their bodies were touching helped to keep Reyna focused and moving.

But they still had miles to go before they reached the coast.

"We'll make it," he said as if reading her mind.

She nodded. "Of course, we will."

"I'll find us a car soon."

"I'll walk as far as I need to."

This time, he was the one who turned his head to her. "The strength you gained at Helge's is evaporating quickly."

"I won't be a burden."

He stopped and brought her to a halt with him as he faced her. "I'm not worried about that. I'm more concerned with your loss of blood and the fact you haven't had time to recover."

"I can handle it. And if it gets too bad, I'll tell you."

"No, you won't," he replied.

She smiled because she wouldn't.

He lifted her hand and kissed it. "It'll be dawn soon. I'd like to find a car before then."

Reyna looked toward the lights of the town that was still a few miles away. They were walking slowly because of her. If she weren't injured, they could easily jog there in half the time.

"Go ahead of me." When he started to argue, she quickly said over him, "I'll keep walking and stay out of sight. But if we continue at this pace, we'll get to town after the sun is up. You know it's the right thing for you to go."

"I don't like it."

She smiled and nodded. "I know."

"Promise you'll keep walking to me."

"You won't get rid of me that easily," she teased.

He held her gaze, refusing to return her smile.

Reyna licked her lips and squeezed his hand. "I promise. Besides, I want more of your kisses."

Finally, he grinned. "Just my kisses?"

"I want all of you."

"Damn good thing, woman, because I feel the same about you."

"Now that we've got that settled, get moving," she said and slapped him on the butt.

She bit back the groan that simple movement cost her. He gave her a quick kiss and then took off running toward the town. Reyna watched him until he disappeared over a hill. Then she sighed and looked longingly at the ground.

If she sat, she likely wouldn't get back up. So, she stayed on her feet. Without Lev beside her, she found it difficult to keep going, but she didn't have any other choice.

"Move, Harris," she told herself.

That first step was the hardest. She maneuvered farther from the road they had been following to keep out of sight of any vehicles that might pass by. All the while, her mind was filled with thoughts of Lev.

She couldn't help but think about life with him next week, next month. Next year. What would happen when they returned to the States? She didn't allow herself to think of the alternative.

Would she remain with Lev? Would he still want her? She had nowhere else to go, but she didn't want him to think that she stayed with him because of that. Then there was the question of how Sergei would receive her.

If Sergei didn't like her, there was a chance that Lev would bend to the will of his boss's opinions. Lev seemed the type that forged his own way, but a man didn't become a *Brigadier* to a Russian mob boss by not doing what the *Pakhan* wanted.

Then there were the Loughmans. Reyna and Lev could go there. Those at the Loughman ranch had already done a deep-dive into her background. Unless the Saints had added false information—which she knew they did from time to time.

Reyna grew anxious as she thought about the lies the Saints had no doubt told about her. Would the Loughmans believe them? She hoped she had a chance to dispute any that might come up, but the fact remained that the Loughmans might choose not to trust her.

So, again, where did that leave her? She didn't want Lev choosing between Sergei, the Loughmans, or her. But she couldn't walk away from him either. What she'd found with Lev was something unique and special. And it had very little to do with the fact that they were running for their lives.

She'd seen sides of him others never would in such situations, and she liked what she saw. They had to trust and rely on each other heavily.

Still, she didn't discount the importance of any of that. But she knew what she felt in his arms. It was...wonderful. Almost like she'd discovered the other half of her soul. She hadn't wanted to become attached to him, but there had been no denying the enticement he presented her with.

In his arms, she got a taste of what life could be like. And she wanted to seize it with both hands. In fact, that's what she intended to do. Saints be damned.

Her thoughts took her to the person who'd given her access to the building—the Saints' headquarters. She hadn't even known that's what it was, or what to look for in the archives room. She didn't know who had helped her, but she wished she'd been able to find out. They had risked a lot to get the information and urge her three different times to go.

She'd tried to investigate who the material had come from, but they had covered their tracks very well. The fact that someone inside the Saints wanted the organization's dirty laundry aired gave Reyna hope. Because where there was one, there were more.

———

Lev was winded by the time he reached the small town. He hadn't slowed since he left Reyna. He stopped and scrutinized the buildings and cars for several minutes as he caught his breath.

He zeroed in on a sedan and made sure that no one was near. Then he walked to it and tested the door. It was locked. He looked around until he found a rock and used that to bust the window.

After he'd scraped the glass out of the seat, he got inside the vehicle and reached under the dash to pull out the wires. In seconds, the engine roared to life. He put the car in gear and turned it around to head back for Reyna.

He hated stealing stuff, but it wasn't as if they had a choice. Once he got back to Texas, he would have Callie do her thing and find out who owned the vehicles they'd stolen. He'd make sure they were compensated.

The sky continued to lighten, but he still had trouble locating anything moving in the trees along the road. He worried that Reyna had been more tired than she'd let on. He'd seen the fatigue on her face, which was why he'd gone to get the car. Now, he wondered if that had been a good idea.

His gaze was on the side of the road they'd been walking on as he slowed the vehicle. There were few other cars and trucks on the road, so he didn't bring any attention to himself. Then, he saw a figure step out of the trees.

He recognized Reyna's jacket immediately. Lev did a U-turn on the road and pulled up alongside her. She smiled and got into the car. He didn't say anything about the dark circles under her eyes.

"Get settled in," he told her. "You sleep while I drive."

The fact that she didn't argue told him how exhausted she was. She crossed her arms over her chest and leaned her head back. With one last smile in his direction, she closed her eyes.

Lev pressed the accelerator and picked up speed. He drove back through the town without slowing and kept on the same road toward the coast. He'd been doing some thinking about that. He wanted to talk it over with Reyna, but it would have to wait.

He heard a buzzing that sounded like a cell phone on silent. He looked in the cupholders and slid his hand between the seat and door and the seat and the center console, but he didn't find anything. Then he opened the center console and found the phone.

Lev accepted the call but quickly ended it. That allowed him to get into the cell and place a call of his own. He dialed Sergei first. As the line connected and began to ring, Lev glanced at the clock, calculating the time difference. Since Sergei liked to go to bed early, he likely wouldn't hear the ringing.

The call went to voicemail, so Lev hung up. Then he dialed the number to the Loughmans. On the third ring, he heard a feminine "hello."

"Callie?" he asked.

"Um. No, this is Natalie. Hang on. I'll get the others."

Lev frowned. Why couldn't she talk to him herself? He realized that she might not know everything. So, of course, she'd go get Callie.

Except it wasn't Callie who answered. It was the middle Loughman brother, Owen. "Lev? How are things?"

"They're shit," he stated.

"Where are you?"

He looked around for a sign but found nothing. "Somewhere in Norway. We're not being trailed right now, but that's because they know we're headed to the coast."

There was a beat of silence. "How do they know?"

"We had a bit of a run-in. Reyna was shot in her left side soon after we entered Norway. The bullet went through, and it took me some time to stop the bleeding. The bastards managed to find us in a cabin. There was a confrontation where they attempted to carry Reyna's unconscious body down the mountain."

"I gather you stopped them."

Lev snorted. "Damn right, I did. Reyna and I moved as quickly as we could in the dark. An old man found us and gave us shelter so I could see to her wound properly. We also got clothes and food, but they found us again. They killed the old man and tried to pin me and Reyna down in the house."

"Obviously, you escaped."

"They were shooting near us, but not at us."

Owen grunted. "They want you alive. No doubt

to torture you until both of you give up information on us."

"Exactly. So, we ran. They started to follow but stopped shortly after."

"Is your plan still the same?"

Lev glanced at Reyna. "We've got to get out of here, but I honestly don't know where we'll be safe. And Reyna needs time to recover."

"Getting on the water will help as long as they don't know what ship you're on. Do you intend to head to a large port?"

"Right now, I'm just driving as Reyna sleeps. I've been going back and forth on large versus smaller ports. They're all going to be watched."

"Then don't go to either."

Lev paused as he thought over Owen's words. Then it dawned on him. "Private slips."

"That's the way I'd go. The homeowners won't be watched like the ports. You'll have an easier time getting a boat and getting on the water."

"Until the owners report the vessel missing."

"It still gives you time."

And Lev needed more of that. "Is there any way Callie can take the number I've called from and hack into the carrier?"

"I can ask."

"I'd like to be able to communicate with you rather than be without when we get on the water."

Owen said, "I'll make sure Callie gets on that right away."

"One more thing. Can you let Sergei know I've made contact? I tried to call him, but he didn't answer." The silence that followed Lev's request made him anxious. "Owen? What is it?"

"Fuck, man. I didn't want to be the one to tell you."

Lev gripped the steering wheel tighter as his stomach clenched in fear and dread. "Tell me what?"

"Sergei is dead."

Lev couldn't process the information. "What happened?"

Owen sighed loudly. "His car blew up."

Fury raced through Lev because he knew who was responsible—the Saints. Lev had warned Sergei that this would happen, but Sergei hadn't cared. He'd told Lev that helping the Loughmans was the right thing to do.

"Lev?" Owen called.

"When?" Lev demanded in a half-growl.

Owen hesitated before he said, "A couple days ago. We had no way to contact you, or we would've made sure you knew."

"I know."

"You and Sergei were close. We all know that, but don't do anything stupid."

Lev issued a bark of laughter. "You mean like going after the Saints? Isn't that what I did by traveling to Kiev?"

"Lev," Owen began.

"I took this mission because Sergei wanted to help you. Now you're going to help me. You make sure no one dismantles what Sergei spent his life building. When I get back—and I *will* get back—I want everything intact."

"We'll see to it," Owen promised. "Cullen and Mia have already headed to Dover for the funeral. We all wanted to go."

Lev wanted to hit something. Hard. "But you can't. I understand."

"We all liked Sergei. And we will get revenge for what they've done to him."

No. Lev would get the revenge, but he didn't tell Owen that. "I'm going to turn the phone off when we hang up. I'll turn it back on in two hours. If I don't hear from Callie, then I'll repeat the procedure until she manages to get into the phone."

"Be safe."

Lev shut off the phone and glanced at Reyna. He wanted to get her as far from the Saints as possible. Then he was going straight for them.

26

Reyna knew something was wrong the moment she opened her eyes and looked at Lev. He stared at the road as if it were his enemy. A muscle ticked in his jaw, and his body was tense.

He glanced her way when she sat up. "How are you feeling?"

"Better. Where are we?"

"About forty kilometers from the coast."

She licked her dry lips and glanced down to find the cell phone in the cupholder. "What happened?"

"I called the Loughmans."

"Is everything all right? They didn't get attacked, did they?"

"They didn't."

Her body was cold from sleep, so it took her some time to slowly shift to see him better. "Who did, then?"

"Sergei."

She put her hand on his arm. He didn't need to say more. She knew by his tone and attitude that Sergei was dead. And she knew who was responsible. "I'm so sorry."

"The phone was in the car," he explained.

It seemed like he needed to talk, so she didn't reply.

"I tried Sergei, but he didn't answer. I assumed he was asleep. So, I called the Loughmans. That's when Owen told me Sergei's car had blown up."

Reyna closed her eyes to block herself from the agony she knew Lev felt. She wanted to wrap her arms around him and try to take some of his pain, but she couldn't at the moment.

Lev's blue eyes briefly slid to hers. They were filled with torment and anguish. "He was an old man."

"It was a way to get to you, that's why they went after Sergei."

"They're cowards."

"Yes, they are," she said. "Sergei wanted to join the fight against the Saints. He knew he physically couldn't, which is why he turned to you."

Lev took her hand and squeezed it. "I wasn't there when he died. I should've been there."

"He wanted you in Kiev."

"I should never have gone. I should've remained with him. Maybe then he'd still be alive."

Reyna glanced at their intertwined fingers. "Or you would be dead with him."

Lev didn't respond, but he was no longer as tense as before. That was something.

"Sergei saw what I do," she continued. "You're the type of fighter who gets under the skin of groups like the Saints. They underestimate you, which gives you an advantage. The kind that will help to topple them."

Lev gave a small shake of his head. "You give me too much credit."

"No, I don't," she said with a laugh. "I've been doing this for years now. I've worked with and encountered all kinds of people who are highly trained. You have their skills, yes, but you come at things differently. It makes you unpredictable. That scares them."

"Until someone comes along who stops me," he said as he glanced her way.

Reyna shrugged her right shoulder. "Maybe. Maybe not. Look what the Loughmans have done. You're now a part of that, and that scares the Saints."

"You don't know that," he said, a frown of disbelief on his face.

She quirked a brow. "Have they attacked the Loughmans?"

"Not since the first time."

"That's because they want to make sure they are able to wipe everyone out the next time. They're testing each of you. You've put a kink in their plans."

Lev released a long breath. "Good. Because I intend to do much more than that."

"It's easy to get lost in the anger and grief of losing someone. If you do, you let the Saints win. Focus everything you're feeling on bringing them down."

"No."

She was taken aback by Lev's succinct statement.

Then he turned his head and met her gaze. "I'm also going to think about you."

She smiled, her heart melting as he looked at the road again. "I could get used to you saying those kinds of things."

"Then you better get used to it because I'm going to be telling you all the time."

She leaned her head back against the headrest and sighed.

"Are you feeling okay?" he asked, worry in his tone.

"A little peckish."

He grinned. "I've been hungry for a few hours. I'll stop up here and see about getting food and petrol."

Reyna wanted to get out and stretch her legs, as well as go to the bathroom, but she knew they took a huge chance every time they stopped. "We need to avoid cameras. They'll use them with facial recognition to try and pinpoint our location."

"I saw a cap in the back."

"You use that. I'll find some way of disguising myself."

He nodded and fell silent as he drove. Reyna found herself thinking about Sergei. She had really wanted to meet the man who Lev considered a father. It broke her heart that she wouldn't get to do that. And she hated that the Saints had taken him from Lev.

It was just another reason for her to hate the group. She'd spent five years with them. She'd thought she would go in and find they were evil people who'd joined a cult.

The sad part was, some of them were really good people. Human beings she would be proud to call friends. If she hadn't known their true motivations, she might have trusted them with her life.

How could seemingly normal people be turned to such an organization? What had been the keyword that switched them from a 'no' to a 'yes?' And why didn't it work on everyone?

Though she should be thankful for that. Yet it seemed that there were more and more individuals joining the ranks of the Saints. For decades, the Saints had built their shady society in the darkest shadows when they would've been small enough to squish like a bug.

Now, it felt as if they were the giants wearing the boots.

Before they reached the town, Lev pulled over and rummaged through the trunk and back seat. Reyna wanted to help him, but her pain was minimal at the moment, and she decided to conserve her energy since there was no telling when she and Lev would be actively running for their lives again.

Her door suddenly opened, and Lev squatted down beside the vehicle. He placed a scarf in her hands as well as a fedora. Both would be perfect to hide her face and hair.

"I'm fine," she told him with a smile as she eyed the baseball cap he'd put on.

He leaned forward and put his lips on hers. "I just wanted a kiss."

She was falling more in love with him every day. And if the Saints killed him, Reyna knew her poor heart would never survive.

"Hey," he said worriedly. "What is it?"

"I don't want to lose you."

His lips turned into a crooked grin. "That should be me saying that since you were unconscious with a bullet wound a bit ago."

"I'll give you that."

They laughed, but it was obvious that they were

both trying to keep things upbeat instead of facing the reality that the Saints were outnumbering and outgunning them.

Lev rose and shut Reyna's door before walking around the car. She wrapped the scarf around her head, making sure to tuck it beneath the ends of her hair so nothing would show. Then she set the fedora on.

He got into his side and started the engine. They reached for each other as he pulled back onto the road toward the city. Six miles later, he slowed the car as he turned into a petrol station and stopped beside a pump.

"I'll try to hurry," she told him. "But my bladder is about to burst."

"Do you want food here? Or should we try our luck somewhere else?"

She looked into the store and thought of the bags of chips and other items and turned up her nose. "I'd rather wait if we can."

"Then we'll wait."

Reyna took a deep breath and opened her door. The first movement of her legs caused pain to shoot up her body. And twisting to get out of the vehicle made her break out in a sweat.

She tried to walk as if she weren't injured, but she knew it was still slower than a healthy person would move. Once she was on her feet and the door was shut behind her, she looked over the car roof to see Lev stand. Their gazes met, and they shared a smile.

They had an unspoken pact. They had come this far together, and they would face whatever was to come—together.

Reyna turned and began walking to the door of

the store. When she was inside, she saw the signs pointing to the restrooms and went straight there without looking at the register.

The toilet was only for one, so she was able to lock the door. She took her time lowering her pants and relieving herself, and then took more time getting her clothes back on. She looked at herself in the mirror to ensure that the scarf and hat were in place before she unlocked and opened the door.

A woman stood outside with an infant strapped to her front with a blanket over its head. She said something in Norwegian. Reyna only knew a few basic words. She smiled and moved to the side so the woman could get in.

Out of the corner of her eye, Reyna saw the edge of a pistol. She hesitated in pushing the woman because of the baby, and that small delay gave the woman time to pull out the gun with a silencer.

Reyna slammed her hand into the woman's right shoulder, which caused her to stumble backward and the blanket to fall off the baby. Except it wasn't an infant. It was a doll.

"You bitch," Reyna said and grabbed the woman's hand holding the gun.

They wrestled in the small alcove of the bathroom. Reyna kept trying to turn the gun away from herself and toward her attacker. The woman was a little taller than Reyna, but she didn't have the same anger and need for retribution that Reyna carried.

That's what made the difference in the end. Reyna managed to twist the gun right before the woman pulled the trigger. Her attacker's eyes widened in shock as she stepped back into the wall while the life drained from her. Reyna released her and walked away before the woman could slide to the floor.

Reyna was breathing hard when she strode from the store and to the car where Lev waited. She got in and said, "Drive."

He didn't ask questions as he put the vehicle in gear and drove off.

"There was a Saint outside the bathroom. She pretended to have a baby," she explained. "A baby!"

"Is she dead?"

"Yes."

Lev nodded. "Good."

"They'll know we were here."

He shrugged and changed lanes. "Knowing where we are and catching us are two different things."

"We can't stop for food. I should have gotten something at the store."

Lev glanced at her and smiled calmly. "We're going to get whatever food you want."

"Why aren't you upset that the Saints found us?"

"Because I know we're going to get away."

She laughed, she couldn't help herself. "How is that?"

"We're going to find a private residence that has a boat and take it."

"To cross the North Sea and the Atlantic, we're going to need a good-sized vessel."

He grinned. "Wealthy people tend to have exactly those types of ships."

"That's actually a good idea. I was thinking ports again. The Saints won't be able to keep track of all residences. However, you know the owners of the ship will report it stolen. And I know the Saints have at least two submarines, so they can track us from below."

Lev shrugged. "We'll worry about all of that once we have the boat. I'm sure we can come up with some way to change the numbers and name."

"That will require boating stickers."

"Just one more stop we'll have to make. But first, food."

27

L   ev was happy when they finally reached the coast. With Reyna's belly full, they focused on finding a boat. They drove up and down, looking at the homes and surveying the areas before stopping at a store for boating stickers.

To his surprise, Reyna easily picked a man's pocket, taking out a couple of banknotes before tapping him on the shoulder and giving the wallet back to him.

"What?" she asked with a grin. "We didn't need it all."

"We will need to stock the boat with some items."

She lifted the money. "We'll have enough."

With her scarf and hat still in place, they walked into the store and found the stickers for the boat. Then they got some bottled water and other necessities. They barely had enough cash to cover it.

Lev eyed everyone to see who was watching them and who wasn't. They kept their heads down to make it difficult for the cameras to catch a view of their faces. No other Saints made themselves known. Lev wasn't sure if there weren't any in the area, or if they had been ordered to pull back.

Either way, it worked for him and Reyna.

Back in the car, they made another couple of passes along the coast to narrow down the house choices to two.

"I like the Sunseeker," Reyna said as she pointed to the boat tied to a dock.

"How big is she?"

Reyna shrugged. "It's a Tomahawk 41 with a fiberglass construction, two engines with a cruising speed of twenty-two knots per hour, and a max speed of thirty-three."

He raised his brows when she looked his way. "Really?"

"I almost bought a Sunseeker. I love boats. And to answer your first question, she's forty-four feet. We'll have plenty of room."

All Lev could think about was hoping that he didn't get seasick again, but he knew he would. Reyna's love of the water was obvious. He liked it, too. He just didn't feel the need to be on it. Looking at it was enough for him.

"Then the Sunseeker it is," he said.

They pulled over, and he checked the time. It had been two hours, so he turned on the phone and waited five minutes to see if Callie would text. When she didn't, he turned it back off.

"What was that?" Reyna asked.

"I'm having Callie hack into this phone and erase all of the owner's info so no one can track it."

Reyna smiled. "That was smart. I missed a lot while I slept."

"You needed it."

"And now I need to get to the boat."

He frowned, not liking her words. "What are you thinking?"

"I swim to it while you wait for me down a few miles like we did last time."

Lev was shaking his head before she finished. "We do this together. Besides, what are the chances that the keys will be in the boat?"

"You don't intend to break into the house to get them, do you?"

"If I have to."

She pressed her lips together. "It's daylight. We can't do that."

"Why not? Look around? It's the middle of the week. People have already left for work. The house should be empty."

"What choice do we have?"

"None," he replied.

Reyna nodded, her gaze on the house. "If we can get to the back of the house without being seen, we should be good. It's getting over the iron fence that concerns me."

"Your idea of swimming sounds good."

She cocked a brow. "Does it now?"

He laughed. "I'll swim to the back and get in from the water. Then I'll unlock the house and let you in."

"What about this car? I don't want to walk up to the house."

She had a point. Lev thought about it a minute before he came up with another plan. "I'll unlock the house, then swim back and get in the car. I'll then drive you to the house where you can go inside and get the boat ready while I ditch the car."

"And you swim back out to me?" she asked skeptically.

"Yep. Then we take the boat."

Reyna touched her wounded side. "Since I'm all but useless, I think it's the best plan. I hate that you'll be doing most of the work, though."

"I'll be quick. I saw a house a few hundred yards back that had access to the beach. I'll use that to get into the water. Until then, we need to move the car."

She pointed behind them. "I saw a place that'll be perfect."

He turned the vehicle around and drove to the abandoned store and parked in the back. Lev gave her a quick kiss and made sure the guns were within easy reach for her. Then he headed down to the beach. He rotated his injured shoulder, hoping that it wouldn't hurt too badly when he tried to use it.

Lev kept an eye out for others as he walked to the water. He took off his shoes and hid them behind some rocks before he walked into the water and started swimming.

The water was cold, and his shoulder hurt like a son of a bitch, but he didn't stop. He clenched his teeth together against the chill and put his face in the water. Others were swimming, so he didn't look so out of place. As hot-natured as he was, even this was a bit much for him.

He looked up often to gauge his distance to the boat. Lev was breathing heavily by the time he reached it and the house. He swam up to the dock and peeked over the boards to make sure no one was out back. Just as he was about to climb the ladder, he heard a child's shriek.

Lev ducked back down just as a toddler came

running out into the backyard, followed by a woman. The sound of something breathing heavily made Lev frown. When he looked up, he saw a large dog standing on the edge of the dock looking down at him.

The dog barked, his tail wagging. Thankfully, it wasn't going after him. The dog continued to make noise, so Lev lowered himself back into the water. No sooner had his head gone under than the woman, now holding the toddler on her hip, walked over to the dog. She said something to the animal and tugged on its collar. Finally, the dog relented and turned around.

Lev broke the surface of the water and listened as the trio walked farther away from him. He could hear the woman talking as they walked into the house, but he didn't understand her. He was about to look for another home and boat when he heard a jingle that sounded like keys.

He peered over the edge of the dock and saw the woman and toddler walking to the garage. It wasn't long before the car started and they drove away.

Lev looked around to see if anyone was watching him. When the coast was clear, he climbed up the ladder, water sliding off him. He kept his head forward, but his gaze swept the area from one side to the other. A quick check showed him that the house didn't have an alarm. However, it did have a dog.

Said animal was standing at the glass door, tail wagging, watching him. Lev stared at the pooch, and he could've sworn the dog smiled at him.

"You going to bite me?" he asked.

The dog barked and backed up, his tail still wagging.

"I don't have time for this," he mumbled.

It didn't take him long to pick the lock. The moment the door was cracked open, the dog's snout was there, sniffing and licking him. Lev opened the door wider and scratched the dog behind his ears.

"Good boy," he murmured.

Lev slipped inside then walked straight to the front door and unlocked it. After another rub for the dog, Lev hurriedly retraced his steps and dove into the water to swim back to the beach. He slipped on his socks and shoes. He was shivering by the time he reached Reyna and the car.

"Your lips are tinged blue," she said with a smile.

He grunted as he started the engine. "That water is fucking cold. How the hell can anyone stand it?"

She chuckled. "It's what they're used to."

He checked the road for oncoming cars before pulling out. "They're crazy."

It took only a few minutes before he pulled up to the house and looked at Reyna. "It's open. There's no alarm. But there is a dog. He doesn't bite."

"That's good news. I'll be quick," Reyna said as she grabbed the bags of supplies and the boat numbers. "You be safe."

"Wait," he called. Lev removed his shoes and socks again and handed them to her.

Reyna winked at him and turned away, but he saw the wince on her face. She was still hurting, and no doubt would be for a while.

He waited until she reached the front door before he turned on the heater and drove away to ditch the car. Lev was just beginning to thaw out some when he hid the vehicle and made his way to the beach once more.

Lev hated the way his wet pants, now cold, stuck

THE DEFENDER | 221

to his legs. He ignored it and waded into the water to make his final swim.

Reyna hated the weakness of her body that caused her to make several trips because she couldn't carry as much as she normally would. And following her each step of the way was the most precious dog she'd ever seen.

"You're such a sweetie," she told him, giving him lots of love.

On her first trip with the bags with food, the boat numbers, and Lev's guns, shoes, and socks, she quickly looked over the boat.

It was semi-stocked, but not nearly what would be needed for their voyage. There were places they could dock and fill their stores, but the less they had to do that, the better.

With her mental note in place, Reyna went back into the house to look for the boat keys. She found them near the back door, hanging on a hook. After slipping them into her pants' pocket, Reyna located a reusable grocery bag. She went through the kitchen pantry and fridge, taking everything that she could. When the bag was full, she brought it to the boat and unloaded it before making a third trip.

That jaunt included some clothes she'd found washed in the laundry room. She didn't know if they would fit Lev, but anything was better than wearing the same items for weeks at a time.

After that, she went through the house, wiping down anything she'd touched to obscure her fingerprints, as well as locking the front door. She kept the towel in her hand as she walked to the back. The dog tried to go out with her.

"No, buddy, you can't," Reyna told him.

She bent over, ignoring the pain, and gave him a good rubbing before she slid the glass door closed, locking it with the dog inside. With the bag of clothes in hand, she turned to the boat.

Her wound was hurting, and she was becoming fatigued, but she was determined to get on the vessel and find Lev. Reyna's hands shook from the pain and nausea that had set in while she was untying the boat from its moors. It took her a couple of tries to get the key into the ignition. She started up the engine and looked back at the house where the dog was barking and pawing at the glass. She gave the animal a wave.

She caught sight of Lev swimming toward her and made straight for him. It worried her how slow he moved, but she knew it had more to do with the cold water than his wound, though she was sure that had something to do with it, as well.

Thankfully, he looked up as she slowed the boat to pull up alongside him. He treaded water until she stopped. She put the engine in idle, and as she turned to go to Lev, she jerked to a stop because she thought she heard the retort of a rifle. Lev then climbed up into the back unharmed, and she thought it must have been her imagination. She met him with a towel and a smile.

"We did it," she said.

He grinned and wrapped the towel around himself. "Let's put some distance between us and the Saints."

Reyna didn't need to be told twice. She returned

THE DEFENDER | 223

to the wheel but pointed at the bag behind her. "There are some clothes you can change into."

She gunned the throttle, propelling the boat forward. The more they moved away from Norway, the better she felt. But she knew it was temporary. The Saints would find them.

When she couldn't stand it anymore, she sat in the chair and kept the boat at a steady speed. It wasn't as fast as she wanted to go, but she didn't want to draw unnecessary attention to them either.

After thirty minutes, Lev came up beside her and held out a plate of food. "You need to eat and rest. I can handle this."

She looked over his face. He didn't appear to be as seasick as he'd gotten the last time. She didn't want the food, but she had to build up her strength.

"Thanks," she said and took the plate as she got to her feet.

She stayed with him, sitting behind him as he took the wheel. After the first tentative bite, she realized she was famished and devoured the rest of the food.

Lev's chuckle caused her to raise her head to look at him. "What?" she asked.

"I can fix you some more. I didn't realize you were that hungry."

"Neither did I," she replied with a smile. "This is fine for now. How are you doing?"

He shrugged. "So far, so good. This boat is huge. I had no idea they could be so luxurious."

"This is a smaller one. Wait until you see a big one. I'm surprised Sergei never had a yacht."

Lev shook his head. "Sergei did his business at the

docks because it was accessible, not because he liked the water."

"I can understand that."

"But you like the water."

She grinned as she looked out the window at the dark waters of the sea. "I don't love it like some people, but I enjoy being on the water. The longest I've been out is a week, so this should be interesting. I might go stir-crazy."

"Oh, I'm sure we can come up with some activities to keep you entertained."

Reyna saw the desire in his eyes and nodded. "That could be fun."

28

The funeral home was somber. Then again, they always were.

"You doing okay, babe?" Cullen asked.

Mia looked into his hazel eyes and smiled sadly. "No."

"Me, either."

She leaned her head on his shoulder when he put an arm around her. They sat at the back of the room, squeezed in between a crush of people. Mia was amazed by how many had shown up for Sergei's memorial.

Though she shouldn't be.

He might have been a mob boss, but he'd had one of the biggest hearts that she'd ever encountered. And she was going to miss him dearly. However, there was someone who would miss him more—Lev.

"It's not right that Lev isn't here," she whispered.

Cullen shifted his head so that his mouth was by her ear. "Don't say his name too loudly."

Her head jerked up as she frowned. "Why? Everyone knows how close they were."

"Yes, but only Sergei knew why Lev went away. The others think he's gone on business."

"So?" she said with a shrug.

Cullen blew out a breath as he met her gaze. "I heard some of Sergei's men talking."

"About?"

Cullen looked at her pointedly.

"Oh," she said, realizing he meant Lev. "What were they saying?"

"Some claim that he was the one who killed Sergei."

"But that's not true."

"And when he gets back, Lev will make sure they know."

If Lev returned. The obstacles surrounding him and Reyna multiplied every day. Mia and the others might know how good Lev was, but against so many Saints? The odds weren't in his favor.

"Don't worry about him," Cullen said.

She rolled her eyes as she looked at the giant picture of a smiling Sergei set up at the front of the room surrounded by dozens of flowers. "Right. As if you aren't concerned about him."

"Not as much as I was."

Mia raised a brow and swiveled her head to him. "What did you do?"

He lifted a shoulder in a shrug. "Just sent a message."

"To who?"

"Maks."

Her eyes widened. "What? You know how to get ahold of him?"

"No, but I know he's been keeping tabs on us. He'll get the message."

"And what did you tell him?"

Cullen's lips turned up in a smile. "I just said that one of us was being hounded and might need a hand. If Maks can, he'll help Lev and Reyna."

Mia twiddled her thumbs anxiously. "We should've flown out to Norway."

"That would've been suicide."

"And sending Lev was signing his death warrant," she whispered.

Cullen tightened his arm around her shoulders. "It was his choice to go. No one, not even Sergei, could've made Lev do anything he didn't want to do. And if any of us could get out of the situation he's in, it's him. Maks is good at blending in, but Lev is good at getting out of jams."

"I would've agreed before this," Mia said, jerking her chin toward Sergei's picture.

"Yeah," Cullen agreed with a sigh. "I'm also concerned that Lev will focus on revenge instead of getting back to us."

"Do you blame him?"

"Not in the least. We saw them together, and even in that brief time, it was obvious they were close. It wouldn't surprise me to find out they were closer than we imagined."

Mia blinked to stop the tears that threatened. "The last time I talked to Sergei, he called Lev the son he'd never had."

Cullen kissed her temple and pressed his forehead against her hair. "I had my reservations about Sergei and Lev, but they saved us. I owe them both. Even if I didn't, I would still seek revenge for what was done."

The lines of retribution and fighting for what was

right were getting blurred. Then again, with a group like the Saints, they would hit anything that hurt those that opposed them.

Mia couldn't imagine them killing Cullen. She'd never survive without him. The Loughman family had so much at stake. The entire world did, but so few realized it. She wanted to stand up and tell them the truth, even if no one believed her. At least they'd hear it.

She and Cullen grew quiet as the memorial began. The walls on either side of them were lined with members of Sergei's *Bratva*. The brotherhood. Mia didn't need to check their coats to know that they were armed. At the front of the room, the first couple of rows were for those in the top tier of Sergei's crew.

A tear leaked down Mia's cheek when she saw a space reserved for Lev.

The target was locked through the scope. Maks sighted Anatoli Kozel in his crosshairs. Maks then shifted the rifle and zeroed in on Lorraine as a group of Saints milled about the car Lev and Reyna had last stolen.

Anatoli looked bored as he messed with the cuticle on one of his nails. But Lorraine looked like a woman at the end of her rope.

Maks smiled. He couldn't wait for Lorraine or her men to discover the dead body of the Saint floating in the water. Maks had found the sniper before he even saw Lev or the woman with him. Maks took out the gunman without hesitation, allowing the couple to get away.

He might have blown his own cover to help out, but he didn't mind. There were so few of them standing against the Saints. If they didn't remain united, then they didn't stand a chance against the group.

Maks wished he knew what Lorraine was saying to Anatoli, but he couldn't get closer. It would be so easy for him to take out a half-dozen of them before they even realized what was happening. As much as he itched to do just that, it wouldn't do any good.

The Saints would send even more people. Right now, they were on Lev's trail. Maks had another path he had to walk. And if everything went to plan— along with some luck—then he and his friends just might be able to hit the Saints with a hard enough blow that it would wake up the rest of the world.

It was a long shot, but that was the only kind he'd ever known.

He wouldn't reply to whichever of the Loughmans had sent him the message. It was too risky. Soon enough, he'd be back with the rest of them in Texas. And, hopefully, Lev and his woman would be, as well.

Maks moved his finger to the trigger and contemplated putting a bullet in Lorraine's head. She would hound Lev and Reyna relentlessly. There was nothing more Maks could do now that Lev was out on the water.

It would be up to the *Brigadier* and the spy to stay alive until they reached America. Once they entered the States, the Loughmans could help them.

Maks was rather impressed by Lev and Reyna making it as far as they had against two dozen Saints hot on their trail with more of the group searching for them. Lev had shown the Saints that they weren't invincible, and that made Maks smile.

In fact, Lev had all but flipped them off. And he'd done it with a smile on his face.

Maks moved his finger from the trigger and sat back as he started to dismantle his rifle to pack it away. In no time, it was in its metal suitcase. He stood and walked to the BMW 8 Series coupe and put the briefcase on the floorboard behind the driver's seat as he got in.

The engine roared to life as he turned the car back toward Russia.

This can't be happening.

Lorraine repeated that over and over in her head, but the proof was right before her. The car was empty, and Lev and Reyna were nowhere to be found. Which meant they had already gotten on a boat.

Or were hiding.

Lorraine pivoted and stormed back to Anatoli, who was looking at his nails. "We have a leak."

Several seconds passed before he looked up at her. "You have to be joking."

"I'm not. That's the only explanation."

"It could be that Lev and Reyna are just lucky. If the woman hadn't been found at the petrol station, we wouldn't have known to come this way. If there was a leak somewhere, don't you think that would've been taken care of?"

"Not if the person didn't know about it."

Anatoli rolled his eyes. "You want to blame

anyone and everyone instead of accepting that you might very well have met your match. I warned you to send men after them when they left the house. You chose to call them back. Reyna is trained in our ways. It was obvious when we realized where they were headed, and they knew that, as well."

"I've not been outsmarted," Lorraine replied—and then inwardly winced at how childish she sounded.

"They hid the car here. What does that tell you?"

She didn't want to play this game. Lorraine put her hands on her hips. "It means they didn't go far because they wouldn't want to be out in the open."

"Precisely. Check around to see if any boats are missing."

She laughed. "They wouldn't be able to steal any of the vessels around here. Take a look at this part of the community."

"So, what if those around this area are wealthy?" he said with a shrug.

"Fine. I'll send out men to look." Lorraine barked out the order, and men spread out to begin asking questions to homeowners.

Anatoli was smiling when she looked at him. "What are you going to give me if I'm right?" he asked.

"I won't hit you like I've longed to do," she retorted.

He laughed. "You always were passionate."

"Stop," she said in a low voice while looking around to see if anyone had heard him.

"No one cares."

"I care."

Anatoli shrugged, the smile still in place. "And that's the problem."

"Smug bastard," she mumbled when he walked away.

Lorraine turned and looked at the water. If Reyna and Lev had managed to steal a boat, radar could locate them, as well as other, larger ships that the Saints controlled.

If the couple thought they could get away on the water, they had another thing coming.

Lorraine's cell phone rang. She lifted it to see that there was no caller ID and a blocked number. Her hand shook as she accepted the call. "Hello?"

"I understand you have more bad news."

She closed her eyes at the sound of Lester's voice. "They're slippery. Both are highly trained, and it doesn't help that Reyna knows our protocols."

"That doesn't excuse you from continually disappointing me. I assured the elders that you would succeed. You're making me look bad."

"Do you think I'm doing this on purpose?" she said, letting her anger get to her. "Trust me. I want them as much as you do."

"The elders' patience is running thin. You really don't want to make them wait much longer."

"I'll find them."

"So you keep saying."

Lorraine closed her eyes and searched for patience. She almost told Lester about her theory of a leak, but she decided against it at the last minute. "I will."

"Don't make me call again, Lorraine. You won't like the consequences."

The call disconnected.

29

L ev shook the water from his face and swam to the back of the boat. He'd spent the last hour removing the old numbers and replacing them with the new ones. It wouldn't keep the Saints off their trail completely, but it would make life difficult for them, that was for sure.

He climbed up the ladder and got out of the water. His gaze scanned the back of the boat as he dried off. Lev had left Reyna sleeping. As she had been for the six hours prior. The fact that they were relatively safe allowed her to get the rest her body so desperately needed.

When she woke, he would take a look at the wound. He'd wanted to inspect it before she went to sleep, but he hadn't had the heart to wake her when he found her curled up on the bed.

Lev checked the map and the compass to make sure he was headed southwest. They had decided to skip stopping in Scotland or Ireland. Iceland was on the way, but Lev would prefer not to stop there either.

He started the engine and throttled the boat

forward, headed toward Dover, Maryland. No doubt the Saints were waiting for him, which is exactly what he wanted.

For the third time, he turned on the cell phone and checked the clock. Barely one minute had passed before the phone vibrated with a text.

All clear.

He smiled when he read it. Right after, the device rang. He didn't hesitate to answer. "Hello?"

"I'm sorry it took so long," Callie said.

Lev chuckled and sat back in the chair as he kept the boat on course. "No need to apologize. I knew you'd figure it out one way or another."

"I don't like that it took me so much time. The Saints began attacking us virtually, which is what slowed me down."

His smile disappeared. "Should I be worried that they're tracking this."

"Oh, please. You know I would never have called if that was a possibility."

He did, but he couldn't help but worry. "How did you stop them?"

"I haven't yet. At least, not completely. I focused on separating this line from everything else, which will allow you to check in when you need to."

"You mean they're still attacking you?"

Callie laughed. "They sure are. I set up several layers of firewalls and malware because I knew they'd come at us this way. It's keeping them busy, but I'm having to add more and more layers so they can't get through."

Lev knew the Saints had a team, while Callie was working on her own. "Is there anything we can do?"

"Stay alive," Callie stated. "I'm hoping you'll

come around the States and come into port at Galveston, but I suspect you're about to tell me you're headed somewhere else."

"You'd be right."

"I figured. Just thought I'd put my hope out there."

"I don't want any of you there when we come in. All of you need to stay at the ranch."

Callie barked with laughter. "Wow. You've totally forgotten who we are. As if we'd leave you and Reyna hanging."

"Callie, I'm serious. They'll be waiting for me."

"And we'll be waiting for them. Cullen and Mia are going to stay in Dover."

Lev shook his head, twisting his lips. "That's a bad idea."

"Hmm. Maybe you should have told Orrin and Yuri that, as well. They left this morning."

"Please tell me the rest of you are staying in Texas."

There was a beat of silence. "If I'm perfectly honest, I'll say that we're still debating that."

In other words, Wyatt and Owen wanted Callie and Natalie to stay behind while the girls wanted to go. Lev knew who was going to win that fight—the men. Wyatt had already locked Callie in the bunker once to keep her safe. He wouldn't hesitate to do it again. But Lev didn't tell her that.

"Lev," Callie said, her voice deepening in seriousness. "Cullen said that some of Sergei's men think you're the one who killed Sergei."

"Because I wasn't there," he said. "Yeah, I figured as much."

"You won't be able to trust any of them."

"I trained those men, Callie. I know them."

She made an unintelligible sound. "I've learned that when it comes to the Saints, you can't trust anyone."

"That's the truth. I'll know when I look into their eyes which I can and can't trust."

"They might turn on you, as well."

"Let them try."

"Damn, but I want to be there to see that," she said, a smile in her voice.

He grinned. "Do what you can to keep Wyatt and Owen in Texas. I don't guess you've heard from Maks?"

"Actually, Cullen sent him a message about you and Reyna."

"I didn't see him. Then again, if he was there, he wouldn't have made himself known." Lev thought about the shot he'd heard when he was swimming.

Callie sighed loudly. "We won't see or hear from Maks until he's ready for us to. But if he was able to help y'all, he would have."

"I know."

"You can keep the phone on. I've got it so highly encrypted that the Saints couldn't even find it."

He chuckled. "Good luck with the cyber-attack."

"Oh, they don't even know what I'm about to unleash. They chose wrong coming at us this way. I've stayed away from their computers, but that's about to change."

Lev suddenly had an idea. "You might want to get in without them knowing and have a look around."

"Why wouldn't I take them down if I could?"

"Because it'll be better if we hit them

simultaneously via their computers and their personnel."

"Oohhh," Callie replied. "That's good. We've been on the defensive since we began this. I'm ready to be offensive."

Lev was, too.

They ended the call. Lev yawned as he realized that his stomach was grumbling. He input the coordinates for Dover into the GPS to keep the boat on course and then set the autopilot. He then took his hands off the wheel for a few minutes to see how it did. When the vessel stayed on course, he rose and went to empty his bladder, check on Reyna, and grab some food.

He was gone less than ten minutes. Still, he returned to the helm and ate the cheese and crackers instead of staying below. He wasn't worried about running into anything. No, Lev was more concerned about other boats coming his way. He wanted to be able to spot them first and prepare. The great thing about being out on the water was that you could see a potential enemy from miles away.

Happily, the seasickness had been kept at bay. Maybe because his gaze remained on the horizon as much as he could, but he wouldn't chance getting sick. Reyna needed him. And he needed to be ready for an attack.

The rest of the day remained quiet with nothing to see but water and sky. Lev checked the weather every few hours to see if they would encounter a storm. Everything seemed to be staying to the north of them for the moment, thankfully.

By the time night fell, he needed more substantial food. He slowed the boat and let it drift as he went below to check on Reyna. He felt her head, but there was no fever. She slept deeply, so he left her alone.

Lev went to the galley and sautéed some spinach and then cooked the two chicken breasts Reyna had found at the residence. He left one on the stove for her while he plated the other for himself.

He remained below to eat and look at something other than water for a little while. The food did wonders to revive him. He grabbed a soda and a bottle of water from the fridge after washing his plate and then went back up top.

A part of him wanted to anchor the boat and climb into bed with Reyna. But he decided against it because she needed to be left undisturbed, and because they had to cover as much ground as they could.

He went another forty miles or so when the rain started. The lights from the boat directed on the water showed that the waves were still pretty calm. He knew little to nothing about ships. If the storm got too bad, he'd have to wake Reyna.

After about ninety minutes, the rain tapered off, and the clouds cleared. He found himself gazing at the stars. They were so clear and bright out there that they were mesmerizing. Even the moon was hypnotic.

He was beginning to understand people's love of the water. If he didn't have the Saints chasing him, he'd really be enjoying himself. Especially on a boat like this with Reyna.

Sergei would laugh at him. At the thought of his friend and mentor, Lev got choked up with emotion. He hadn't gotten to speak to Sergei since he'd left for Kiev. Nor was he at the funeral.

Lev could almost hear Sergei telling him that funerals meant nothing to the dead. They were for the living, and that Lev shouldn't feel bad about anything.

But he did.

He wanted to honor Sergei and the life the old man had given him. Lev could well imagine the sendoff Sergei got. He had been feared, yes, but more than that, he'd been respected. He was known for being fair—though not forgiving.

Even if Lev had been at the funeral, he wouldn't have said anything. It wasn't his way. He'd have told Sergei privately.

Lev cleared his throat and tried to put his thoughts into words, but they were all jumbled. His pain was too fresh, he supposed. He needed time to get it all straight in his head before he went to Sergei's grave and spoke to him.

"I miss you, old man," he murmured to the stars, wondering which one was Sergei's.

Lev shut off that train of thought and began planning for when he and Reyna reached Dover. They had about a week of traveling, and he had to have everything sorted out by then. Callie was right, there was a chance that Sergei's men would come at him. There was also a chance they wouldn't.

He knew the port at Dover better than anyone else. There were ways of getting in that no one knew about. He'd used it a few times to smuggle Sergei's friends in and out of the States. Never had he thought to need it himself.

By the time the sun came up, Lev had figured out where the Saints would station themselves at the port to locate him. Then, all he had to do was take each of them out.

The problem with that was that there were always Saints you didn't know about. All it would take was one of them seeing him and sounding the alarm. Yet the fewer bodies he had to fight, the better.

He stared in wonder at the beauty of the sunrise. It turned the water almost gold, and the sky scarlet and orange. After staring at the marvel for a few minutes, Lev grabbed the binoculars and checked behind him, on either side of him, and in front of him for vessels.

When he lowered the binoculars, Reyna was standing there. He smiled at her mussed hair and sleepy eyes.

"You should've woken me," she told him sternly, then ruined it with a yawn.

Lev bit back his laugh. "You needed the rest."

"We needed to cover the distance. If things had gotten bad, I would've stopped for the night."

She rubbed her eyes. "You seem to be taking to the water much better."

"I'm coming to understand the love of it."

"Are you?" she asked with a grin.

He nodded. "How's the wound?"

"Sore still, but better."

"I need to check it. And then how about some breakfast?"

"You sit. I'll do that."

Lev gave her a dry look. "Sit and steer, if you must. I'll cook."

She saluted him, but she wore a smile. "Yes, sir."

"Hmmm," he replied with a wink. "I could get used to that."

30

She was healing, but not as fast as she'd like. Reyna and Lev might be in a fight for their lives, but at the moment, it seemed as if they were the only two people on Earth. And she quite liked it.

The solitude out on the water gave them a false sense of security. It could be shattered at any time. Hell, for all she knew, they were being tracked under the water. It wasn't as if a plethora of vessels made the trip from Norway to the States daily. In fact, they had only glimpsed one, a cargo ship that had been miles away.

Lev seemed to really enjoy driving the boat. They took turns, but he was always eager to take the helm. In the three days they'd been out on the water, he hadn't exhibited any signs of seasickness.

They kept the engine opened up, eating up miles of water in a day. But it was taking a toll on their gas stores. They had already used one of the cans stored on the boat, and they were on the second and last. They had no choice but to make a detour to Greenland.

Reyna glanced over her shoulder as Lev appeared

from below with both gasoline cans in hand. Two hours ago, she had altered their course toward Greenland. Lev had taken that time to check the guns and get everything ready for when they reached land.

"If we fill up these cans as well as the tanks, will that get us to Maryland?" Lev asked as he set down the cans.

She shrugged. "I honestly don't know. We could always stop in Canada if we have to."

"That's just it. I don't want to stop."

"Neither do I, but that's the choice we made when we decided to run the boat at eleven knots an hour."

He glanced out the front of the boat. "Is there anything else we need since we're stopping?"

"We could restock the food."

"Only if there's a store near."

She nodded in agreement. "You get the gas, and I'll get the food."

"I'll take care of all of it."

Reyna shot him a hard look. "Just because I'm injured doesn't mean I can't pull my weight."

"I know that."

"Do you? Because you're not acting like it."

Lev ran a hand down his face. "I just...there will be Saints everywhere."

"I'm aware."

"You could get hurt again."

She held out her hand, waiting for him to take it. When he did, she wrapped her fingers around his. "So could you."

"Maybe."

"Don't," she told him. "The minute you begin putting my life above yours, you hurt us. We've survived this long because we've worked together, pulling our own weight."

Lev's lips thinned. "You haven't healed."

"And I won't for weeks. I can do this, and you need to let me."

He looked away once more, a muscle ticking in his jaw. "I don't have a choice, do I?"

"None."

Lev issued a slight laugh and swung his gaze to her. "All right. Which do you want? To stay with the boat? Or get supplies?"

She might have won a small victory, but she wasn't blind to why Lev had wanted her out of harm's way. "Which would you rather I take?"

His lips turned up in a smile as he brought her hand to his lips and kissed her knuckles. "Stay with the boat."

"I can do that."

"Thank you," he whispered as he leaned down and kissed her lips.

Heat instantly filled Reyna. She and Lev hadn't made love since Sweden. He'd kept his distance because of her wound, but at least they'd shared a bed for a few hours each night. She liked having his arms around her. Being held by him was the best way to end each day.

They remained holding hands as she looked back out the window as Greenland drew closer.

"You know, we might have enough to reach Newfoundland."

He quirked a brow. "You want to take that chance?"

"Maybe."

"Why Newfoundland instead of Greenland?"

She licked her lips. "We could head back over land again."

"That means crossing another border. I think I'd rather take my chances on the water, even if it means there are few places to hide."

"Then that's what we'll do."

They grew silent as they slowed in their approach to the southernmost point of Greenland. Prince Christian Sound was stunning with its mountains, glaciers, and deep blue water. A tourist destination that even cruise ships used, the beauty drew everyone.

"Damn," Lev murmured as his gaze moved over the glaciers. "It's gorgeous."

"I love the fjords. We didn't get to see much of them in Norway."

Lev nodded, his gaze never leaving the view.

Reyna took her hand from Lev's to maneuver the boat toward the small port village of Aappilattoq. The brightly colored Nordic-style houses were a pleasure to look at. She pulled her gaze from them and made her way to a dock. As soon as she got the boat close enough, Lev leapt out and tied it off.

He looked around before coming back onto the boat to get the gas containers. "You sure?"

"Yes," she told him.

Lev took the cans to the dock and helped her off the boat. They walked together to the petrol station, but Lev diverted toward the store as she smiled at the young man who greeted her.

In no time, the boat tanks were being topped off, and the cans filled. She then bought a third one and had that filled as well, just to be safe. After she'd paid, she bent to pick up one of the cans and winced when her side pulled.

"Let me," a young man said with a Greenlandic accent.

She let him take two of the cans to the boat as she waited with the third. When he returned, she walked with him. He made idle conversation, but his accent was so thick that she couldn't understand much of what he said.

Reyna stopped him when he started to get on the boat. A moment later, she heard her name and looked over her shoulder to find Lev making his way to her.

The young man smiled and nodded before he walked away. He and Lev exchanged a pleasant greeting as they passed. Reyna eyed the bags in Lev's hands as he approached.

"Everything good?" he asked.

She smiled. "Absolutely. You?"

"I got us stocked. Why don't you get in, and I'll hand you the bags? Then I'll get the cans."

Reyna eagerly climbed into the boat and reached for the bags. She brought them down to the galley and began unloading them. She smiled when she saw the bag of peanut M&Ms. They were one of her favorite candies. There was some vegetables, chicken, shrimp, and crab, as well as a baguette of bread. And to her delight, two individual sandwiches, and snack-sized bags of chips. But it was when she saw the two bottles of Coca Cola that she squealed.

She heard the engine start up, and a moment later, they were moving.

"How'd I do?" Lev asked as she came up with the sandwiches, Cokes, and chips.

"Perfect."

"I was getting tired of water and coffee," he said with a shrug as he took a bottle of soda from her.

She sat opposite him at the helm and unwrapped his sandwich before she handed it to him. Then she opened the bag of chips and placed it in between his legs so he could easily reach it. After he was settled, she got her food ready.

The first drink of the soda was like Heaven. She sighed loudly, which caused Lev to chuckle.

Reyna couldn't hold back her smile. "What? I have a weakness for soda."

"You won't hear me saying anything about it. How's the sandwich? I didn't know if you liked ham or turkey."

She looked down at hers before she glanced at the sandwich Lev held. "I'll eat either. Do you want mine?"

"I'll eat either, as well. Just wanted to make sure you had a choice."

A man who looked out for her. Yeah, she could certainly get used to such treatment.

They ate as they slowly made their way back out to sea. In just a few days, they would reach Maryland. The quiet solitude they'd enjoyed would be gone.

Until then, she was going to enjoy every second she had with Lev. It might very well be their last. But she'd been saying that since they first ran from the Saints.

"What are you thinking about?" Lev asked.

She smiled. "You."

"Good things, I hope," he said with a grin and a wink.

"Very."

"We're going to be fine."

She flashed him a bright smile because she knew his words for the lie they were. He was telling himself as much as he was telling her. Perhaps if they said it enough, it might come true.

The Saints thought they had struck a damaging blow to Lev by murdering Sergei. They had no idea that it strengthened his resolve. Nor did they realize— yet—what it meant for them.

Lev was the type of man who would evade death itself in order to carry out judgment against those who had taken his friend and mentor from him.

Reyna hadn't understood people like that before. But she did now. And she wondered what it would feel like to have someone like that love her. Then she remembered that he did. She stared at his profile, amazed that they had found each other out of the billions and billions of people on the planet, in a country that neither of them was from.

It defied the odds. But it also meant that they were supposed to be together. She wouldn't have made it this far alone. And neither would he have. However, as a team, they had managed to evade capture again and again. Hopefully, their luck would hold once they reached the States.

Reyna had no idea how long it would take them to find Mia and Cullen. Despite the excitement of knowing that she and Lev wouldn't be alone in Dover, she agreed with him. The Loughmans should've remained in Texas.

But the fact that Mia and Cullen had gone to Sergei's memorial said a lot about what the family thought of the Russian.

"Tell me about Yuri," she urged Lev.

He shrugged at the mention of the Russian

general. "He killed Orrin's team after they stole the bioweapon from Russia. And he kidnapped and tortured Orrin for weeks."

"Yet they're working together now?"

"Orrin's entire team worked for the Saints. Yuri thought Orrin did, as well. He was looking for the bioweapon to destroy it."

Reyna nodded, understanding. "That's when they began working together."

"They've actually known each other for years. They worked closely together back when Orrin was still in the military."

"It's lucky that Yuri is on our side."

Lev met her gaze. "Absolutely. But it's hard to trust anyone."

"Because you're always wondering if they're really working for the Saints," she said with a nod. "I understand. I hope to one day discover who it was that leaked me the information to get into the headquarters building. I'd like them on our side."

He grunted and finished off his soda. "You'll probably never know."

"But anyone willing to take that kind of chance against the Saints is exactly who we need on our side. I bet there are more of them out there. We have to find them."

"If we survive this, then we will."

31

"I don't like this," Cullen said, his voice carrying into the ear COMs his father, Mia, and Yuri wore.

A chuckle came through the COM before Yuri said in his thick Russian accent, "Still upset that your woman won?"

"He knows better," Orrin replied.

Mia sighed loudly. "I'm fairly certain Cullen is referring to the number of people we've determined are Saints."

Cullen was high up on a crane that unloaded the containers from the ships. It gave him the perfect vantage point to Sergei's office and anyone coming and going. "We have no idea when Lev and Reyna will get here. It could be two days or five. It'd make life a hell of a lot easier if I could start removing some of the Saints now."

"I agree, son," Orrin replied. "Right now, they believe we're in Texas. It's going to give us the element of surprise."

Mia said, "And by the ten I count on my side, we're going to need every bit of that surprise."

"Do not forget the ones we haven't picked out yet," Yuri cautioned.

In other words, they were fucked. Cullen was happier than ever that he and Mia had come to Dover. Not just because of Sergei, but because Lev and Reyna wouldn't stand a chance without them.

"They're setting up, just like we are," Orrin said. "No doubt many are at the Canadian border just in case Lev and Reyna take that route. As soon as one group lets everyone know they've seen the couple, the others will come this way."

Cullen adjusted his rifle and peered through the scope. "It's going to be a bloodbath."

"*Da*," Yuri replied.

Mia grunted. "I don't regret being here, but we need to come up with a better plan than just picking off the Saints one at a time. They'll find us."

"I've been thinking about that," Orrin said.

Cullen watched as a car drove up to Sergei's office. "Me, too."

"It's four—well, six if you count Lev and the woman—against dozens. It will have to be one hell of a plan."

Orrin laughed. "With our four brains, we'll come up with something."

"We are not making use of Mia's skills," Yuri stated.

Before Cullen could balk, Mia hastily said, "I agree. Choppers fly around the docks all the time."

"But, honey, they aren't equipped to fire weapons," Cullen added.

"Unless you're the weapon," Orrin said.

Cullen pulled his eye from the scope. "I thought you wanted me in a sniper position?"

"No, no, no." Yuri blew out a long breath. "Orrin, you get in the chopper with Mia. Cullen, you take position near the office where the majority of the Saints are congregating. I will take your sniper position."

"Huh. I actually like that," Mia said.

Cullen had to admit that it put everyone in the best positions. He'd taken the crane spot so he could get a view of a large portion of the docks. All of them had locations around the port to pinpoint the Saints.

"I agree with Mia. We need to hire a helicopter now," Orrin replied.

Cullen laughed and peered back through the scope. "One phone call to Callie should get that taken care of."

"You're right," his father said with a chuckle.

"I'm calling her now," Mia told them.

While she took care of that, Cullen asked the other two, "What are the odds that Lev even reaches the docks?"

"Slim," Yuri said.

Orrin made a sound at the back of his throat. "I'm more worried about once he and Reyna get here."

"We're going to need a place to hide," Cullen said.

Yuri made a sound of disagreement. "That would be foolish."

"So would trying to get back to the ranch right away."

Orrin cut in before the argument could escalate. "Both of you have a point. We've all been in tricky situations before. We'll come up with several plans tonight. It may come down to us splitting up."

"This isn't a battle we're planning. This is an all-out war," Cullen said. "This kind of operation would be planned for months, not days."

"This is all we have. Deal with it," Yuri stated.

Cullen ignored the hard bite to the Russian's words. "My point is that we have a lot of work to do in order for this to succeed."

"What we need is more people," Orrin said.

"No." Cullen wasn't going to call his brothers in. They were already pushing things with the four of them there.

Yuri said, "I agree with your son."

Cullen looked to his right where he saw activity near him. "I've got to move. Sunset isn't far off. I'll get Mia, and we can meet back at the house to plan."

"Be careful," his father said.

Cullen pocketed his scope in the backpack and slung it over his shoulder as he began to climb down the crane. He kept an eye on the individuals coming toward him. He got away just before they got to the crane.

He found Mia at the back of one of the warehouses that had a view of the gate into and out of the port. She held up a finger when she saw him to let him know that she was still on the phone. A moment later, she ended the call.

"Callie called Lev while I was on the phone."

That piqued Cullen's interest. "Does he have any idea when they'll be here?"

"Two days. He said they'll come in at night. Apparently, there is a place where he can get in and out of the port without anyone seeing him."

"Great. Where is it so we can get to him?"

Her lips twisted as she shrugged. "He wouldn't tell us."

"He's afraid it'll get to the Saints. I can't blame him for keeping it secret."

"I told him our plan, and he liked it. He said he'd find you at the offices."

Cullen sighed as he thought over everything. "I was hoping he'd let us take him straight to Texas."

"He can't. And neither would you," she said.

He nodded. "Did you tell him how many Saints were here?"

"I did."

"This is something Lev has to do." Even if it put the rest of them at risk. "Mia, I have a favor."

She shook her head and wagged a finger at him. "Oh, no you don't."

"What?" he asked with a frown.

"You want me to take Reyna and leave."

He shrugged. "Maybe."

"That's going to be a might bit difficult if I'm flying the chopper."

"Well, I actually have another plan."

"Do you?" she asked and folded her arms over her chest. "I'm one of the best pilots around. Why not use me?"

"Because that's what they expect. The Saints know we're here. Even though we led them to believe we returned to Texas, they'll hedge their bets. I guarantee they'll have helicopters of their own."

Mia dropped her arms, defeated. "So, I can't fly?"

"Not this time, sweetheart. We're going to hire a chopper, but we're also hiring a pilot. Let them lead the Saints on a merry chase."

"While we get away," she said with a grin.

"In another chopper."

Her smile widened. "Now you're talking."

"Come on. We're meeting Dad and Yuri at the rental house. We've got a lot to discuss tonight."

"Please tell me you're cooking pancakes. I'm famished and craving them."

He wound his arm around her shoulders. "For you? Anything."

They made their way back to the motorcycle they'd hidden and put on their helmets. Cullen revved the engine and drove them out of the docks.

The door to the plane opened after it had come to a stop on the tarmac. Lorraine was the first to exit. It had been over ten years since she had been to the States, and she wasn't exactly thrilled to be back now.

"Happy to be home?" Anatoli asked from behind her.

She ignored him and proceeded down the steps of the plane. A black Suburban awaited them. She climbed in with Anatoli right behind her.

"Ma'am." A young, blond woman in a navy pantsuit turned from the front passenger seat and handed her a file.

"Thank you." Lorraine opened it and read the reports from the soldiers combing through the docks.

Anatoli asked the blonde, "Has there been any trouble?"

"A few made a ruckus about our numbers, but we quieted them soon enough," she replied with a smile.

Lorraine caught the woman's eyes. "What's your name?"

"Monica."

"Well, Monica, how about you tell me if any of the Loughmans have been seen."

Monica shook her head. "Nothing, ma'am. We had eyes on Cullen and Mia when they came for Sergei's funeral."

"As I expected."

"But they went home that same day before we could get close enough to them."

Lorraine rolled her eyes. "Your orders were to grab them."

Monica exchanged a look with the male driver who had remained silent. "Mia and Cullen were never far from Sergei's men."

"We have members embedded in the mob."

"And they tried to get to the couple," Monica said. "There just wasn't a right moment."

Anatoli didn't hide his smile, which infuriated Lorraine. She blew out a frustrated breath. "It shouldn't be that difficult to take down two people."

"They've been trying for some time," Anatoli stated.

Monica jerked her chin to the file in Lorraine's hands. "In the back, you'll find a detailed account of each encounter with the Loughmans, as well as Natalie Dixon—now Loughman—Mia Carter, and Callie Reed."

"You forgot Major General Yuri Markovic."

"No, ma'am," Monica said and handed her another file. "He has his own."

"I've read everything about this family and those who have joined forces with them. It doesn't explain why none of them have been taken down."

Anatoli cleared his throat. "You mean caught."

Lorraine jerked her gaze to him and glared. "Up

until a few days ago, the elders wanted everyone dead. And as far as I know, the only ones they want brought in are Lev and Reyna."

Anatoli winked at Monica before he said, "Oh, I'm fairly certain the elders would be happy to talk to any of those we're after."

She made her fingers loosen on the files when they started to bend. She didn't care that Anatoli was flirting with a much younger, pretty woman. It didn't bother Lorraine at all. And if it did a little, she wouldn't deign to give it a second thought.

"I want an update from those leading the men," she ordered. "Tonight."

Monica gave a quick nod. "Of course."

With a motion from Monica, the driver pressed the accelerator.

Lorraine wouldn't admit it to anyone, but she was scared. Terrified actually. She'd honestly believed that she would get Lev and Reyna before they reached the coast. Then she'd believed she would get them on the water, but that had proven more difficult than she'd imagined. Even with the submarines at her disposal and many cargo vessels searching on their voyages, none of them had spotted the boat.

The closest she came was when there was a sighting on Greenland. She'd immediately jumped on a plane for Maryland then. There was no point chasing the boat. She would be there waiting when Lev returned home.

And she would end this nightmare she'd found herself in once and for all.

32

"Are you ready?" Lev asked Reyna.

She took a deep breath and nodded as she kept her hands on the wheel of the boat.

For the past two days, they had gone over their plan again and again. Lev had told her about the secret entrance into the docks and how she could get out if things got tricky—because things were certainly going to get very hairy.

Reyna had wanted to pass on their plan to the Loughmans, but Lev refused. While he trusted Callie that the phones were encrypted, things still happened. He didn't want to get this close and have everything go sideways just because the Saints happened to hear something during their phone call.

"We'll get a slight advantage," Lev continued. "But it won't be long until the Saints know we're there."

"And they call in reinforcements."

He kept his gaze on the water. They had turned the boat's lights off. Since Reyna was better at driving the vessel, he'd let her have the helm, directing her when and where to turn.

"We could easily slip out," Reyna said.

Lev glanced her way. "I've thought about that option often. With all of your knowledge about the Saints, I think you should do exactly that."

Her head snapped to him. "Don't."

"Think about it, Reyna."

"I am. I'm also thinking about you."

Lev shook his head. "I knew what I had to do the minute I learned about Sergei's death."

"And you're playing right into their hands. This is what they want you to do. To go barreling in, guns blazing so they can take you down."

"They won't catch me."

She snorted loudly and focused on their path through the water. "You're full of shit."

"Sergei needs to be avenged."

"I agree," she stated, anger lacing every syllable. "Getting yourself captured or killed isn't the way to do it. You want to hurt them, then you have to stay alive."

Lev put a hand to his lips as he looked at her. It was the signal for her to turn off the engine and let the boat coast with the current.

They remained silent, passing huge cargo ships, workers on the docks, and even other boats without being seen. Reyna had to maneuver quickly to avoid hitting a vessel coming at them, but she did it with ease and finesse.

He gave her a thumbs up and a smile to let her know he was impressed. The woman constantly amazed him. She was cool under pressure, calm when everything went crazy, and a force when she needed to be.

Lev held his breath when they came to the turn-in. He motioned with his hand, and Reyna immediately turned the wheel, steering the boat into the narrow channel.

His hand fisted at his side when he saw the other boat docked. It was a small one, but it would still make it difficult for them to pass. Reyna saw it too and put their vessel as far to the side as she could without running into the dock.

No matter her skill, the area was too narrow for two boats. And when they reached the other vessel, theirs scraped against it. The sound was loud to his ears, and it caused them to lose a lot of momentum. Lev looked around, waiting to see someone come running, or even a body come out of the tied craft. But there was no one.

In order to keep moving, he had to push against the dock. There was more scraping, and even their hull bumping against the dock. But, finally, they got through.

Lev palmed a pistol. One of the rifles was already slung across his body. The other leaned near Reyna, waiting for her to grab it.

Lev motioned for Reyna to move the boat to the right in between two lights so they would be in shadow. There was a small alcove that appeared to dead-end. Lev kept his gaze on the area as she pulled up alongside the dock. He jumped out and grabbed one of the lines to hold the boat as Reyna gathered her guns.

Once she was beside him, he handed her his gun as he tied off the boat. He turned back to her and took his weapon.

"Why are you staring at me?" she whispered.

"Because I love you. Because you've made my life better."

She smiled and touched his face. "I love you, too. Your words were moving, but I'm still not leaving without you."

He sighed and glanced at the ground. "Sergei wanted me to take over upon his death. I need to do that."

"Since you knew how to get us to the port without being seen, I'm guessing you know how to get to Sergei's building without being seen, as well."

Lev nodded. "I do."

"That's what I thought. Let's go there and take care of that business. Then we can find Cullen and the others and leave."

"Without killing any Saints?"

She dropped her hand to his chest. "Honey, I want them dead as much, if not more, than you. But we have to be smart. There are few of us fighting against them. If we go up against them now when their numbers exceed ours and they're waiting for us, then we've already lost. You're too cunning to make such a mistake."

Damn. She was right, and he hated it.

"It's a good opportunity to take some of them out," he argued.

She dropped her hand to her side. "I don't want to win a skirmish. I want to win the war. And it's going to take all of us."

"I can't run Sergei's business from Texas."

"Yes, you can."

He shook his head. "No, I really can't. The moment the Saints realize I'm gone, they'll destroy every one of my men as well as the building. I have to stay."

"Then I'll stay with you."

"It's too dangerous."

She laughed as she took a step closer and rose up on her tiptoes to place her lips against his for a quick kiss. "That's the life I've led for many years. The only difference now is that I'll be doing it with the man I love."

"You know too much about the Saints," he argued, hoping that he could convince her to go to Texas. It wasn't that he wanted her gone. It was about keeping her safe and alive.

"And from what I've learned about Callie, she can do wondrous things with the information I can share. I go where you go. And that's final."

Lev turned his head and looked out over the docks. The workers there were loyal to their union. They fought to have their jobs and everything that went with it.

"What are you thinking?" Reyna asked.

He grinned at her as he realized the answer had been right in front of him the entire time. "I'm thinking if we're going to stay, then we need to show the Saints who owns the docks."

"They'll have people there. Dock workers who give them information."

"Yeah, but they won't have Tommy."

She quirked a brow. "Who?"

"I need you to go find Mia like we planned."

"And where are you going?" Reyna demanded.

He smoothed back a strand of hair that had flown into her face. "I'm going to get an army. Once you're with Mia, alert the others that something big is coming."

"Where do you want us?"

"Sergei's office."

She touched his cheek. "Be careful."

"You, too."

Lev waited until she was out of sight before he made his way toward Tommy Sullivan's office. He and Sergei had once been enemies, but when the dock workers had fought for better union wages, Sergei had joined them. Their feud had shifted to an uneasy truce. Not long after Tommy had gone to Sergei for help with someone stealing from the docks, Sergei had found the culprit and turned them over to Tommy so he could alert the police.

After that, their friendship continued to develop over the years until they were as thick as thieves. If anyone were going to help Lev, it would be Tommy.

Lev stayed out of sight, keeping to the shadows and noting the men not doing a good job of hiding as they hunted him.

He slipped into the office and immediately found four guns pointed at his face. Lev held up his hands, letting his gun dangle on a finger as he stared into the faces of two of Tommy's guards.

"I need to see Tommy," he told them.

The big one on the left snorted as he finished chewing a bite of his meatball sandwich.

The one on the right shook his head. "Not going to happen."

"It is if you want to get the men who have taken over your docks this past week."

Tommy's disembodied voice came out of a room at the back. "Bring him!"

The guns were lowered, and the two men escorted Lev to Tommy. Lev tucked his pistol into the waistband of his pants and walked into the small office. Tommy had an ego, but it didn't equate to a big office with a nice view of the docks. His main concern was the workers and how he could get them more as the union president.

Unlike his guards, Tommy was as thin as a reed. Age spots covered his face and bald head. He steepled his gnarled fingers and eyed Lev as he leaned back in his chair behind the desk.

"I wondered when I'd be seeing you," Tommy said. "We missed you at the funeral."

"I wasn't in the country," Lev explained.

Tommy shrugged. "You should've gotten back."

"I just did. It was Sergei who sent me to Kiev on a matter that he felt we had no choice but to be involved in."

Tommy sat forward, his face lined with worry. "Was this about the Saints?"

Lev's knees nearly buckled he was so glad that he didn't have to try and convince the man. "You know about them?"

"Sergei told me all about them after he returned from Texas. I didn't believe him at first, but it didn't take much digging to learn that he told me the truth." Tommy motioned for Lev to take a seat.

Lev lowered himself into the chair. "They're the ones who killed Sergei because I went to Kiev. I encountered another American who had been working with them for the last five years, spying on them after they killed her partner. The Saints came after both of us. We traveled across Poland, Sweden, and Norway before we got on a boat and came here."

"Damn," one of the guards said behind Lev.

Tommy rested his arms on the desk. "I had no alert that you'd arrived at the docks."

Lev shrugged. "I have my ways, and I had to keep hidden because the Saints are looking for me. I counted ten of them on my way here."

Anger contorted Tommy's features. "Where?"

"Wait," Lev cautioned. "If Sergei told you about this group, then you know they infiltrate everything. There are no doubt Saints in your union. If you call up any men now, you'll alert the Saints that you know about them."

"Then what do you suggest?"

Lev smiled. "Get ahold of your strongest and most loyal and have them come here. Can you call a meeting with the union members?"

"Yes. Why?" Tommy asked, frowning.

"If we get them all in one room, then we might be able to sort out who is a Saint and who isn't."

Tommy rubbed his hand along his jaw. "Do we have time for that?"

"No, but we need your men."

Tommy jerked his chin to the guards, who quickly walked from the room. "They'll get the word out that I've called an impromptu meeting to take place in an hour. I've done it before so it won't raise any suspicions. As for the other request, there are eight men I know I can trust without a doubt. I'll call them now. Two are already working."

"Get them here and armed. And I need a map of the docks so I can show you where I've spotted the Saints."

33

The Saints were everywhere. The closer Reyna came to Sergei's building, the more of them she saw. They had set up a perimeter that would make it impossible for anyone to get in—or out.

Reyna ducked beside a barrel and tried to find a route to the building as she looked for Mia. The location where Mia had told her to meet was now guarded by a Saint. That meant that Mia had either moved or the Saints had her.

Reyna didn't want to take the time searching for Mia if she could get into the building and help Lev. More than anything, Reyna didn't want the Saints to find her.

If only she knew what Lev had planned.

She put her hand over her wound, hating that it prevented her from moving freely. The last week had done wonders for healing it, but it wasn't enough. And she refused to allow it to prevent her from saving herself, Lev, or his friends.

Reyna turned on the balls of her feet and started to stand when she caught a brief glimpse of a woman near her. She rose, remaining bent at the waist, and moved to another set of barrels. Closer and closer she got until she came up behind the female.

Reyna lifted her pistol and aimed it at the back of the woman's head. "Drop your weapons."

There was a beat of hesitation before the woman swiveled her head to the side. "I can't do that."

"You don't really have a choice since I have a gun aimed at you."

The woman slowly turned to face her. "If you're going to kill me, then I'll face my murderer. You Saints don't scare me."

That drew Reyna up short. "Who are you?"

"My name doesn't matter."

"Actually, right now, it really does. You say the right one, then I won't pull the trigger."

The woman's eyes widened. "Reyna?"

She instantly lowered the weapon. "Mia?"

"Yeah. It's me."

"Holy shit. I nearly shot you," Reyna said.

Mia's long, black hair was gathered in a ponytail at the back of her head. Her dark eyes were large as she looked Reyna over. "I've been searching for you. Callie sent a picture, but it's difficult to see anything in the shadows."

They both ducked down when they heard someone approach. Reyna spotted two men, heavily armed as they did a sweep of the area. They remained silent until the two Saints were gone.

"Where's Lev?" Mia whispered.

Reyna shrugged. "I don't know exactly. He said he had to go see Tommy."

"Tommy? Tommy who?"

"Hell if I know. Lev said that Tommy could help."

Mia touched her ear. "Did you guys hear that?"

That's when Reyna realized Mia had a COM in her ear, likely with Cullen, Orrin, and Yuri listening. If only she had one to talk to Lev.

"What else did Lev tell you?" Mia asked.

Reyna shot her a crooked smile. "Just that something big was coming."

"It'd be nice to know what that is," Mia said with a laugh.

"Agreed. For now, we need to get to the office."

"Any ideas?"

Reyna eyed the discarded bottles of liquor near them. "How are your acting skills?"

"Pretty good. What do you have in mind?"

Reyna smiled as she hid her pistol in the back waistband of her jeans. She messed up her hair and altered her shirt so that it was unbuttoned enough to show cleavage.

"Oh, I like this," Mia said. Then she frowned. "Honey, it'll be fine."

Reyna let Mia convince Cullen as she grabbed two of the bottles. Reyna was wondering how to keep the rifle with her when she turned back to Mia and let out a whistle.

The fighter pilot had taken down her hair so that it fell in waves around her face. She had shifted her jacket so that it hung off one shoulder. "I'll pass then?"

"Definitely. Are Cullen and the others on board?"

Mia chuckled. "Orrin and Yuri think it's a good plan. Cullen will after a little convincing."

"All right. We've got some distance to pull this off.

Let's make our way from the cars so it looks as if we came from that direction."

They crept quickly and quietly to the parking area, avoiding the Saints. Once there, Reyna decided to hide the rifle in case she needed it later.

"Ready?" Mia asked.

Reyna nodded and threw her arm around Mia's shoulders. "I should warn you, I can't sing."

Mia slung her arm around Reyna's shoulders and began belting out a song. They stumbled, half from acting drunk, and half from being linked to each other. They laughed, missing words to the song and singing off-key, all the while appearing entirely soused.

Reyna dropped her head forward, causing her hair to cover her face. It allowed her to look in specific locations for Saints. She tapped twice on Mia's shoulder to let her know she'd spotted two.

A heartbeat later, Mia tapped once when she found another. They continued in that vein, waiting for someone to stop them. And then it happened. They were within thirty feet of Sergei's building when a Saint stepped out of the shadows.

"Ladies, you're going to have to stop," he said in a loud, deep voice.

Reyna jerked to a halt and looked at Mia. "We can't. We're expected," she slurred.

"Expected," Mia agreed and lifted the bottle to her lips. Then she looked at it oddly. "It's empty. Again. How does that keep happening?"

"I don't know. Sergei will have more," Reyna said.

The Saint held up both hands to stop them. "You need to turn around and go home. Now."

Mia laughed loudly. "I can't drive. I'm dru...drunk," she said on a hiccup.

Reyna nodded hard, then leaned so that it appeared as if she were about to fall. She faked losing her grip on Mia and ended up stumbling forward toward the Saint. Reyna then dropped to her knees, the bottle she held shattering when it hit the ground. She kept her hand on the neck of the bottle that remained in her hand.

"Ooooopssssssss," she said with a laugh and looked back at Mia. "I think I'm just going to lay down right here."

"No, you don't," the man said as he rushed to her.

As soon as he leaned down to help her, Reyna lifted the bottle and slid the broken glass into his skin, severing his jugular. He grabbed his neck, his eyes going wide.

"The Saints are going to lose," Reyna whispered to him before his life drained away.

She reached behind her and pulled out her pistol as she got to her feet. Mia fired twice. In moments, both of them were shooting as they raced toward the building. They were steps away from the door when it was thrown open, and several burly men came storming out firing—but at the Saints.

"In here," one of them said to Mia, who rushed inside.

Reyna followed. In moments, the men were back inside with them. Bullets hit the door, but they bounced right off.

The same man who had urged Mia inside looked at Reyna with black eyes. He was a tall, hulking man that reminded her of Arnold Schwarzenegger. His light brown hair was cut short on top and cropped on the sides. "It's an armored door."

"Thank God, Sergei thought of that," Mia said.

The man shrugged, his face becoming sad. "It was just put in a week ago."

Reyna looked at the hallway and the men staring at her. "Those men out there are looking for me. And Lev."

At the mention of Lev, all of the men straightened.

She cleared her throat and said, "Lev is coming. He had to make a stop, but those people out there can't get him."

"He should've been here for Sergei," someone behind her said.

"It's not my place to tell you why he wasn't," she said as she looked at each of them. "If you know Lev, and you knew Sergei, then you knew their bond. You should also know that if it had been in Lev's power, he would've been here."

Mia moved to stand beside her. "She's not lying. Lev will explain it all when he arrives."

"And," Reyna continued, "the people out there now are the ones that killed Sergei. They're called the Saints."

The man in charged nodded. "I'm Arnold."

She held back her chuckle after having compared him to Schwarzenegger. "I'm Reyna."

Arnold jerked his head for them to follow him as he walked past. He ordered two men to inform the others to get armed. Reyna and Mia followed him into a back room where he left them.

Reyna looked around at the large office where a desk was situated, as well as a sofa, tables, and chairs.

"Every time I came into this office, Lev stood there," Mia said.

Reyna turned to where she pointed and found herself looking in a corner near the desk. That's when she realized that they were in Sergei's office. "Lev intends to take over."

"It's what Sergei wanted, so I'm not surprised. But is Lev doing it because he feels obligated, or because he wants it."

"I think it's a little of both."

Mia blew out a breath and walked to the sofa where she sank down. "Cullen, we're inside and unharmed." She smiled. "Love you, too, babe."

Reyna turned away, feeling odd listening to Mia's conversation. She thought of Lev and hoped that he had made it to Tommy's and had gotten what he needed. She'd gotten so used to having Lev near that she didn't like being without him. Not to mention, she was worried that the Saints would find him.

"If anyone can get around these docks, it's Lev," Mia said.

Reyna looked at the woman over her shoulder. "Is my worry that obvious?"

Mia grinned. "Only because I've had that same kind of concern before. And now," she added, brows raised.

They shared a laugh as Reyna turned to face her. Then she walked to the sitting area and chose the chair opposite Mia. "Thank you for trusting me."

"I've not known Lev long," Mia said. "He saved my and Cullen's life. We owe him a huge debt. In the short time I've known him, I've realized that he is a man of few words but of action. If he trusts someone, it's because they've earned it. You did that, and because of that, we trust you."

Reyna swallowed. "I almost killed him in Kiev."

"Almost doesn't count. You two were meant to be on this journey together."

"I wouldn't be here without him."

Mia chuckled. "A lot of people can say that about Lev. He doesn't expect or want any praise. That sets him apart from others."

"And his skill. He would've made an excellent spy."

"I think he found his calling with Sergei."

Reyna leaned back and began reloading her gun. "I've been in the middle of the action for so long that it feels weird to sit back and let the others do it."

"Oh, I take full advantage of these times. Soon enough, we'll be in the middle of the fray again."

"I just wish I knew where Lev was."

Mia checked her pistol and pulled out bullets from her pocket to reload the magazine. "By the way he talks about you, I have a feeling he'd move Heaven and Earth to get to you."

Reyna smiled at hearing that. "I fell in love with him while running for my life."

"The two of you have been through something terrible and came out better for it. Lev doesn't do anything halfway. So, if he's in, he's all in."

Reyna slid the magazine into her gun and pulled back the slide to cock it. "So am I."

34

L ev was done hiding.
   He was finished with running.

It was time he came face-to-face with those who thought they could suppress him, rule him. Make him cower.

It was time he showed them just who they had fucked with.

He stood in the shadows, staring at the building that had become his home, his sanctuary while he worked for Sergei. His friend was gone, but Lev would see his legacy live on.

Sergei hated regrets. He'd always told Lev to live life without any, and Lev had tried. Yet he had one regret. That he hadn't told Sergei that he would take over once the old man was dead.

Lev's gaze lifted to the sky. "But you knew I would, didn't you?"

He drew in a deep breath and slowly released it as he returned his gaze to the three-story edifice. While he didn't know where Cullen, Yuri, or Orrin were, he did know that Reyna and Mia had made it to the building. The knowledge that Reyna was safe lifted a huge weight from his shoulders.

Not that she would remain that way. As soon as the bullets started flying, she would be right in the thick of things. But that's what made her who she was.

And it was why he loved her.

Well, one of the many reasons.

Lev had left Tommy's office and stopped off at his secret cache of weapons and ammunition to load himself up for the battle. He wasn't going to lose simply because he'd run out of bullets. Besides, he just needed to get to the building.

He shifted his shoulders, adjusting the bulletproof vest he'd had made specifically for him. The Saints might want him alive, but he was sure there would be some who fired directly at him.

With a knife in one hand, he walked along the path he had driven several times a day for the last decade and a half. Lev remained in the shadows and crept up behind the Saint nearest him. The bastard hadn't even realized that Lev was near. And he was paying for it with his life.

Lev slit his throat and lowered him to the ground before he bent low and ran to his next target. In minutes, he'd taken out nine.

He hid behind a crate and eyed the fifty feet between his location and the door of Sergei's building. Lev cleaned the blade of his knife off on the clothes of the Saint he'd just killed and sheathed it. Then he palmed a pistol in each hand.

From his count, there were another thirteen Saints between him and the door. That wasn't counting the soldiers with sniper rifles or those hidden behind the building that he couldn't see. He wasn't worried about them. It would take them time to come around to the front. The snipers, however, might be an issue. They could wound him, making him immobile. Lev was counting on Orrin, Cullen, and Yuri to handle those.

Lev usually had the patience of a saint—no pun intended—but he was fast running out, waiting for Tommy. If the union men didn't show within the next five minutes, Lev was going in on his own.

The minutes ticked by excruciatingly slow. He'd taken a chance with Tommy. It wasn't that the union leader had backed out. Most likely, Tommy had had a hard time convincing the others to join him.

Tommy and his men had been the ace up Lev's sleeve, but he hadn't counted on them. He, along with his friends and Reyna, could handle this problem. And Lev would make sure the Loughmans and Yuri were able to get out of Dover and make it to Texas.

Lev tightened his grip on his weapons and started to rise when there was an explosion to his left. His head jerked in the direction as a smile pulled at his lips.

"I knew you'd come through, Tommy," he whispered.

Lev smiled again when he heard the shouts of the dock workers as they encountered the Saints. He watched as the Saints near him turned their attention to the disturbance that was rapidly making its way toward them.

Lev stood and raised his weapons as he began walking toward the building. Lev pulled the trigger on the first Saint that looked his way, his aim dead center mass. After that first shot, the Saints nearest him turned his way.

Lev fired round after round as bullets flew near him. He dove to the ground and rolled as he ejected the empty clips and loaded more. He then got to his feet and began firing again. It was when he saw a Saint go down that he hadn't aimed for that he knew the Loughmans had his back, just as he'd expected.

He was fifteen feet from the door to the building when the Saints pinned him down. The door suddenly opened, and his men filed out, along with Reyna and Mia. The moment he saw his woman, Lev smiled.

"Get inside," Mia told him.

Lev shook his head as he got to his feet and kept firing. His men fanned out around him. Several went down, but more Saints were lying dead.

The sound of a chopper approaching drowned out some of the shots, but it was an all-out war on the docks with Lev, his men, and the Loughmans fighting the Saints on one side, and Tommy and his men on the other.

The helicopter flew over them, a spotlight on the Saints to make it easier for them to be taken out. Unfortunately, that didn't last long as two other choppers flew in and began firing at the first.

"What the hell?" Lorraine asked.

Anatoli discreetly withdrew his gun from the holster while Lorraine and the four men she had with her looked on at the scene before them.

Anatoli had told Lori repeatedly not to

underestimate Lev or Reyna, and yet she had done it time and again. Now, she saw just what that had wrought.

Despite his plan after secreting the information to Reyna to get into the headquarters and the archive room, he'd never imagined that he would end up with Lorraine. The time he'd spent with her had shown him that she hadn't changed at all. She never stopped to look at the small things.

All she saw, all she wanted, was world domination. With her leading it.

He'd discovered that about her within the first few months of dating her, but he'd already been in love with her by that point. She had done them both a favor by leaving.

"Who is the other group?" Lorraine demanded of anyone who might answer.

Anatoli remained slightly behind her and the Saints. "I did warn you about bringing so many to the docks and not talking to the union president."

"Oh, please," she stated sarcastically as she glanced at him over her shoulder. "We're the Saints. We do whatever we want."

"And that's why you're going to die." He fired four shots, killing the guards before they realized what he'd said.

Lori whirled around. Shock filled her face as she looked from the guards to the gun he held pointed at her, and then she finally met his gaze. She squared her shoulders and lifted her chin. "So, the elders sentenced me."

"No," he said with a snort.

Her brows drew together in a frown. "If not them,

then...?" She shook her head as she realized what was happening. "You won't kill me."

"I will. Without hesitation."

"You still love me. I can see it in your eyes."

Anatoli laughed. "You see what you want to see. I stopped loving you long ago, Lori. Right about the time I came to understand exactly what the Saints were planning."

"You agreed with their rhetoric. You said someone needed to handle governments so the silly wars, the killings, and the famine would stop."

He shrugged, twisting his lips. "The Saints managed to do a few of those things, but I'm talking about Ragnarok."

She snorted loudly and looked at him as if he were the dirt beneath her shoes. "There are too many people in this world. Babies who have no one to raise them because the mother was too stupid to make the man wear a condom and she didn't want her life hindered by a child."

"We're not God, Lori. No one has the right to decide if a person can have a child or not. We've created our own sins, and it is up to the human race to fix it. Not one group who believes they know best."

"But they do," Lori argued.

Anatoli shook his head in disbelief. "We kill because people speak out against the Saints. We silence them, we take away their right to free speech. We stop people from forming their own opinions. We threaten and murder to take over governments and military so we can run countries."

"So," she stated with a shrug. "It's all done for the betterment of this planet. Sure, some innocents will be killed in the process, but nothing ever worthwhile has been done without consequences."

"I won't have any more dead on my conscience."

She raised a brow. "And my men? Me?"

"The world will be a better place without the Saints."

Her mouth went slack. "Oh, my God. You're the one who leaked the information to Reyna."

"There are more of us in the organization. More than you can possibly know. And we're going to take down the Saints."

"If you think I'm going to let you get away with that, then you're wrong."

As soon as she reached for her gun, he pulled the trigger, the bullet piercing her heart.

Anatoli rushed to her, gathering her in his arms as she fell. Her eyes stared up at him as she clung to him.

"I don't want to die," she whispered.

He watched blood run from the corner of her mouth. "We could've been good together."

She smiled then. "I knew...you...still loved...me."

Anatoli continued to hold her after her hand went slack and her eyes closed. He kissed the top of her head and gently lowered her to the ground. Then he rose and stood beside the car as he pulled a mobile phone from his pocket.

He dialed the only number in the phone and waited for the line to pick up. There was no voice on the other end, there never was.

"Lorraine is dead. The Saints in Dover are being taken out as we speak. In another ten minutes, none will be left standing."

The line went dead. Anatoli pocketed the phone

and turned his gaze to the building that Sergei had occupied for decades, a building that would house a new boss—Lev Ivanski.

Lev and his group didn't know they had allies. It was better this way. The Saints were relentless in their pursuit of taking out anyone they believed went against them—especially one of their own. And it was going to take those within, as well as those outside of the organization to bring them down.

Anatoli wanted to remain and see the outcome of the battle. He would also love to meet Lev and Reyna, but that could never happen. Just as Reyna would never know that he was the one who'd given her the details to get into headquarters.

The brutal and aggressive strike against the Saints this night would reverberate through the organization for weeks to come. And just like with the Loughmans at their ranch in Texas, the Saints would pull back, lick their wounds, and figure out how to attack next.

That left Anatoli and the others in the society fighting against the Saints little time to plan. But they would pull something together. They didn't have any other choice. Each of them was all in and prepared to give their lives in this ambitious showdown.

Anatoli had once had a dream for the planet. He'd wanted an end to war, hunger, and poverty. To have peace. That's what had led him to the Saints, and it was that same dream that had him standing against such a malicious and criminal organization now.

He got into the car and drove to the airport where the jet awaited to take him back to Kiev.

35

Reyna held her arm against her bad side as she continued to fire until the last of her ammunition was gone. Lev then shoved her behind him as he continued to fight.

Suddenly, there was silence.

Lev turned his head to look at her. "You good?"

"Yes. You?" Reyna asked.

He winked at her before looking at the men around him. Over half were dead, with a handful more wounded. Reyna peered around Lev, but she didn't see any more Saints standing.

"Are they all dead?" Mia asked.

Lev motioned for some of his men to go around the building and check while the rest of them inspected the area. Reyna accepted a magazine from Lev and ejected her empty one, replacing it with the full one. She held her gun up, ready to shoot should an enemy jump out. Mia was on her other side, and she had also gone through a fair share of ammunition.

By the time they finished looking over the bodies, the men Lev had sent to the back had returned and gave the all-clear.

"We got them all," Mia said with a smile.

Lev turned as someone said his name. Reyna looked over to find a short, skinny man with two hefty men flanking him. The short one was smiling as he and Lev shook hands.

"Thank you, Tommy," Lev said.

The union boss shrugged. "It was my pleasure. I think these Saints will think again before they come back here."

"Don't get your hopes up," Reyna said. "They will retaliate."

Lev grabbed Reyna's hand and said, "Tommy, this is Reyna. Reyna, Tommy Sullivan."

"Nice to meet you," she said as she shook his hand. "And thank you again for helping us."

Red stained Tommy's cheeks as he smiled at her. "We've always stood with Sergei, and we will stand with Lev."

Tommy and Lev exchanged nods before Tommy turned on his heel and went back to the rest of the workers who had begun to return to their homes now that the threat was over.

Behind them, Sergei's men waited for Lev to turn around. Reyna didn't push him. She simply stood in the arms of the man she loved, marveling that they had won a major victory over the Saints. But she feared that they had only angered the titan.

And the retribution would be vicious.

Lev kissed her temple. "You can still leave."

"I'm with you," she told him, meeting his gaze. "I'll always be with you."

He smiled at her before he turned them to face those remaining. "Thank you all for fighting with me. I've heard that some of you believe I was responsible for Sergei's death. The men we fought today were the ones who took his life."

"Reyna and Mia told us," Arnold said as he held his wounded arm.

Lev's gaze moved over the men. "Sergei asked me to take over upon his death. I told him no repeatedly, but he never gave up hope that I would take his place. I'm here to tell you that I will honor his wishes."

A loud cheer went up, causing Reyna to smile as she beamed proudly at her man.

"It's not going to be an easy road," Lev continued when the cheering died down. "Sergei was determined to see the Saints ended, and so am I. Our business is going to extend from the normal port dealings. We're fighting a global giant that has people everywhere. We have to trust each other. The minute that ceases, we have a problem."

"We're with you," Arnold told him and was joined by a chorus of agreements.

Lev grinned at them. "Let's see to our dead and wounded."

The men wandered away to do as ordered. Lev dropped his arm and walked to the left where a huge black mark scorched the concrete. She didn't have to ask to know it was where Sergei's car had blown up.

Mia moved closer and said, "Lev is staying here, isn't he?"

"He thinks having two locations shows the Saints that we're not afraid."

"It's what Sergei would've wanted. Oh," she said and hurried away.

Reyna watched her rush toward three men walking their way. The youngest jogged to meet her, wrapping his arms around Mia and swinging her about.

Lev returned to her side and retook her hand as the foursome walked up. He and Cullen nodded to each other. However, the older man who looked similar to Cullen held out his hand.

"Glad to have you back safe and sound."

Lev laughed and shook his hand. "It's good to be back."

"And you brought a friend," the Russian said as he grinned at her.

"Yuri, Orrin, Cullen, I'd like you to meet Reyna Harris. Reyna, these are my friends."

"We're her friends, as well," Mia said with a wink.

Reyna greeted each of them, shaking their hands as they welcomed her. They stood around, laughing and talking for a few minutes before one of Lev's men said that they'd found five more bodies, one a woman.

They followed the man to the dead, and Reyna found herself staring at the body of her old boss. "That's Lorraine," she told Lev.

Orrin knelt beside her and looked at the wound. "She was killed at point-blank range."

"She knew her killer," Cullen said.

Lev looked at Reyna. "Do you think it might be the same person who helped you?"

She shrugged. "Anything is possible. Are there cameras around here?"

"Behind us," Lev said, pointing to them. "I'll ask Tommy for the footage."

Mia walked around the bodies. "It looks like the woman who has been chasing the two of you is gone. Maybe you can stop running."

Reyna met Lev's gaze. "We'll all be running until the Saints are brought down."

"Come on," Lev told them as he tugged on her hand. "There's vodka waiting in Sergei's office. I mean, my office. Damn. That's going to take some getting used to."

"But it fits," Yuri said.

Lev smiled and gave Reyna a quick kiss. "That isn't the only thing that fits."

"I'll be damned," Cullen said with a wide smile. "Lev has himself a woman."

"Keep talking, Tex, and I'll kick your ass," Lev promised.

Reyna looked at Cullen and said, "He's pretty good. I think you should zip it."

"Hey," Mia exclaimed, unable to keep the smile from her face "My man is just as good."

"Ooooh. Do I see a fight coming on?" Yuri asked, rubbing his hands together excitedly.

Orrin sighed loudly and looked up at the sky. "I'm too old for this shit."

They all laughed, enjoying the interlude of peace because they would need to start planning soon. But they had earned a few hours of rest and celebration.

EPILOGUE

Three days later...

"There's nothing to see," Reyna said.

Lev stared at the video of the night Lorraine and her men had been killed. The man responsible had his back to the cameras. He'd kept his face hidden at all times, but there was no mistaking the phone call he'd made.

"It looks like we have a friend," Lev said. "At least, I hope he's a friend."

"I'll send this over to Callie. She might be able to get something off of it that we can't," Reyna said.

Lev nodded in agreement. He leaned back in the chair Sergei had occupied for years. It felt weird to sit here, but also right at the same time. Lev wasn't a fool. He knew that things wouldn't be smooth with the men. Most had accepted him taking over, but there would be some who objected.

And he already had his eye on three of them. Moreover, he suspected that the Saints had at least one person within his ranks. He'd need to ferret them out.

Reyna suddenly sat in his lap, looping her arms around him. "We did it."

"We certainly did," he said with a smile.

She glanced away and licked her lips. "What now?"

"We prepare for the war."

Reyna swallowed. "I finished writing down everything I learned from the Saints during my years there. Names, locations, events. All of it."

"What about what you discovered at headquarters?" It was the first time he'd asked, though he'd been curious from the moment he learned of it.

Her lips split into a grin. "I wondered if you'd ask."

"I wasn't sure you wanted to tell me."

"I don't have any secrets from you," she said and gave him a quick kiss. She straightened and sighed. "The instructions were explicit on how to get into the building and down to archives. I was directed to one file specifically."

"And that was?"

"A location," she said.

He smiled slowly. "Looks like we've got more traveling to do."

"I was hoping you'd say that."

Maks wanted it finished. The Saints had done enough damage, destroyed enough lives, and controlled too much. It was time for them to come to an abrupt and violent end.

And he was happy to be the one to do it.

The phone in his pocket vibrated with an

incoming call. He pulled it out without bothering to look at the screen. He didn't say a word as the line connected, and he listened to the voice on the other end.

When the caller finished, Maks hung up and turned to walk to the car he'd parked on the side of the road. He got behind the wheel and turned around. He wasn't leaving Russia anytime soon.

ABOUT THE AUTHOR

New York Times and *USA Today* bestselling author Donna Grant has been praised for her "totally addictive" and "unique and sensual" stories. She's written more than ninety novels spanning multiple genres of romance including the bestselling Dark King stories, *Dark Craving, Night's Awakening*, and *Dawn's Desire*. Her acclaimed series, Dark Warriors, feature a thrilling combination of Druids, primeval gods, and immortal Highlanders who are dark, dangerous, and irresistible. She lives with her two children, a dog, and three cats in Texas.

Connect with Donna online:

www.DonnaGrant.com
www.MotherofDragonsBooks.com

www.facebook.com/AuthorDonnaGrant
www.twitter.com/donna_grant
www.goodreads.com/donna_grant
www.instagram.com/dgauthor
www.pinterest.com/donnagrant1